M. LEIGI

—*Nette's Bookshelf*

AND "SERIOUSLY SCANDALICIOUS."

—*Scandalicious Book Reviews*

PRAISE FOR M. LEIGHTON'S BAD BOYS NOVELS

Down to You, Up to Me, AND *Everything for Us*

"Scorching hot . . . insanely intense . . . and it is shocking. *Shocking!*"
—*The Bookish Babe*

"I definitely did *not* see the twists coming."   —*The Book List Reviews*

"Brilliant."
—*The Book Goddess*

"Leighton never gives the reader a chance to catch their breath . . . Yes, there is sex, OMG tongue-hanging-out-of-mouth, scorching sex."
—*Literati Literature Lovers*

"Well, I drank this one down in one huge gulp . . . and it was delicious . . . seriously *scandalicious.*"
—*Scandalicious Book Reviews*

"Delicious . . . I stopped reading in order to grab a cold beer and cool off . . . The twists and turns on the plot line are brilliant."
—*Review Enthusiast*

"OMG! It was freakin' hot!"
—*Nette's Bookshelf*

continued . . .

"Steamy, sexy, and super hot! M. Leighton completely and absolutely knocked [it] out of the park." —*The Bookish Brunette*

"Scorching hot . . . an emotional roller coaster." —*Reading Angel*

"I devoured it, and I'm pretty sure you will, too."
—*For Love and Books*

"Prepare yourself to be blown away." —*My Keeper Shelf*

"I loved it . . . bring on the Davenport boys." —*Smexy Books*

PRAISE FOR M. LEIGHTON'S WILD ONES NOVELS

There's Wild, Then There's You

"Engaging and charismatic." —*Kirkus Reviews*

"Will leave readers enthralled by the intriguing and emotional infatuation Jet and Violet share. This story is hot enough to start a forest fire, yet will keep readers cool, calm, and collected as they attempt to decipher the characters' complicated personalities . . . This one is swoon-worthy." —*RT Book Reviews*

Some Like It Wild

"*Some Like It Wild* left me feeling breathlessly happy . . . the exact same feeling I had when I read *The Wild Ones*. M. Leighton has done it again—she's written the perfect, sexy love story!"
—*New York Times* bestselling author Courtney Cole

The Wild Ones

"This book is worth every second I spent reading it. Ms. Leighton is a phenomenal writer and I cannot give her enough praise."

—*Bookish Temptations*

"Hands down one of the hottest books I've read all summer . . . Complete with love, secrets, dreams, and hidden pasts! *The Wild Ones* is romantic, sexy, and absolutely perfect! Drop everything and read this RIGHT NOW!"

—*The Bookish Brunette*

"I can honestly tell you that this is one of my top books of the year and easily one of my new all-time favorites. I couldn't put the book down."

—*The Autumn Review*

"You will laugh, swoon, and even shed a few tears. M. Leighton knows how to write an amazing story. Get your copy of *The Wild Ones* today. You will not regret it."

—*Between the Page Reviews*

"This book was one of the best books I've read this year. It may sound like just a love triangle on the surface but inside there's so much more going on."

—*The Book Vixen*

"One of the best books I've read this year so far."

—*Sim Sational Books*

STRONG *Enough*

M. LEIGHTON

BERKLEY BOOKS, NEW YORK

BERKLEY

An imprint of Penguin Random House LLC
375 Hudson Street, New York, New York 10014

This book is an original publication of Penguin Random House LLC.

Library of Congress Cataloging-in-Publication Data
Leighton, M.
Strong enough / M. Leighton.—Berkley trade paperback edition.
p.   cm.
ISBN 978-0-425-27946-5
I. Title.
PS3612.E3588S77 2015
813'.6—dc23
2015016257

PUBLISHING HISTORY
Berkley trade paperback edition / August 2015

PRINTED IN THE UNITED STATES OF AMERICA

10 9 8 7 6 5 4 3 2 1

Cover photo of couple by Miz Watanake / ImageBrief.
Cover design by Leslie Worrell.
Interior text design by Laura K. Corless.

Penguin
Random
House

STRONG
Enough

PROLOGUE

Jasper

Seventeen years ago

"What's he gonna do, Mom?" I try to wriggle away from her, but she holds me too tight. I feel like something bad's gonna happen, but I don't know why. "Maybe I can make him not be mad. Let me go!"

"Shhh, baby. It'll be okay. You have to stay here with me or he'll take you, too."

My heart's beating so hard it hurts, like it did that time when Mikey Jennings punched me in the chest. Not even my mother's arms around me makes the pain go away, and her hugs usually make everything better.

My eyes water as I stare out the window. I can't blink. I'm afraid to. I don't want to see what Dad's going to do to my older brother, Jeremy, but I can't look away either.

The longer I watch, the less I can move, like my feet are glued to the floor and my arms are strapped to my sides. It feels like I can't even breathe. I can only stare at the cold, gray water and the two shapes moving closer to it.

I see Jeremy's fingers clawing at my dad's hand where it pulls him by his hair. It's not doing him any good, though. Dad isn't letting go. Jeremy's feet sometimes drag along the ground, his ratty tennis shoes kicking up mud and grass, but my father never slows down. I can tell by the way his other fist is balled up that he's mad. Madder than usual, maybe.

Jeremy got in trouble at school again today. They called Dad at work instead of Mom, so she didn't even know until Dad brought Jeremy home. By then it was too late.

"No kid of mine's gonna act like a monster. There's something wrong with you, boy," Dad was saying when they walked through the door. Jeremy was in front of him. Dad pushed him so hard, my brother fell and slid across the kitchen floor.

There *really is* something wrong with Jeremy. The doctor said so. He said Jeremy needed medicine, but Dad doesn't care. It just makes him mad, makes him lose his temper with Jeremy even more.

I was standing at Mom's side when Dad stopped in front of her. He put his finger in her face until it almost touched her nose. His eyes were that red color all around the edges like they are when he's getting ready to whip Jeremy. "You'd better hope this little shit doesn't turn out the same way." He slapped me in the side of the head when he said it. It made my ear sting like a bee got me, but I didn't even say "ouch." I didn't say *anything*. I knew better than to open my mouth. "One's enough."

Dad went and grabbed Jeremy by the back of his shirt, pulled him up to his feet and threw him out the kitchen door. Jeremy fell again, but that didn't stop Dad. He followed him into the yard.

"Get up, you worthless little asshole," he yelled. There was something not good in Jeremy's eyes when he looked up. Then I saw him spit on Dad's work boots. I knew he shouldn't have done that. I knew it even more when Dad kicked him in the ribs. Now we're watching my older brother get dragged away for punishment.

Rather than stopping at the old stump that he bends Jeremy over to whip him, Dad keeps walking right out into the lake. He doesn't even stop at the edge.

My eyes hurt while I watch, but I can't close them. Something about this time looks different. Feels different. Something about the hot tears streaming down my face tells me that this time *is* different.

Dad's boots splash through the shallow water. He drags my brother behind him like he does a bag of trash when he's loading up the truck to go to the dump. Jeremy falls and gets back up, falls and gets back up. He's fighting for real now. He's kicking and hitting. I see his mouth open wide like he's screaming, but I can't hear it. The only thing I can hear is my heartbeat. It's like drums in my ears, it's so loud.

Dad stops when the water is up to his waist. He pulls Jeremy to him. I see his face from the side, my father's. It's so red it looks purple. Veins are standing out all down his neck. My brother's face is almost white, like he's wearing ghost Halloween makeup. His eyes are dry, though. He stopped crying over the stuff Dad does to him a long time ago.

Dad yells something at Jeremy, his mouth stretching so wide it looks like he could eat him. Like a snake, just swallow him whole. Jeremy just stares up at him with his pale face. Dad shakes my brother hard enough to make his head snap back, and then he dunks him under the water.

I suck in a breath. I've never seen Dad do this before, no matter how mad he gets at Jeremy. Something in my chest burns while I watch Dad hold him under, like *I* can't breathe either. Like air is stuck in there, burning. Just like I'm stuck in *here*. Hurting.

I taste salt from my tears. I lick them away, ashamed to be crying.

Something starts pecking the top of my head. A wet trail, like snail slime, slides down the side of my face. I wipe it away and look at my hand. It's just water. Warm water.

Tears. But not my tears. They're Mom's.

I count. *One Mississippi, two Mississippi, three Mississippi.* I wonder how long Jeremy can hold his breath. My head feels like it might explode.

Four Mississippi, five Mississippi, six Mississippi.

Air and sound push past my tight throat to make a weird garbled scream. It lands in the quiet room like a crack of thunder. It's the only noise I make. It's the only noise I *can* make.

I watch Jeremy's hands, beating against my dad's wrist. Dad never budges, though, never lets up. His arm is straight and ruthless, holding my only brother under the water.

Mom's arms squeeze me tighter. It's getting even harder to breathe.

Seven Mississippi, eight Mississippi, nine Mississippi.

I count, even though time stopped moving. When I get to *twenty Mississippi,* I start over at one, start over for Jeremy, to give him more breath. To give him another chance. But he doesn't use it. He can't. His time already ran out. Like his breath did. I know it when I see his hands drop away. They fall into the water and float, like there's nobody attached to them. Like my brother just . . . left.

Dad lets him go. Sort of pushes him out into the deeper water. Jeremy just drifts there, like he's playing dead. Like he used to do when Mom took us swimming on summer afternoons when our father was at work.

I don't watch Dad walk out of the lake. I don't watch him walk across the yard. I don't even look up when he walks through the back door. I just watch Jeremy, waiting for him to move, waiting for him to wake up.

"Get your purse. We're going out to eat. The boys can have a sandwich here."

Boys? Does that mean Jeremy's okay?

I start toward the door, but Mom grabs me. "Jasper, be a good boy and get my purse for me, sweetie. It's beside the front door."

Her eyes are different. They look scared and they make *me* scared, so I just go get her purse and bring it to her like she asked. When I hand it to her, she takes it and pulls me against her. I feel her arms shaking and when she lets me go, she's crying. But she's smiling, too, like she's not *supposed* to cry. None of us are supposed to cry.

"You sit right there in front of the television, okay? Don't you move a muscle." Her voice is warning me about something. I don't know what's going on, but I'm afraid. She's afraid, too.

"Okay."

I turn on cartoons and sit on the couch until I hear Dad's truck start. When I do, I get up and run as fast as I can, through the kitchen, out the back door and across the yard toward the lake.

It's raining now and the grass is slick. I fall twice before I can get to the edge of the water. When I do, I holler at my brother.

"Jeremy!" He doesn't move. He just floats on the surface like my green turtle raft does. "Jeremy!"

I look back at the house and then back to my brother. I know nobody can help me. Nobody will stand up to my dad. Not even my mom. If I don't help Jeremy, he'll die.

My hands are shaking and my knees feel funny when I step into the water. It's so cold it stings my skin, like when I fell off my sled last winter and snow went up my pants leg. I couldn't get it out fast enough. It was so cold it almost burned. But this time, I keep going no matter how much it hurts.

When the water is up to my chin and my teeth are chattering so hard I bite my lip, I think about turning back. Jeremy is so far away, I can barely see him and I can't catch my breath enough to holler for him.

"J-J-Jer—" I try again.

I paddle out farther. My arms and legs weigh so much I can hardly move them through the water. It's like trying to run in cold, thick soup. I fight to keep my chin up, gulping down the water that laps into my mouth.

I swim and swim and swim, watching the back of Jeremy's head until he's close enough for me to touch. It's raining harder now. Big, fat drops are splattering on the back of my brother's neck, and it's running down my forehead and into my eyes.

I grab a handful of his dark hair and raise Jeremy's face out of the water. His eyes are open, but they aren't looking at me. They're looking at something else, something I can't see. I take his arm. It's cold and feels kind of like that fish Dad brought home and made Jeremy skin.

My stomach hurts and my eyes burn. I feel like somebody's squeezing me around the middle, squeezing me so hard I can't even cry.

I take my big brother's hand and I pull him toward me, toward shore. He floats pretty easy, so I swim a little and tug, swim a little and tug.

After a while, it gets harder and harder to move, harder and harder to keep my face above the water. The shore, the grass, the back door of my house . . . they're all getting farther away, not closer. I'm scareder than I've ever been before. Even scareder than that time Jeremy made me watch *The Evil Dead*.

Jeremy seems heavy now, like he's trying to drag me down every time I pull on him. "Swim, Jer, swim," I mumble through a mouthful of water. "Please."

I go under. When I try to scream for help I know won't come, water goes down my throat. I try to cough, but I can't. There's no air.

I can see light above me and I use my heavy arms and legs to crawl toward it. When I finally get my face out of the water, I grab for my brother's hand. I hold on to it tighter than I've ever held on to anything before, even my favorite G.I. Joe soldier.

I paddle as fast and as hard as I can, pulling Jeremy behind me until I can touch the squishy bottom of the lake. I pull and tug and drag me and Jeremy to the shallowest part of the water and I roll him over.

His lips are blue and his face is still so white. But it's his eyes that scare me the most. They don't look like he's awake. But they don't look like he's asleep either. They sorta look like mine feel—scared. Like he saw something that made him want to hide, but he didn't get away fast enough and now he's just . . . froze.

I shake his shoulders. I scream my brother's name. I cry even though I don't want to.

I give in and pound on his chest. I know that if he gets up, he'll punch me in the back of the leg until I say "uncle," but I don't care. I just want him to get up. But he doesn't. He doesn't get up. He doesn't move at all. He just slides in the mud until he's back in the water.

I try to reach for him, but my feet slip and I almost fall in. That scares me so bad I scream my head off. I can't go back in. I won't come back out if I go in the water again. I just know it.

Don't make me go back in! Don't make me go!

But what about Jeremy? What about my brother?

I cry as quiet as I can as he floats away from me again. I watch his white ghost face until the only thing I can see is black. And nothing else.

ONE

Muse

I shake out the three-hundred-dollar sweater I just folded for the third time and I start over. Somehow keeping my fingers busy seems to calm my brain. It gives me something to think about other than the man I'm waiting on and how worried I am about taking this step.

When the icy blue cashmere is folded perfectly—for the *fourth* time—I lay it on top of the others in the stack and check the time on my phone again.

"It's almost noon, damn it!" I mutter, as if my friend Tracey Garris can hear me all the way across town. She's the one who knows this guy. I should've gotten more information from her, but she was in a rush this morning and she's in a meeting now, so I'm stuck waiting. Information-less. I only know what she muttered so briefly before she hung up, something about a guy coming by and his name being Jasper King.

I let out a growl of aggravation and grab another sweater, flicking it open with enough force to cause one sleeve to snap against the table like a soft crack of thunder. For some reason, I feel a little better for having taken out a bit of my frustration on *something*, even if that something is an innocent piece of very pricey material.

Rather than climbing right back onto a ledge of frustration, I purposely tune out everything except the words of the song playing overhead, "If I Loved You." It always reminds me of Matt, the guy I left behind. The guy who should've hated seeing me leave. The guy who *would've* hated seeing me leave *if* he'd loved me like I wanted him to. But he didn't. He let me go. Easily. And now, even after eight long months, it still makes my heart ache to think of him.

I don't shy away from the pain. In some twisted way, I bask in it. Like most artists, I welcome all kinds of emotions. Good or bad, they inspire me. They color my life and my work like strokes of tinted oil on pristine white canvas. They make me feel alive. Sometimes broken, but still alive.

After I finish the sweater, I move through the store, lost in thoughts of my ex and how much it hurt to say good-bye. I'm straightening a rack of ties when the chime over the door signals the arrival of a customer. I catch movement in my peripheral vision and absently throw a polite greeting in that direction. "Welcome to Mode: Chic," I say, feeling both resentful and relieved at the interruption.

I get no response, so with a deep sigh I even up the last row of ties and smooth my vest before turning to find my visitor. When my eyes settle on the interloper, all thoughts of Matt and the past and every trouble in the world melt away for the time it takes me to regain my breath.

A man is standing behind me. I didn't hear him approach, didn't smell cologne or soap, didn't sense the stir of the air. He was just coming through the door one second and looming right behind me the next.

He's tall, very tall, and dressed in black from head to toe. Other than his lean, dramatically V-shaped physique, that's all I notice about his body. It's his face that captivates me. From an *artist's* standpoint, he reminds me of a bronze sculpture, something strong and ancient that was carved by the talented hands of Michelangelo or Donatello, Bernini or Rodin. From a *woman's* standpoint, he's simply breathtaking.

His face is full of angles and hollows—the ridge of his brow, the slice of his nose, the edge of his cheekbones, the square of his chin. Even his lips are so clearly defined that I find myself wanting to stare at them, to reach up and touch them. Find out if they're real. If *he's* real. But it's his eyes that I finally get stuck on. Or maybe stuck *in*. They're pale, sparkling gold, like a jar of honey when you hold it up to the sun. And they're just as warm and sticky, trapping me in their delicious depths.

Despite all my worries, worries that have consumed me for several days now, I am only aware of the raw, primal power that radiates from him like heat from a fire. He doesn't have to say a word, doesn't have to move a muscle to exude confidence and capability. And danger. Lots and lots of danger.

I don't know how long I've been staring at him when I become aware of his lips twisting into the barest of smiles. It's minimally polite, but somehow anything more would seem a betrayal of the intensity that oozes from his every pore. The tiny movement is potent, though, and I feel it resonate within every one of my female organs like the echo of a drumbeat in the depths of a hollow cave. *God, he's gorgeous.*

As much as I enjoy the rubbery feel of my legs, the tingly fizz in my stomach, I pull myself out of the moment. Not necessarily because I want to, but more because I have to. I'm at work. Men don't come in here to be ogled. They come in here to be outfitted.

Unless they come here to see me. The thought hits me like a slap. Could this possibly be the bounty hunter Tracey was telling me about?

"Pardon me," I eventually manage, taking a step back as reality and worry and purpose crash back into my mind in a multi-colored tidal wave. "How may I help you today?"

Dark head tilts. Tiger eyes narrow. Silence stretches long.

I wait, part of me hoping this is the man who will help me, part of me praying he's not.

When he finally speaks, it's with a voice that perfectly mirrors what he physically projects—dark intensity, quiet danger. "I need to be measured for a suit."

I let out a slow breath, oddly more disappointed than relieved. "I can do that for you." I take yet another step away, clasping my hands together behind me, determined to find some equilibrium in his presence. I glance at Melanie, the other person working the store today. She's the owner's daughter and for the fourth hour straight, I find her holding down the chair behind the cash register, typing into her phone. I should probably tell her that I'll be in the back getting measurements, but I obtusely decide to let her figure that out for herself when she can't find me. It won't take her long to realize I'm gone when someone else comes in and I'm not out here to do her job for her. "This way," I say, turning toward the rear of the store.

All business now, I ask questions as I make my way toward the dressing rooms. Even though his rich, velvety voice warms my belly, I find it easier to concentrate when I can't see the man following quietly along behind me. He answers all my queries politely, seemingly oblivious to the way he affects me.

I take him to the larger dressing room, the one with a platform that rests in the center of a crescent of mirrors. It has enough space for a desk and computer to one side, so we use this room to measure for tailored clothing. That and for special fittings like bridal parties and other groups.

I glance to my left as we enter the scope of the mirrors. My gaze falls immediately on the figure behind me. I look quickly away, but not before I notice the lithe way he moves. With the fluidity of the jungle cat his eyes remind me of.

Like a tiger. Surefooted. Silent. Deadly.

Without turning, I sweep my arm toward the dais. "If you'll stand there, I'll get the tape and be right with you." I don't doubt that he's following my instruction, even though he doesn't respond. I still can't hear him, still can't even detect a disturbance in the air, but now I can *feel* him, as though my body has become perfectly attuned to his within the five minutes he's been in the shop. It's beyond ridiculous, but it's the absolute truth. I've never been more aware of a man before. Ever.

I busy myself gathering the cloth tape, a small notepad and a pencil, doing my best to keep my mind on the task at hand until I'm able to control my thoughts to a small degree. Those wayward thoughts scatter and my mouth goes bone-dry when I turn and see him standing on the platform, muscular arms hanging by his sides, long, thick thighs spread in a casual stance. It's not his posture that catches me off guard. It's his eyes. Those intense, penetrating eyes of his. He's watching me like a hunter watches prey. I feel them stripping me bare, asking all my secrets, exposing all my weaknesses.

"Ready when you are," he murmurs, startling me from my thoughts.

"Right, right. Okay," I say, dragging my gaze from his and focusing on his body. As disconcerting as it is to appraise him so openly, it's not nearly as disturbing as eye contact, so I go with it.

As I take him in, I realize that he's a magnificent male specimen. I'd wager that his dimensions are perfect for every kind of clothing, from formal to sleepwear. And, dear God, I can only imagine what a striking figure he'd make in a tuxedo. He'd look like a model. For guns, maybe. Or bourbon. Something dangerous and thrilling or smooth and intoxicating.

I clear my throat as I approach, careful of my feet as I step up to stand beside him. I sense his eyes on me as I move, making me feel clumsy and slightly off balance.

I lay the pad of paper on the thin podium to my right and I clamp the pencil between my teeth as I stretch the tape out straight. With movements that I'm relieved to find swift and sure, I measure his neck and over-arm shoulder width, his chest and arm length. I jot down the numbers then make my way to his waist, cursing the fine tremor of my hand when my knuckles brush his hard abdomen.

I note his measurements, mathematical proof of the flawless way he's put together. What I don't write down are things that no numbers could convey. I don't need to. They'll be seared in my brain for all eternity, I think.

Wide, wide shoulders, the kind a girl can hang on to when she's scared. Strong, steely arms, the kind that can sweep a woman off her feet. Long, hard legs, the kind that can tirelessly chase down what he wants.

It's when I get to his inseam that things get . . . tense. Surprisingly, despite all the other worries that hover at the back of my mind, I can't overlook the heaviness that presses against the back of my hand as I measure. My belly contracts with a pang of desire that rockets through me. *Good Lord almighty!*

I snap into a standing position, turning away to write down the last of his measurements before he can see the blush that heats my face. Normally, I'd love all these "feels," but not now. Not today. Not like this. It seems like a betrayal.

Without another word or glance, I take my pad and step off the platform, moving to the computer to enter them into a New Client form. My pulse settles more and more the longer I keep my eyes to myself. "What's your name, sir? I'll set up a profile for your order." Still, I don't glance back at him. I keep my gaze glued to the lighted screen.

"King," he replies, his voice so close that I jump involuntarily. I don't turn when I feel his hulking presence behind me; I just stiffen.

I type in the name. It's as I'm hitting ENTER that it clicks. *King. The last name of the bounty hunter Tracey told me about.*

I whirl to face him, ready to pin him with an accusing stare, but I stop dead when I see that he's not looking at me. He's looking down at what he's holding. Between his fingers is the pencil that was stuck between my teeth. I can see the tiny bite marks as he rubs over each one.

I watch him move his thumb over the indentions, gently, slowly. Back and forth, like an intimate caress. It's hypnotic. Erotic. A fist clenches low in my core, causing me to inhale sharply at the sensation. It feels as though he's rubbing *me* with those long fingers. Touching me, arousing me. It's so physical, so tangible, so *real* that I have to reach back to steady myself against the edge of the desk.

"What sharp teeth you have," he says quietly, Big Bad Wolf–style. When he glances up at me, his eyes are a dark and serious amber. "Do you bite?"

"No," I whisper. "Do you?"

"Only if you ask nicely."

TWO

Jasper

I watch her lush lips part, her breathing already shallow. She's off-kilter. Just the way I like. "Are you Tracey's friend?" she asks, finding a coherent thought and clinging to it.

"I am," I reply, reaching around her to lay the pencil on the desk. The action brings my face to within an inch of hers and our arms brush. I hear the soft gasp of her inhalation.

"Why didn't you just tell me? You didn't have to pretend to be a customer."

Anger. It rushes in to clear away the cobwebs. I can see it in the way her sleepy green eyes start to flash like two fiery emeralds.

"I wanted a few minutes alone with you before you went on guard. Like you are now."

"Why? Am I being interviewed or something? I thought *I* was the one hiring *you*."

"You are. But I like to know who I'm working for when I take a job like this."

While the look on her face says she doesn't approve of my tactic, she's too curious to let it go. "And?"

"And what?"

"And what did you find out? What do you *think* you figured out about me in ten minutes of silence?"

I hold her gaze for long, quiet seconds before I speak. I sense how uncomfortable it makes her. I'm used to it. Such directness makes *most people* uncomfortable, but that doesn't stop me. Keeping others off balance is always a benefit to me. "I don't need to *interrogate* you to learn things about you. Being *with you* is enough."

"Yeah, right," she scoffs, trying for casual.

"For instance, you're a hard worker who takes her job seriously, even though I don't think it's really the job you *want to be* working. You're good at this, but you're not quite at home here, which tells me that this isn't permanent. You looked sad and distracted when I came in, like you might be missing someone. Maybe *that* is where home is. And then there's the fact that you're trying to hire me. I'd say that accounts for the worried frown I keep seeing between your eyebrows."

Her mouth drops open for a few seconds before she snaps it shut. "Is that all?" she asks sarcastically, pulling her vest tighter around her middle like she feels naked. I'm used to that, too. No one likes to feel exposed, like their secrets aren't theirs to keep anymore.

"No, that's not all, but I doubt you want to hear the rest."

She eyes me warily for a few seconds before she raises her chin, eyes locked bravely onto mine. "Of course I do."

She's courageous. Ballsy. I like that.

"Well, just off hand you have a good eye for color, which makes me think you're artistic. Artists are usually very . . . emotional. I'd say that when you're not consumed with concern you have a tendency

to throw yourself into the way you feel regardless of potential outcomes."

"You can't possibly know that."

"I can. And I do. Just like I know you wash your hair in something that contains lilac." Her eyes widen, but she says nothing so
I continue, leaning in ever so slightly. "And then there's the fact
that you're attracted to me. You don't want to be. You probably even
think that you *shouldn't be*, but that's like catnip for you, isn't it?"

She's shaken. Visibly shaken, but I don't back off. I don't give her
a centimeter of the space I can see that she needs. I want her this
way—off balance, uncertain. She's the kind of woman who would
rather *feel* than *think* if she has a choice. And that's good for me. Not
only will it serve my purposes *very* well, it's also sexy as hell.

Her cheeks blaze with a rush of blood and I think about running my finger over her skin to see if it's as silky as it looks. But I
don't. At this point that would be too much. I'm nothing if not
intuitive. And controlled. In my line of work, I have to be.

I actually smile when she steps out from between the desk and
me. I can see by her expression that she's choosing to ignore my
assessment altogether. It's much easier than trying to deny the truth.

"You, um, you said 'take a job like this.' A job like *what*? I thought
this is what you do."

I cross my arms over my chest. "My jobs aren't *exactly* like this,
but they're close enough. The main thing is that I . . . find things.
And I'm damn good at it. So tell me, beautiful, what can I find
for you?"

THREE

Muse

His voice, his intensity . . . *God!* Is he really just asking me an innocent question? Because it *seems* like he's asking me so much more.

"Uh, it's not a 'what.' It's a 'who.'"

He nods once. Slowly. His eyes never leave mine, constantly boring, examining, searching. "Okay, then who can I find for you, Muse?"

Goose bumps spread down my arms as though he touched me when he said my name. He didn't, of course, but he might as well have.

Who the hell is this guy? And what the hell is wrong with me?

Maybe the stress has finally driven me over the edge. Or maybe it's just been so long since I've connected with someone—*really connected*—that I'm making more out of this than there actually is. Either way, it's not a good thing. I can't be thinking like this, *feeling* like this. There are more important things I need to focus on.

I clear my throat, mentally shaking off the spell that his eyes are weaving around me. "A man."

One dark brow shoots up. "A man, huh? Who is he?"

"A . . . friend," I hedge, not wanting to give him any more information than I absolutely have to. It's too dangerous.

He nods slowly again. "And does this man know you're looking for him?"

"Probably." Surely my father would know that I'd come looking for him when I didn't get a response.

"And does this man have a . . . significant other that I should know about?"

I frown. "A significant other?" I'm confused.

"Yes. Wife, girlfriend? *Boy*friend?"

"No, but why would that matter?"

"Just wondering if I'm likely to run into an angry lover along the way."

"What?" And then it dawns on me what he must think. "No! God no! It's not like that."

"No? Then how is it?"

"This guy is older."

Jasper raises his hands in surrender. "Hey, I don't judge."

"No, no, I mean . . . He—he's not *that kind* of a friend."

He watches me wordlessly, neither refuting nor accepting my explanation. "I'll need some information, of course. A place to start."

"Okay. Whatever you need."

He glances around. "Is now a good time?"

As much as parts of me would like to, I can't hide in the back forever. Melanie probably still has no idea I'm gone. "Well . . . not really. Can we, uh, can we meet after work?"

Jasper glances down at a chunky black watch. It looks like something a Navy SEAL or someone like that would wear, something that tells time in a million countries and can synchronize with a death squad. "I've got some things I need to do. Can I come by your apartment later?"

I find myself frowning. Again. "How do you know I live in an apartment?" Jasper gives me a withering look that says, *Really?* "Oh, right. I'm sure you . . . looked into me first." On the one hand, the thought makes me feel a tad violated, like my privacy has been compromised. But, perversely, on the other hand I find it a little thrilling to think that he might've been by my place, that he might've watched me from afar. Were my blinds not fully closed? Did he see me eating breakfast or getting dressed?

I shiver in response. That's twisted, but no more twisted than the way I'm reacting to the mere thought of being stalked by the likes of him.

I doubt that's the case anyway, what with all that information being obtainable via the Internet, but still . . . it's possible.

"Tonight then?" he prompts.

"Oh, uh, yeah. That would be fine. I'll be there."

"I'll see you later, then."

I give him a tight, cool smile, anything to belie the jittery, anxious, excited feeling that's jumping from synapse to synapse.

I watch Jasper as he walks away, noting everything from the liquid way he moves to the way the light gleams off his short, inky-black hair. My entire being seems to slump when he disappears from sight, the absence of him bringing an empty chill over me.

I've never met someone more stimulating and handsome and intriguing than Jasper King. I've never met someone who makes me want to ask so many questions. And I've never met someone who makes me feel like I'll never get any of the answers.

FOUR

Jasper

Lilac. I smell it as I raise my hand to knock on the closed door of her apartment. It's like a delicate shroud that surrounds her, permeating the air wherever she is. It reminds me of a small town that I traveled through just outside Paris. It had somehow remained untouched by most things modern, a single white thread in an otherwise dingy, yellowed tapestry.

It takes Muse almost two full minutes to answer the door. She flings it open and glares at me, pulling her flamboyant turquoise and pink robe tighter around her waist. She's angry again. Not only can I see it in her eyes, it's there in every rigid line of her body as well.

She starts in without preamble. "You'll have to excuse the way I'm dressed. Silly me, but I just *assumed* you'd come by at a decent hour."

"Are you always like this?" I ask.

Another frown. "Like what?"

"So high-strung."

Her mouth drops open in aggrieved surprise. "I am *not* high-strung."

To this, I say nothing. I like that I throw her off yet she still grapples for control. I like that she's so rigid around me when everything else about her screams that she's dying to let go. I like that she fights. I like that a lot. And I like her fire. Everything about my life is cold and calculated. Sometimes fire feels good.

"Well, as to your complaint, *I* can still be decent at this hour, but if *you* feel the need to be *indecent*, don't let me stop you."

"I didn't . . . that's not what I . . . grrrr. Just come in," she snips, standing to one side of the opening. When I walk past her, I inhale her clean, floral smell. It's definitely lilac, but there's a darker, muskier undertone that takes it from innocent to seductive. I can't imagine a scent more perfectly suiting a woman, suiting *this* woman, with her brisk mood swings and complete inability to hide what she's feeling. She's hot and cold, fire and ice, sexy and wholesome. She couldn't be any more different than me if she tried, and I find it oddly refreshing. For the most part, people are predictable, but not this woman. I get the feeling she's *anything but* predictable.

I wait for her to shut the door and I follow Muse into a cozy living room. The palate of the room is surprisingly bland with its dark hardwoods and grayish furniture, but it makes her use (and obvious love) of color that much more noticeable. From the bold red throw pillows to the various sizes and shapes of vibrant paintings scattered all over her walls, I'd wager that Muse has bled all over this room, right from the bottom of her soul.

I cross to a fireplace that apparently hasn't worked in some time. The cool cavern of its interior is clean and holds a couple dozen ivory candles rather than wood. But that's not what draws me. It's the painting that rests above it, propped on the mantel to lean against the wall.

The piece depicts a tree, one simple tree, but it's the way the branches list to one side and hang downward that catches my eye. When I look closer, I see that pale yellow raindrops trickle from the dark leaves like tears, falling into puddles on the ground. Those shallow pools reflect a half-full moon suspended in a midnight sky. The image, while stunning in its use of contrasting color and shadow, is poignant and somehow tragic.

I turn to find Muse watching me. She doesn't look angry anymore; she looks . . . nervous.

"What's the matter? Afraid I'll see too much?"

She raises her chin and tries to act nonchalant. "I don't know what you mean."

"Do you still feel this way?"

"What way?"

"The way you felt when you painted that?" I ask, nodding toward the mantel.

Her eyes widen and her mouth drops open for a tenth of a second before she snaps it shut. "How . . . how did you know that I . . . ?"

"I'm observant."

"But . . ." She glances at the canvas behind my head as if searching for what gave the artist away. What she probably can't see, what probably *no* artist *can* see, is that she is all over that painting. All over it and all *in it*.

"Do you?" I prompt, returning to my question.

Her eyes flick back to mine and she shrugs with one shoulder, her toes digging rhythmically into the plush pile of the area rug. "Sometimes." Her voice is quiet. Small. She looks quickly away from my eyes.

"What made you feel that way?"

"I miss the people I love." Her eyes make their way back to mine, a ghost of a frown floating across her forehead. "Doesn't everyone?"

It's my turn to shrug. "I guess if you have people you love."
Before she can say anything else, I get down to brass tacks. "So, tell
me about this man you're hoping to find."

She takes a deep breath. Sighs. "His name is Denton Allen
Harper. He lives in Treeborn, South Carolina."

"Job?"

"He's retired from the military. He consults for some private
security firm now and then, but . . ."

"What is his relationship to you?" Her lips thin. She doesn't
want me to ask personal questions. And that only makes me want
to ask them even more. "Look, if you want me to find the guy, you
need to be honest with me." When she still hesitates, I add, "It's
not like I'm a cop or anything, if he's into something illegal."

"It's not that. He's not a criminal, for God's sake!" she defends.
"He's a good man."

"You sure about that?"

"Of course I'm sure. He—he's my father."

I nod. "How long has it been since you've talked to him?"

"A month. A month ago Friday."

"Just a month? I take it that's unusual."

"Yes. We have a . . . routine, sort of. We talk once a month, like
clockwork."

"A month ago Friday. Obviously you've tried calling over the
last five days." She nods. "You've tried his friends, associates, people
who might know where he is?"

"Ummm, not really. I mean I can't really . . . I can't . . . It's
complicated, but I know that if everything was okay, he'd have
been there when I called."

"Been where? At home? On his cell phone? Where?"

"Where he is when we talk."

"Which is . . . ?" She doesn't answer. I study her in silence for two full minutes, long enough to make her fidget uncomfortably. "You realize that the more you keep from me, the less likely it is that I'll find him."

"I thought you could find anyone. In fact, didn't you say you were damn good at it?"

"I did. And I am, but I'm not a psychic. I still need something to go on."

"And I gave you that. I'm telling you everything I know that might help you find him."

"Where do you call once a month?"

She breathes out noisily, obviously perturbed. "We use pay phones, but they're all in different places around Treeborn." Muse shakes her head, her thick hair teasing her shoulders. "Look, that's not important. What's important is that he wasn't there when I called and he *always* is. Something is wrong and I want you to find him."

"Why not just call the police? Place a missing persons report? It's been long enough."

"I can't . . . We . . . That's just not an option. That's why I'm hiring you. You do this for a living. You should be able to find him, right?"

I pause. "Yes. I can find him. It just might take me a few days."

"A few days? Is that all?"

"Yeah, I think so. Doesn't sound too complicated. That's after I get there, of course."

"Which will be . . . when? Will you fly out tomorrow?"

"No, I'll drive."

"Drive? You're going to drive from San Diego to South Carolina?"

"Yes. Is that a problem?"

"I . . . No, I don't suppose. I'm just . . . surprised is all."

"Does it matter how I get there?"

"No, not really. It's just that . . . the thing is, I want to go with you."

This I wasn't expecting. Maybe she really *is* unpredictable. "And why is that? If I need something from you, I can call."

"Because I need to see him, I need to talk to him. Face-to-face."

I say nothing for a while. I couldn't be happier with this turn of events, but, obviously, I can't let Muse know that. Finally, I speak to lay down some ground rules. "I'll agree to that on a few conditions."

She arches one smooth brow. "Which are?"

"I work alone. If I let you tag along, don't expect me to include you in details, conversations, or sources. Don't expect me to answer a bunch of questions or explain why I do the things I do. Just trust that I'll find your father. I'll find him and I'll take you to him. If you do that, let me do my job, no questions asked, we won't have any problems."

I can tell by the expression in her green-green eyes and the twitch of her full-full lips that she wants to say something. Probably argue. But she won't. I have the upper hand and she knows it. Normally, she'd probably have a lot to say, but she's controlling herself for the sake of finding her father.

"Okay. I can do that." A pause. "What about money? How much do you charge?"

"A thousand-dollar retainer. We can talk about the rest when I find him."

She blanches a little. "Okay. I . . . That'll be fine."

I don't feel guilty for taking her money. It's not like I'll be keeping it.

"Look, I know it's late. Why don't you jot down the target's last known address and telephone number so I can get to work and you can get back to . . ." I glance at what's playing on the television. "Whatever that is."

"It's *Dirty Dancing*."

"Am I supposed to know what that is?"

"It's a classic," she defends weakly.

"By whose standards?"

"Mine. And every other woman, girl and child who has ever seen it."

"Whatever you say," I rejoin mildly. "While you're at it, I'll need the make and model of his car and where he spent his last vacation. And the names of any companions he spends time with."

She nods and turns to leave the room. She stops in the doorway where the hardwoods give way to tile. I assume it's the entrance to the kitchen. Her sober eyes plead with mine. "Please don't call him 'the target.' He's the most important person in my life. The only thing I have left in the world." With that, she disappears around the corner.

And just like that, I feel the first pang of guilt that I've had in seven long years.

FIVE

Muse

By seven in the morning, I'm perched on the edge of the couch, watching the street through the filmy black scarves that cover my living room window. I've been sitting here for eleven minutes, mainly because I slept very little and have been up since five packing. I had no idea what kind of clothes I might need. I mean will this be like a spy movie where we'll be sneaking around, all covert and stuff? Will we be visiting questionable biker bars and beating information out of lowlifes? Or is this a case of I watch too much television, our trip will be nothing like that and I'll spend a lot of time in the car? I don't know because Jasper didn't tell me. *Big surprise!* And I've never had to search for someone like this before—or *hire someone* to search for someone like this either—so I packed a little of everything plus a couple of days' worth of travel clothes. That's the one thing I could find out for sure. We'll be on the road for approximately thirty-six hours. *That* requires a lot of yoga pants.

My phone rings in my hand. It's my boss, Miran. I called her to tell her I need some time off. Her return call reminds me that I forgot my charger. I answer as I scramble up the steps to retrieve it. "Hello?"

"Are you okay? Are you hurt? Are you in jail? Did you get mugged?" comes the machine gun–like fire of questions.

"Yes, no, no and no," I reply.

I hear her sigh of relief. "Thank God. It's too early to be bailing someone out of jail." I hear the rustle of covers and I can imagine the tiny blonde burrowing back down into the obscenely thick goose down comforter that covers her bed.

"I wouldn't call so early if it weren't important, but . . . I hired someone to find the Colonel. And I'm going with him." I brace myself for her outburst, but it never comes.

Miran knows my father, which is why he sent me here when I had to leave Treeborn. Without giving me a single detail about their relationship, he gave me her phone number and address and told me that he trusted her, then he sent me on my way. But trust works like that for the Colonel. He trusts sparingly, yet when he does, it means something. In fact, it means everything. That's how *I* trust *him*. Implicitly. Without question or hesitation. And that's how I now trust Miran.

She doesn't know everything that happened, and she's never tried to find out. She just took me in because the Colonel asked her to. End of story. But she knows enough to realize that going back to South Carolina is *not* something I should be doing. My father would kill me and she knows it. Yet she hasn't said a word.

The line is so quiet, I wonder if she's hung up or fallen back to sleep. "Miran? Are you there?"

"You know he'll be furious."

"Yes."

"And you know he'd expect me to stop you."

"Yes."

"But I won't because I love him, too. And if he were my father, I'd do the same thing."

I smile. I have no doubts she would. Miran is the type who would fight to the death for those she loves. And she'd fight dirty, too. She might be little, but what she lacks in stature she more than makes up for in ferocity. Obviously, she and her daughter are polar opposites. Melanie is two steps up from a slug.

"I appreciate that."

"Just promise me one thing."

"Anything," I respond. And I mean it. In the short time I've known her, Miran has become a bit of a mother figure to me and there isn't much I wouldn't do for her.

"Be careful. If something doesn't feel right, turn tail and haul ass. I know some people. If it gets ugly, you call me."

I know some people. I shudder to think what kind of people she'd send to help me, people fiercer than she is.

"Okay. I will." I have no idea how she (or the people she knows) could help me if I get into trouble two thousand miles away, but if it makes her feel better . . .

"Who did you hire, by the way? To find him, I mean. A private investigator or something?"

"No. Actually he's a bounty hunter. I guess he does stuff like this on the side. He's a friend of a friend."

"What's his name?"

I roll my eyes as I grab my charger from the dresser drawer in my bedroom. Miran thinks she knows everybody. Or at least that she knows everybody worth knowing.

"Jasper King."

"J—" She barely utters the consonant before she stops abruptly. I hear more rustling followed by Miran's low voice. "Keep your guard up, Muse, you hear me?"

I frown at the steps as I descend them. Her tone is different, more alert, more sincere. More dire. "I will. There's no need to worry, Miran. He's a friend of Tracey's."

"That girl wouldn't know a decent guy if he bit her in the ass."

"No, but she's probably known a lot of guys who *have* bit her in the ass," I tease with a grin. Tracey likes sex and she likes men. The combination of the two tends to blind her to some of the more important facts, like whether he's married. Or a criminal.

But Jasper doesn't seem like a criminal. Surely he couldn't be a bounty hunter if he was. They work with law enforcement. Surely they're . . . regulated somehow. I figure I'm safe. All set. I'm paying him to do a job. He'll do it. End of story.

"I'm not kidding, Muse. You be careful."

"I will, I will. Try not to worry. I'll call you in a couple of days."

I stuff my charger in one of the zippered compartments of my suitcase. My fingers pause mid-zip when I hear Miran's next words.

"I love you, kid. I'll be mad as hell if you mess around and get yourself killed."

"Miran, why in the—" A knock at the door pulls me up short. I rush to the window and see a sleek, black Mercedes sedan parked at the curb. "I've gotta go. I'll call you when I get there, 'kay?"

"Leave your phone on and make sure it's charged at all times, got it?"

"I know, I know."

"Be safe. I'll see you when you get back. Give my love to the Colonel."

"I will. And, Miran?"

"Yeah, babe?"

"I love you, too."

With that, I hang up and reach for the doorknob. I can't help noticing the fine tremor in my hand and the slight tingle down my spine. I try to use reason and common sense to talk myself into a calmer state.

I was uptight yesterday. I'm sure he's not nearly as heart-stopping as I thought he was. No man can be that gorgeous, that sexy, that intense.

I take a deep, cleansing breath and I swing open the door.

And realize how very, *very* wrong I am.

Standing on my stoop is a man that is quite possibly even more disturbingly handsome than he was yesterday. His arms are crossed over his broad chest, a casual gesture that belies an unmistakable impatience I feel rolling off him.

"Ready?" he asks in a no-nonsense way that fits him as perfectly as the lightweight black T-shirt he's wearing. The long sleeves are pushed up his forearms, revealing golden skin, ropes of sleek muscle and thick, bulging veins. I've never wanted to stare at forearms before today.

I feel my frown appear again. I'm baffled that anything could distract me so much from my worries, yet it seems that every millisecond that I'm around Jasper, my focus is pulled inexorably in his direction. He fills my thoughts and warms my blood. I suppose I should be thankful for something to take my mind off my concerns, but Jasper is almost *too* consuming. If he affects me this way when I've got so much else to consider, God help me when I don't.

"Hello?" he prompts, bending slightly to put his face in my line of sight.

I shake off my thrall. Or at least I try to. "Sorry. Yes, I'm ready."

I roll my suitcase over the threshold and turn to lock the door behind me. "Got someone to feed your fish for a few days?"

"I don't have fish."

"Cat, then?"

"I don't have a cat."

"Then what kind of pet do you have? You look like a woman who likes animals."

"I do?" I ask when I finally turn to face him, which is a mistake. Jasper's heavy-lidded amber eyes are strolling down my body, studying me in such a way that I feel naked before him, like he's peeling off clothes as he goes.

When they rise slowly back to my face, he answers. "You do. Like maybe you'd take in all the strays. Let them sleep in your warm bed."

I steel myself against the little shiver that trembles through me at his words. The way he said "warm bed," like he wants to be there, too . . . Holy Lord!

I swallow the cotton in my mouth and focus on his observation, which happens to be accurate. All but the bed part.

When I was younger, I'd beg the Colonel to let me keep every animal I stumbled across. He always agreed, but after a few weeks (or sometimes just a few days), they'd disappear and I'd never see them again. I'd search for days and days, hang fliers all over whichever base we were stationed at, but they never turned up. They were just . . . gone.

My father would console me, take me for ice cream, promise me that I'd forget about each one, but I never did. It wasn't until I got older that I began to see a pattern. He never admitted it and I never asked, but I knew that the Colonel was doing something with them. It gives me a cold chill down my spine just to think about it, about what he might've done to all those sweet little animals that he didn't want. I finally stopped bringing them home. I knew they'd have a better chance of survival if I didn't, so I'd sneak off after school and on the weekends to feed them and play with them, wherever they happened to be holed up. It never stopped me from loving them or wanting to take them in. It only stopped me from letting it show.

"Well, I haven't been here very long, and . . . and I'm not sure how long I'll stay, so . . ."

"I would've taken you for the roots kind."

"Most people are the roots kind, aren't they?"

"Most," he answers flatly.

I tilt my head to one side to consider him—the warm skin at home in the sun, the raven hair still wet from a shower, the whiskey eyes that seem both hot and cold all at once. "But not you." It's not a question. It's an observation. One he doesn't bother to refute. He only watches me quietly.

"We'd better get going," he finally says. With that, he picks up my busting-at-the-seams suitcase like it's light as air and starts off down the sidewalk, leaving me to follow in his mysterious wake.

SIX

Jasper

I'm comfortable in the quiet. In fact, I prefer it. I thought I'd made the rules of this road trip clear to Muse in advance.

Evidently I didn't make them clear *enough*.

"So, how did you get started in this kind of work?" Muse asks after less than an hour in.

I shrug. "Just sort of fell into it, I guess."

"How does one fall into bounty hunting?"

"If you have the right skill set . . ."

"And how did you come by the 'right skill set'?"

I sigh. Loud enough for her to hear. "I thought you weren't going to ask questions."

"I thought you said not to ask questions about your methods. You didn't say *anything* about asking questions about *you*."

"I like the quiet," I tell her. She takes the hint.

Two hours later, I can tell she's about to bust. She has filed her nails, organized some sort of list on her phone, cleaned out her purse and turned the radio on at least twice. Each time, I've turned it off.

Muse reaches down to pull off her shoes and tuck her feet up under her on the seat. "This is a nice car. Not quite what I pictured you driving."

"It's a long trip. I thought you'd appreciate a comfortable ride."

I see her head jerk toward me. "You did this for me?"

I glance in her direction. "Don't look so surprised. I'm not completely heartless."

"I—I didn't say you were heartless."

"No, but you were thinking it."

She doesn't argue.

Just after a quick and silent lunch of burgers and fries right outside Tucson, she tries again. "Where'd you get that watch? It looks like something a sniper would wear."

I glance at the black square on my wrist. Not a sniper's watch, but . . .

When I don't answer, she asks more directly, "Were you in the military?"

"Yes," I answer grudgingly.

Encouraged by my answer, she turns in her seat to face me. "Really? What branch?"

"The Army."

"My father served in the Army. He went in because his father and both his brothers served. Did you have family in the military, too? Father? Brothers or sisters?"

I grit my teeth. These are not things that I want to think about, much less talk about. "I really need you to find something else to do with your time. I'm not the talkative, sharing type." I twitch my head to the right and see the wounded slant to her big green eyes. I sigh again and turn back to the road. "Look, I'm not trying to be rude. I'm just being honest."

After a few seconds of silence, I glance back over at her. The twin emeralds are flashing. "Well then let *me* be honest with *you*. It's been a really shitty year for me and now my father is missing. I can't stand sitting here with nothing but time to think about what I might find back home. I'm sorry if polite conversation isn't in your repertoire, but maybe, *just maybe*, you could make an exception *just this once*." Her voice is louder, punchier at the end and I know her temper is on the rise.

Fire.

Damn, I'm liking that!

"I'm doing you a favor, Muse. You don't want to get to know me."

"Maybe I do. You can't possibly know that."

"Maybe I don't *want* you to," I confess quietly.

I hear her huff of frustration before she flounces back in her seat, crossing her arms stiffly over her chest and turning to stare out the window.

She's better off *not* knowing me. She just doesn't know it.

SEVEN

Muse

It's dark when we arrive at our stopping point for the night. I'm relieved to be off the highway.

I ache. Mentally and physically. From too much stillness, I think. The only physical exertion I got all day was wallowing around in the passenger seat, taking two pee breaks and getting out to stretch while Jasper was in the drive-through at lunch. Mentally, the only stimulation I got was wrestling with my own private, tumultuous thoughts. Jasper provided me with . . . well, nothing. Nothing but the services of a chauffer and a heaping dose of frustration.

I've met guarded men before, but none quite so extreme as Jasper. He doesn't even want to share in conversation about other things, mundane things. It's like he doesn't want to participate in life, get even politely close to anybody. Or at least that's the impression I'm getting so far.

Anxious to be able to stand and move, I practically leap out of the car when Jasper parks outside the hotel he chose for the night.

We're on the outskirts of El Paso, a town I've never had the pleasure of visiting. It *could be* a fun and interesting night, a nice diversion from my worries and inner turmoil, but since I'm with a stick in the mud, my expectation now is to crash in my room and be back on the road at an obscene hour.

"You're a terrible road tripper, by the way," I tell Jasper bluntly as I wait for him to come around the front of the car so we can register at the hotel.

"And why is that?"

"You're about as stimulating as a goat. We didn't even play stupid road trip games or anything!"

I wasn't expecting a deep philosophical discussion on the way, but a fun game of "punch buggy" or "ninety-nine bottles of beer on the wall" might've helped ease my mind a little.

He doesn't even glance at me when he responds, just starts off toward the hotel lobby. "A goat? I'm crushed."

I strike out after him, still fussing. "As well you should be. The least you could do is make some small talk occasionally. I mean, *God*!"

He startles a yelp out of me when he stops suddenly and turns toward me. "I didn't realize you needed stimulation. Maybe you should've made your expectations clear from the outset." I crash into his chest and stumble backward. He reaches out to grab my upper arms, hauling me up against him to keep me from falling.

I gasp at the electricity in his touch, in the feel of his body pressed so firmly to mine. My front, from my nipples to my navel, is hot and tingly and . . . aware. Too aware.

His eyes burn down into mine. He's so close I can see the black of his pupils explode to eclipse the amber of his irises. Whatever I'm feeling, it's affecting him, too.

I struggle to keep my wits about me. It's a struggle I lose. His nearness is too much. His emotion, something he has showed so little of, is too overwhelming.

"I . . . I . . ." I don't know what to say. His reaction is so surprising that I'm struck temporarily speechless. I hold his gaze, let it wash over me until I see the golden orbs flicker to my mouth. I lick my suddenly dry lips and when his eyes return to mine, they're full of fire of a *different* kind.

"While I've got you here," he snarls, "might as well get this out of the way."

With no other warning, Jasper lowers his head and crushes my mouth with his own. He's so forceful, so . . . angry, that I remain stiff in his arms. Until the moment that I begin to taste the *real* Jasper, the Jasper that he hides beneath his gruff exterior.

I taste softening in the way his fingers loosen their grip. They caress rather than restrain, coerce rather than demand.

I taste dominance in the way his lips move over mine. He is in control, but he is sure to make certain I enjoy every second of it.

I taste acquiescence in the way he groans into my mouth. He didn't want this, but like me, he can no longer resist it. There's something between us, something that has a life of its own.

And, finally, I taste desire in the way his tongue slips inside to tangle with mine. He is heat, he is gravity. He is the center of all my senses. He is consuming.

Just like those few seconds when he first walked into my life yesterday morning, life ceases to exist outside his presence. He took my breath away then and he's taking my breath away now. There are no fears, no reservations, no other people. There is only Jasper and this insane attraction I feel for him. He is wild and raw, dangerous and tempting. He's a sleek, powerful animal, seeking to thrill and to destroy. He overcomes, he devours, he possesses. He refuses to share his kill with anything else. For a heartbeat, I'm his. His prey. Not necessarily willing, just helpless to fight against him.

And then, God help me, I respond. My body takes over and I lose myself in this kiss, in this moment. In this man. I arch my back, pressing my aching breasts into his chest. With every muscle, every nerve, every fiber, I strain toward him, drinking him in with my body, my soul, my mouth. Unwittingly, I unleash the animal I thought I'd already seen.

With a fierceness echoed in the growl that trembles into my open mouth, Jasper spins, plastering my back to one of the large, concrete columns that support the overhang. He tilts his head and deepens the kiss to a level I've never been before, to a height, to a depth, to an intensity I've never known. He punishes me with the pressure of his body, but he soothes me with the soft lick of his tongue. I feel him everywhere. Within, without, penetrating, radiating.

The kiss comes to a slow, tantalizing end that makes me want to whimper when Jasper breaks the contact. And then I'm free. Free to breathe, free to speak. Free to think and see and hear, but I don't. I don't do any of those things. I can only feel, like the residual sting of a burn. A burn so good.

"Jesus H. Christ!" he mumbles, rasping his cheek over mine, his breath tickling my ear.

I want to beg him for more. I want to know what he's thinking. Why he did that. What's to become of me since meeting him. Because I know I won't ever be quite the same. I have no reason to suspect that, only pure intuition. A feeling. A *strong* one.

He raises his head, but he doesn't push me away, which further surprises me. He just stands, holding me against him, staring down into my eyes.

I watch Jasper watch me, both of us reeling from the heat of that kiss. But then, to my bewildered amazement, I see his expression harden little by little until I can't see what he's feeling anymore. I just watched him bury it. Purposefully. Resolutely. The strange this is, I know it's still there.

It has to be.

Doesn't it?

"Let's go get a couple of rooms," he says in a hoarse voice.

The Jasper of moments ago is now hidden, hidden beneath a matter-of-fact exterior, smothered beneath unruffled feathers. Meanwhile, my world is still rocked and my feathers are still standing on end all over my body.

What the hell just happened?

I've never witnessed such absolute control. It's a bit mindboggling, which is why I pay no attention to the muted greens of the lobby or the broad smile of the twentysomething girl behind the counter when we enter the lobby. It's also why I pay no attention to what Jasper is saying or how the clerk responds. I stand off to myself, a few feet behind him. Thinking.

I'm spinning with sensation, which opens the door to *more* sensation. Thoughts war, feelings battle, guilt descends. I realize with utter dismay that I forgot all about my father, all about my woes twice within a thirty-six hour period. Granted it was only for a few seconds, but that doesn't make me feel any better. What kind of woman lets a man so totally consume her?

One who's never met a man like Jasper.

I'm shaken from my troublesome musings when the object of my turmoil turns and hands me a thin envelope with a number scribbled on the front. "You can have 213. It has a view of the pool."

"Where will you be?"

"Right next door, beside the stairwell." Something tells me he arranged that on purpose. I bet he's one of those guys who likes to sit facing the door in a restaurant, too. It makes me wonder all the more what goes on inside his head. I can't imagine a more complex man. "You can go on up. I'll get our stuff."

I nod, wanting to say something, but knowing it will do me no good. Besides, I don't even know what I'd say. I have only questions. Lots and lots of questions. And Jasper is anything *except* willing to answer them.

I let myself into the cool comfort of my room. I walk to the window and push aside the thin sheer to gaze down at the rectangle of lighted water below. I don't jump when I hear a knock. I was expecting it.

I open the door for Jasper, but he only leans in enough to set my suitcase on the carpeting and give me a curt, "I want to pull out at seven. Be ready." Then he turns, black duffel thrown over his shoulder, and lets himself into his own room.

When his door closes with a soft click, I mutter, "No, no don't worry about me. I'll just order up some room service. But thank you *soooo* much for asking."

I *do* jump, however, when Jasper's door flies open and he pokes his head out. "What was that?"

I just stare at him, wide-eyed and slack-jawed, for a good thirty seconds before I shake my head and duck back inside my own room, closing the door and leaning against it.

Moves like a tiger. Hears like a superhero. What next? Can the guy climb walls?

Determined to push my frustrating neighbor out of my thoughts in favor of more important concerns, I unpack a few things and get settled before ordering something to eat. I let my mind flow once more to the Colonel and what might've happened. Considering that I moved across the country to keep him safe, my distress over his absence is understandable.

Normally, I wouldn't think anything about not being able to reach him for a few days. Aside from the fact that he stays pretty busy, the man hates cell phones. He says they're just another tool that can be hacked and used to violate our rights by those with bad intentions. I've always chalked his paranoia up to the time he spent in the military. Although he never told me much about what he did, it was easy to deduce that it was highly classified. Most people talk about work, at least in a generic way, but not my dad. He's been tight-lipped and guarded (about work, anyway) for as long as I can remember.

I glance over at my phone where it rests on the nightstand. For the millionth time, I contemplate calling Dad at home, but I stop myself. That could end in disaster for him if anyone found out.

Trapped with only my fearful imaginings and the quiet to keep me company, I wander over to the window, parting the curtain to stare out into the darkness. Movement, something disturbing the brilliant blue surface of the water below me, draws my eye. I watch as a lone swimmer cuts through the water with long, powerful strokes, pausing only briefly at each end of the pool before starting back again.

I study the form absently until it stops in the deep end, shaking water from short, dark hair and laying muscular arms along the coping as he rests. That's the very moment when the curling of something warm and inviting in my stomach alerts me to the identity of the swimmer. It's Jasper. Despite the darkness, despite the distance, I know it's him as surely as I know there's carpet beneath my feet and cool glass against my palm.

Without giving it a single thought, I grab my room key and head for the elevator. Following the signage, I make my way to the exit, moving quietly across the cobble decking to perch on the end of a lounger that parallels the pool. Jasper is swimming again, head down, arms slicing ruthlessly through the sapphire liquid like he's got something to prove to it.

Tirelessly, Jasper decimates lap after lap of the rectangle, never pausing in his rhythm until he stops again at the deep end. From my seat, I can hear his ragged breathing. I don't announce my presence. I'm not done watching him.

Finally, after another minute, Jasper plants his palms flat on the edge of the pool and lifts himself effortlessly from the water. The muscles in his back and arms glide under his slick skin like monsters, writhing to break free. When he turns, his eyes come straight to mine. There is no surprise in them, like he knew I was here all along.

Strong and confident, he walks toward me. His legs are long and muscular, encased in dark shorts that plaster to their length as they eat up the distance. I drag my gaze upward, past the granite ridges of his stomach, past the rounded hills of his pecs, stopping only when I reach the black tangle of a tattoo that dominates the right side of his upper body.

When Jasper stops in front of me, I don't bother to hide my stare. I'm too intrigued by the body art to even try. Underneath the water droplets that glisten on his skin, diamonds scattered over smooth bronze, is a series of mean, thorny-looking vines that twist and turn across his right shoulder and upper arm, extending inward onto part of his chest.

Finally, I raise my eyes to his. They're dark and fathomless in the night, causing a shiver to tremble through me. I wrap my arms around my middle, feigning a chill.

I want to ask about the tattoo, but I know I won't get any satisfaction so I don't bother.

"Is the water cold?" I ask casually instead.

"Is that what you came down here to ask me?" he rebuts dubiously.

"I didn't come down here to ask you anything."

"Liar," he whispers.

Jasper is standing so close that I can smell his skin. It doesn't smell like soap or chlorine or sweat or cologne. It just smells . . .

delicious. Natural. Like salt mixed with the barest hint of musk. It's light, but somehow . . . feral. Nearly imperceptible, yet my body is honing in on it as though it's the only thing I can smell at all. Anywhere. Ever. His scent, his closeness is robbing me of my ability to breathe, to think, to *fight*.

I grit my teeth and strengthen my resolve. It's not right that I should be thinking this way, feeling this way. I can't let this guy get under my skin. There's too much at stake, too many other things to worry about. Plus something tells me getting involved with him— *really involved* with him—would be a disaster. At least *for me* it would.

I straighten my spine. "Fine, I *did* want to ask you something."

Jasper crosses his arms over his chest, drawing my eye to the bulge of his bicep. *God, he's built like a dream!* "Well?"

"Why—why did you kiss me?"

"I told you I wanted to get it out of the way."

"I know what you said, but what did you mean by that?"

"We're attracted to each other. I figured it would be best to just get that kiss over with so we're not constantly distracted by thinking about it."

I should be insulted. I should deny what he's saying. But all I can think about is that he's attracted to me, too, and that he's been thinking about kissing me. And how wrong it is that I should care.

"Well," I begin, hating that my voice sounds breathy. "In that case, thank you. I've got plenty to worry about without adding *you* to the mix."

I'm surprised when I see one side of Jasper's mouth quirk into what looks dangerously close to a lopsided grin. "You'd only need to worry about me if you needed something to take your mind off your troubles for a while."

"And why is that?"

I hold my breath as I await his answer, anticipation coiling in my stomach like a slippery, slithering snake.

"Because that's exactly what I'd do. I'd distract you. I'd give you so many things to focus on, so many things to *feel* that you wouldn't have enough energy to think about anything else. That's all I can offer, but what I offer, I excel at providing."

I inhale on a soft gasp.

It's a promise. An invitation. A wicked temptation that I can't afford right now. *Why did you ask him that question? Why did you have to know? Stupid, stupid, stupid!*

"Lucky for you, I don't want a distraction. I need to concentrate. This is too important."

"I won't say that's lucky for me. I'll say that's lucky *for you*."

"And why is that?"

He gives me a long, penetrating look. "I'm probably the worst thing in the world for you. The worst thing that would *feel like* the best." Just when I'm pretty sure my heart is going to leap out of my chest, Jasper moves to step around me. "See you in the morning, Muse."

And then he's gone, leaving me alone in the dark with thoughts I've got no business thinking.

EIGHT

Jasper

When I hear the gunshot, I'm out of bed and on my feet, holding my 9mm before the sleep clears from my eyes. I never rest very soundly. Occupational hazard, I guess.

My brain recognizes immediately that the shot was close, but not too close to me. No immediate threat.

A quick scan of my room tells me that nothing is amiss. My next thought is of the person sleeping a thin wall away, and that she might be in danger. I knew it was a possibility.

I grab the two keys on the nightstand on my way out the door.

Quietly, I let myself into Muse's room. Rapidly, I swing open the door and then shut it behind me just as quickly, ducking into the corner in case she's not alone. The light would've blinded any intruders and since they didn't get a shot off, it would take their eyes a minute to readjust to the dark.

I hear movement to my left. Even if I couldn't see the long waves of hair touching breasts covered in white, I'd know it to be Muse. I can smell her.

I move silently toward her, tucking her behind me and pressing her to the wall. Out of harm's way.

I survey the room, my eyes accustomed to seeing in low light. Nothing seems out of the ordinary. I don't smell gunpowder. I don't sense danger. There is no one in here except Muse.

Muse. I can feel every inch of her imprinted on my back. All I'd have to do is turn and take her in my arms and I could have my fill of her tonight. She wouldn't resist.

But I'm not *that* much of a bastard.

I *do* turn to face her, but I don't touch her. "Sorry if I scared you."

"You didn't," she pants.

I glance down her body. I can see her chest heaving, lush mounds pressing against the pale material of her tank top. One thin, silvery beam of moonlight creates a shadow from the stiff peaks of her nipples. My mouth waters reflexively. "Liar," I whisper.

My cock stirs, a sign of my lapse in control. A rare occurrence for me.

It's been a long time since I've wanted someone this bad. I'm all about restraint, so I wait until it's convenient to slake my baser needs. Convenient, easy, no attachments. That's my type. Or more my MO. I steer away from complications. And this one is about as complicated as they come, especially for me.

"Okay, fine, you scared the shit out of me. What are you doing? And how did you get in here?"

"I heard a gunshot."

"I heard it, too."

"I came to check on you."

"Oh," she says simply.

She pauses, looking up at me with her big wide eyes. I see the shiny tip of her pink tongue sneak out to wet her lips. I can still taste those lips, that tongue. Still feel the untamed response I got when I kissed her. She's all sweet allure and wild abandon mixed with the irresistible tang of forbidden fruit. Unfortunately for her, I've never let the forbidden, the taboo stop me from taking what I want. But something about taking advantage of a woman who I'm using this way . . . well, even someone *like me* finds that hard to swallow.

"Now that I know you're okay," I begin, backing up a step and sticking my gun in my shorts, at the curve of my lower back. "I'll let you get back to sleep."

"H-how did you get in here?" she asks again, stepping toward me as I head for the door.

"A key. They gave you two. I kept one."

"Wow. Thanks for asking."

"I don't often ask permission for anything I do. I hope that doesn't offend you."

"And if it does?"

I shrug. "Then this isn't going to be a particularly pleasant trip for you."

I reach for the door handle.

"Wait." I pause. "You can stay, you know."

"Are you *asking* me to stay?"

She moves back toward the bed, fiddling with her fingers as she goes. "I'm just saying that I trust you not to do anything. I mean, it's not like you can't just come in here whenever you want anyway."

I consider it. It would be so easy . . .

"We both need sleep."

She tilts her head to one side, her long, fiery hair falling over one breast. It's a sexy pose. She probably has no idea just *how* sexy.

"I promise not to keep you awake."

"I can't sleep in the room with someone else."

NINE

Muse

When dawn slices through the clouds, I'm still awake, staring at the ceiling. My body only stopped tingling about an hour ago. For the longest time after Jasper left, I could feel every solid muscle, every warm plane as though my front was still pressed to his back. That's never happened to me before, so I just lay, spread eagle, on top of the covers for the rest of the night. I took turns reveling in the sensation and marveling over what an awful person I am for wanting Jasper so much when my father could be in danger.

I don't think I've ever been so conflicted. I don't *want* to want Jasper. I want to find my father. I want for this whole mess to resolve so I can go back home. To my *real* home. I want a lot of other things, too, but Jasper shouldn't be one of them. He's wrong for me in practically every possible way. He's aloof and stoic, he's a veritable drifter with a dangerous job, he's vague and barely even friendly. He all but admitted to being only one-night-stand material. I mean, could he be a *worse* fit for me?

Probably not.

But still . . . even considering all those cons . . . I want him. God, how I want him! He does something to me. Something powerful and visceral and irresistible. I can feel the heat beneath his cool exterior as vividly as if I were standing in front of a fire, warming my hands.

Not to mention that he's brave and protective. I never expected that. Well the bravery, maybe, but not the protectiveness. I mean, he ran to my rescue when he heard that gunshot, like some kind of hero might. My knees get weak just thinking about him standing in front of me, so tall and fearless, tucking me safely behind him while he faced what could've been a killer or a madman. But he didn't hesitate. Didn't think twice about putting himself between me and danger.

He'd probably laugh if he knew that the only thing about this situation that is offending me is my own reaction to him. It's very much against my will, but that doesn't make it any less fierce.

At just before six, I drag myself from the non-comfort of my bed and set about getting ready to leave. He said seven sharp and I plan to be ready.

Fifteen hours. We've traveled fifteen hours . . . hundreds of miles . . . and exchanged little more than a few polite words. The car has been full of silence since we left. Unfortunately, that doesn't make it empty. Quite the opposite, actually. It's full, brimming with a sensual undercurrent. It's bubbling with want and can't-have, and churning with I-wish and I-wish-I-didn't. Or at least that's how it feels to me.

Dozens of times I've caught myself watching the way Jasper so casually yet so competently grips the steering wheel. I've caught myself studying his long fingers, admiring his thick veins. Even more often, though, I've found myself sneaking glances at his strong profile, following it down the sinew of his throat to his chest, to the wide expanse wrapped to perfection in soft black cotton.

Several times, when I *haven't been* surreptitiously stalking him with my eyes, I've detected movement in my peripheral vision. I've noticed him glancing my way. Each time, he pauses for a few seconds and then looks away. But that hasn't been the bothersome part. The bothersome part has been that I could *feel* the intensity of his stare. I could feel the communication of it as clearly as though words were spoken aloud. It's been unnerving. Maddening. Worse, it's been titillating. It brings the want back tenfold.

All day, I've teetered between obsessive thoughts of the man next to me—what he's thinking, who he really is, what it would feel like to have his lips on my skin—and guilt-ridden thoughts of my father.

I did everything I could to keep him safe, the Colonel, but it's possible that wasn't enough. I reason, however, that if he were dead, I'd have been notified. He had measures in place in the event of his death. At the time, I thought it was excessively morbid, but now . . . now I'm glad he did it. It brings me some small amount of peace in an otherwise gut-wrenching time of worry.

But death isn't the only concern, isn't the only horrific circumstance. If he was just wounded or captured, no one would know to contact me. And he could be either . . . or both.

I stop myself before I can go down that road. Instead, I take some comfort in the reassurance that he's not dead. I hold on to that thought as tightly as my torn mind will allow.

Involuntarily, I shiver.

"Are you cold?" Jasper asks in his raspy voice. "I can turn on the heat."

"The heat?" I feel dazed. Confused. Addled by my chaotic thoughts. I glance around me, taking in the stretch of bland highway illuminated by the headlights. They cut through the darkness in a surgical kind of way. I make note of a sign that reads *Gamble with your money, never your time. Visit the most entertaining casino in Shreveport.*

Shreveport? It's not cold in Louisiana.

"Why would I need heat?"

"You shivered."

I turn to look at Jasper. Immediately I wish I hadn't. No matter how many times I take in his angular face, his mesmerizing eyes, his delectable mouth, I never get used to the fluttery feeling in my stomach that I get from looking at him. It's like I'm awestruck each and every time.

Right now, his face is ethereal in the reddish glow of the dashboard lights. He looks like some fearsome avenging angel, come to take what's his.

Maybe come to take me.

I shiver again.

"I'm not cold."

Far from it.

He takes his eyes off the road just long enough to meet mine, to draw me into the honey of his gaze, to nearly drown me in it. "Then why are you shivering?"

"I'm not. I was just . . . I just had a bad thought. That's all."

He makes no comment, so I turn to stare out the side window, like I've done for a large part of the last fifteen hours when I haven't been covertly watching Jasper. Jasper, the world's most guarded, least talkative car partner.

"Tell me," I hear several minutes later.

I turn back to him, his meaning lost on my boggled mind. "Pardon?"

"Tell me your bad thought."

He tells me this in an almost grudging way, like he wants to know, but then again he doesn't.

Much like I want to tell him, but then again I don't.

A conundrum.

More conflict.

I think about my previous reluctance to tell him much about my father, about *anything* really. But I also think about how hungry I've been for *some kind*, *any kind* of communication from him. Even more than that, though, I find that I want Jasper to know *something* about me, something important. Just enough that he might understand my fear. I desperately want someone to understand, to sympathize. Maybe even to reassure.

So I decide to tell him. Not everything, of course. Not even close. But more than I ever intended to.

"My father was . . . privy to some information that was sensitive. He was working with a guy I was dating. I had no idea it went beyond the obvious casual coworker thing, of course, but . . . it did. I overheard something I wasn't supposed to. I had to leave in order to make sure my father was safe." I pause and sigh. With an explanation like that, Jasper's just likely to think I'm crazy. Or crazily dramatic. "It's a long story. But the main thing is that, every month since I left, we would keep in touch through this one method, this very same method. Every month. Like clockwork. Until Friday."

"So you think something has happened to him?"

"I can't see how something *hasn't* happened to him. I mean, there's no way he would miss that call. There's just no way. Not if he was able to get there. He would know I'd worry. He would know I'd worry and he would know that I'd risk everything to find him."

"Did you think that maybe he's not missing? That he's—"

Jasper's abrupt stop tells me exactly how he was going to finish that sentence.

"What? That he's dead?"

His lips thin and he nods once. Considering how basically

inconsiderate and blunt to the point of being rude Jasper seems some-times, I take it as a compliment that he looks uncomfortable right now. I think this might be his way of being thoughtful and delicate.

"It's okay. You can ask that. And the answer is that I can't be absolutely positive, I don't suppose, but he's put some things in place to where if something happened to him, I'd be notified. So at least I know for sure that his body hasn't turned up somewhere." I swallow the lump that swells in my throat.

Jasper's silence carries with it all the insecurities and appalling thoughts that I've purposely held at bay, things like the fact that people disappear all the time and their bodies are never found. But he at least has the good grace not to say them.

"Maybe he's sick," Jasper finally says. "I mean, if he has . . . pneumonia or something, would he call from the hospital?"

I smile at his choice of illnesses. I guess he didn't want to make matters worse by suggesting a terrible car accident that has left him in a coma, or a brain tumor that has robbed him of his memory, something along those lines. Not that any of those possibilities would be a surprise to me. I think I've gone through every worst-case scenario on the planet.

"No, he wouldn't do that, but . . ."

"Maybe it'll help you to know that I found an electric bill your dad paid recently. It was on a credit card that he hasn't used in years and the address was for an apartment in Atlanta. Do you know anything about that?"

An apartment in Atlanta? What the hell?

I frown. "No, I don't. But why would he . . . I mean . . . ?"

"I can't tell you the why, but I can get you there and you can ask him yourself. How's that?"

Although now I've got more questions, relief washes through me. The payment of a bill isn't concrete evidence that he's okay, but it's pretty damn close. Plus, now that I think about it, this *sooo* sounds like a Plan B my father might have. He'd hide out in some obscure place and wait until I found him. And he knows I would. The Colonel knows that I'd come looking for him and that if I got someone good enough to help me look, eventually I'd find my way to him.

I don't even bother to ask Jasper how he accessed my father's credit card information. Something tells me I don't want to know. Not that he'd tell me anyway. That would be *far too* civil and forthcoming for a man like him.

"You two are close, it seems."

Close, it seems. I love the way Jasper talks. He doesn't use much slang, doesn't curse much. It's like he's too controlled, too . . . precise to take the lazy way out. His voice is very cultured, too, which strikes me as odd for a bounty hunter. But still, it suits him. On anyone else it might seem out of place, but somehow it fits this complex man.

He's got this chameleon-like way about him. It's as though, despite his incredible good looks and a presence so big it could practically suffocate you, he could be anyone from anywhere doing anything. Just Anonymous Joe, someone simply passing through, slipping by under the radar. In a way, it seems like life couldn't find a box for Jasper, a label or a type, so he made his own.

"Yeah, I suppose we are," I finally say in answer to his observation.

"You never mention a mother."

I'm inordinately pleased that Jasper is finally engaging in some sort of polite conversation, even though "polite" might not be the best way to describe it. It feels more like an obligatory interrogation, but I'll take it. I'll take any excuse to talk about my father, to keep him first in my thoughts, which I never dreamed would be a challenge. Doing it with Jasper is just icing on the cake. I imagine that doing *anything* with Jasper would be a pleasure.

When my cheeks warm, I focus on the conversation to keep my mind off . . . other things.

"She left when I was little."

"Left?"

"Yep. She just left."

"Have you ever tried to find her?"

"No."

"Why not?"

"If she didn't *want* us then she doesn't *deserve* us."

Jasper nods with his *humph*. "I get that."

"My father never encouraged it either, which I guess I always took as his way of saying that I didn't really want to know. So I've never looked. Don't plan to either."

There's a short pause, but he keeps the conversation going, which thrills me. If only it hadn't gone in this direction.

"What about this boyfriend-slash-coworker of your father's?"

"What about him?"

"Tell me about him. Maybe he could help me find your dad."

I take a deep breath. I really don't want to discuss Matt with Jasper, but . . . I don't think I have much choice. Because Jasper could be right. Matt might know something, even if it's something little.

"His name is Matt Conklin. He's an engineer for a private defense company. My father was a security consultant for them. That's how we met."

"And what did he think about you leaving to move across the country?"

My smile falters a little, embarrassment and a still-tender wound making my lips tremble. "He didn't like it. At least that's what he *said*, anyway."

"You don't believe him?"

I shrug, trying to act casual. "Well, he let me go, so . . ."

"His loss," Jasper declares. I've tried a million times to tell myself that, but it never takes the sting away from being so easily forgotten. "He's probably kicking himself now."

I appreciate the thought, and I've often wondered if Matt ever thinks of me, ever misses me or regrets letting me go so easily. He wasn't about to uproot his life and come with me into obscurity.

We fall quiet for what ends up being just a few more minutes until Jasper spots the sign for the hotel he was looking for. Once out of the car, we follow much the same routine as we did previously, only this time *I* intend to pay for both rooms, since I was in such a twirl last night that I didn't even get near the counter. The only thing that's missing is that kiss. *God, that kiss!*

My skin feels flushed and sensitive as the memories of having Jasper pressed to my front, his lips devouring mine, burn through me like long, hot flames. *Holy Lord!*

Ruthlessly, I jerk my mind back to the present and I stare, probably a little harshly, at the hotel clerk as she types furiously into the computer, searching for vacancies. She's an attractive blonde who I estimate to be in her early thirties. She has a thick accent and bright blue eyes that continually flicker to Jasper. I can't blame them. He's standing beside me, tall, strong and silent. He doesn't have to say a word to make an impression, though. He just has to show up. He just has to *be*.

I slide a sidelong glance in his direction. He's watching the woman work, his face a blank mask. His expression is neither rude nor open. It's simply blank. Politely blank, I guess. I think again of the chameleon. Dressed in a plain black tee that looks to be of higher quality, his short, jet-black hair in neat disarray (if that's even a thing), Jasper could be a stock broker in casual attire or the bouncer for a high-end night club. He has a dangerous, primal look about him that could be attributed to his lethal actions in a boardroom or to the fact that he carries a gun somewhere in his belongings. The one thing he remains to be at all times, in all situations, and in any attire is attractive. Compelling. Elusive. Fascinating.

And I'm damn sure fascinated.

"The only vacancy we have is a single smoking with two double beds. Will that be a problem?" the attendant asks in her exotic voice.

I don't glance at Jasper. I don't want him to see my blush, don't want him to pick up on my reaction. It's not like it's a big deal, really. It just *feels* like a big deal in some vague, disturbing way. I mean, it's not like Jasper wouldn't just come right on into my room if he had the urge to anyway, just like he did last night. It's just that this seems . . . *intimate* somehow, sharing the same space. A tiny room where he could have unrestricted access to me all through the night.

My reaction to the idea is immediate and visceral, my core bubbling with sensual awareness.

God, you're pathetic! I think before collecting myself enough to answer, "That'll be fine."

From my right, Jasper leans in and utters a smooth, *"Parlez-vous français?"*

The woman's eyes snap up to lock on Jasper

"Oui!" It's clear that she's very pleasantly surprised. "How did you know?"

Jasper spouts off some long answer that sounds like a love letter and makes the woman laugh. Suddenly he's neither a stockbroker nor a bouncer. He's a classy world traveler with the face of a Greek god and the smile of a fashion model. I stare at him, open-mouthed, as he converses fluidly and effortlessly with the older woman.

Finally, in words that I can understand, Jasper thanks her. "I appreciate you moving things around this way. My sister . . . well, she has special needs."

I have to work hard to keep my mouth from dropping open in aggravated astonishment.

The woman glances at me for a split second and then her eyes are once again glued to Jasper. "I completely understand. I'm only happy to accommodate your needs, sir."

Oh, I just bet you are! I think waspishly.

Jasper's answering smile is downright heart-stopping. I can't help staring at him like he's grown a second head, all the while feeling cheated that *I* never get that smile.

Less than ten minutes (of the clerk fawning over Jasper) later, we are dragging our bags out of the elevator. I stop and hold out my hand for a key. Jasper obliges by setting a black plastic card onto my palm.

"Room number?"

"Suite 631," he provides.

I glance at the plaque that tells me in which direction suite 631 lies and I start off in that direction, not intending to say anything else to Jasper. When I stop in front of the double doors, Jasper stops, too. I peer up at him in question.

"I got us a suite."

"Us?"

"Yes."

"To share?"

"Yes." When I continue to stare, he continues. "If that's not okay, I'm sure that smoking single next to the vending machines downstairs is still available. I thought I was doing you a favor."

I sniff, trying not to be angry and not understanding why I am. "I guess I'd have known that if I spoke French."

Jasper shrugs and takes the key from my fingers, letting us into the spacious suite. The colors are soothing blues, browns and beiges. A combo living-dining area is straight ahead and, beyond, a stunning night view of the city is visible through the part in the heavy ecru curtains. There are doorways to either side. I can only assume each is a bedroom.

"You can have your pick. I'll take the one you don't want."

"It doesn't matter. I'll take right, you take left."

Jasper shrugs, walking into the living room to toss his key and his bag on the coffee table. I ponder the mysteries of this man as I start toward the bedroom that will be mine. I pause in my exit. "So . . . how many languages do you know?" I ask.

"Six, but I'm only fluent in four," he admits without even looking in my direction.

I grit my teeth. The man infuriates me. He's so guarded, yet so casual about knowing six, *six* different languages. Who the hell is he?

I don't have the answers, and I don't expect I'll be getting them either. I guess I'll just have to add them to my list of curiosities about the enigma I'll be rooming with.

"Interesting," I say minimally. I get no response, though. Jasper is already paying me no mind as he digs a thin laptop from his bag and sets it up on the table.

I resist the urge to flounce off as I roll my suitcase into the bedroom to the right, leaving Jasper to do . . . whatever it is that he does.

I unpack my toiletries and a few nightly things like my sleep shorts and tank. My belly rumbles for food, so less than an hour later, I'm prowling through a book on the dining table, looking for a room service menu. I hear Jasper in his room, talking to someone on the phone in his low, steady rumble. My eyes fall on a slim MacBook resting on the shiny, wooden coffee table. Casually, the book in my hands laid open to the room service menu, I back up until I can see what's on the screen. I feel bad for snooping, but it's not like I opened up his computer and rifled through it. I'm just glancing at what's in plain sight.

And I almost wish I hadn't.

The DMV picture of a woman Matt used to date is pulled up on the screen. It's zoomed in on some kind of back-end page that has all sorts of details I imagine aren't accessible to the general public. I forget for the moment that Jasper has probably hacked a government site to get this information. I forget it because I'm too busy staring at the address highlighted under Megan's picture. I know it. I spent many a night there, in Matt's arms, listening to him tell me he loved me, wishing I felt that he really did.

And now Megan lives there.

I guess Matt could've moved out and Megan could've moved in. That's *possible*, but highly unlikely. Matt loved that house. His mother had lived there when she was a girl and it was the place she talked about more than anything else when she lay in a hospital bed, dying of cancer. I can't imagine Matt ever letting that house go. People don't throw away things they love. They keep them, fight for them. Ask them to stay. Follow them to the ends of the earth if they must.

I close my eyes against the beautiful, smiling face staring back at me. I knew Matt didn't love me. Or at least not enough. But this . . . this *proof*, it makes it hurt all over again.

As rude as it is to eavesdrop, it's nearly impossible not to when the quiet is so deafening.

"That's okay, Megan. I don't need to leave a message. I can just call back later. Do you happen to know when Matt will be home?"

That's all I need to hear. More than I *ever wanted* to hear.

I toss the room service book onto the couch and go for my purse, not bothering to interrupt Jasper to let him know where I'm going. At the moment, I don't even know myself.

TEN

Jasper

I knew the instant Muse left. There's a difference in the environment when she's around. A vibration almost, like her energy stirs the air when she breathes. The presence of another person also slightly changes the acoustics in any given space, absorbing sound, like pictures on a wall. Besides that, I heard the door click shut as she exited, even over the sultry voice of her ex-boyfriend's new roommate, Megan.

I don't doubt she stumbled upon my laptop. I left it open for a reason. And I didn't close my door for a reason, too. She needs to know the situation before we arrive at her hometown. It's always best to be prepared. Even when it's uncomfortable.

She won't go far, so I wait for two hours before I strike out to look for her. I could call her cell. I have her number from her friend Tracey. I doubt she'd answer it, though, wherever she is.

I take the elevator down to the lobby and I glance down the main hall. Only a coffee shop down there. Not a place she'd go when she's upset, I'm sure, so I push through the glass entry door and step out into the night. There are lights to the left, darkness to the right. I go left. She's not stupid enough to try the right. Not with a cautious father like hers.

The second building I come to is a tavern. It has a heavy antique-wood door and flickering carriage house lights on either side of it. It looks dark and inviting, the perfect place to hide in plain sight.

I pull open the door and scan the interior. Long oak bar straight ahead, small hallway and bathrooms to the left, gallery of mostly-full tables and chairs to the right.

Even though she's facing away from me, I spot Muse within seconds. She's sitting at the bar and her flaming hair, shining like a dark, fiery penny, is a beacon of color in an otherwise bland landscape. As I watch, she throws back her head and laughs, laughs so hard she almost falls off her stool. I twitch, ready to jump forward and catch her, but a youngish blond guy happily steadies her. I clench my teeth when his hand lingers too long at the base of her spine, his fingers dangerously close to the skin visible between her shirt and her pants.

I tune out the muted music and the three-dozen other conversations going on, and I listen closely for the unique sound of Muse's voice. It's a little husky and a lot feminine with a southern twang to it. Sweet charm and sexy stripper, all rolled into one.

I take a step closer when I see the blond slide his palm over her back and pull her against his side. Muse, still laughing, slouches into him for a second before pulling away and signaling the bartender.

"Two more shosh, please," she slurs, tapping two empty glasses on the bar.

I watch blond guy's hand stray down to her waist, pause and then move to cup her ass. Muse seems not to notice, as that's when the bartender sets two more shots of something clear down in front of her.

She sips all of one and then starts in on the other one as her brazen cohort scoots his stool closer and leans in to whisper something

in her ear. Muse laughs again, falling forward over the bar and resting her forehead against it while she slaps the shiny wood with her
free hand.

I bristle as I watch. I don't make a move until I see Asshole turn
his torso toward Muse and reach in with his other hand, presumably
aiming for the inside of her thigh. We'll never know, I suppose.

I'm on him so fast he doesn't even have time to choke out a single
syllable. I jerk him off his stool, slam his head into the edge of the
bar, which makes a satisfying crack, and then I haul him up and
around to stare into his face. I wind my fingers around his throat.

"I think that's enough touching for tonight," I growl.

"What the fu—"

I squeeze my fingers tighter, cutting off his words. He tries to
gasp, but can't.

His face starts to turn red.

"Do I look like the type of man you can question?"

I hear chair legs scratch wood floors as others in the tavern
become unsettled. I don't bother looking. I continue to stare into
the bloodshot blue eyes that are starting to understand exactly what
I mean. And what kind of man I am.

When he manages to nod and relaxes the fingers that were
clawing at my hand, I loosen my grip and shove him aside. He
doesn't bother coming back after me. He just watches me. Warily.
Rubbing his throat and holding his tongue. *Smart guy.*

Slowly, I turn to scan the room. I make eye contact with a few
of the men who stood up. I assume they were preparing to come to
the rescue of the "victim," but none of them makes a move. Some
of them even resume their seat. I know from experience that when
I choose to give people a glimpse of the real me, it changes their
mind about a lot of things. I imagine it's a lot like looking into a
black hole and seeing the eyes of a monster staring back at you.

When I've made my slow turn all the way back to Muse, I find her staring at me in her fuzzy, blurry way. "Jasper? What the hell?" she says quietly, almost uncertainly.

She's trying to sound incensed, but I think she's still lucid enough to have understood what just happened. And to know that I'm not a man to be pushed. *Smart girl.*

"If you're ready, I'll walk you back."

"And if I'm not?"

"Oh, I think you are," I tell her curtly, curling my fingers around her upper arm to help her off her stool.

"Wait, let me finish my drink," she pleads, reaching for the half-full shot glass. She downs it quickly and wipes her mouth with the back of her hand. She makes a gun with her index finger and thumb, points it at me and winks. "Ready, Freddy."

I say nothing as I escort her to the door. I'm only aware of the warm female body pressed to my side and the room full of skeptical eyes that follow us out.

ELEVEN

Muse

I rest my cheek against the cool tiles of the bathroom floor. "The elevator did it," I mumble to the base of the toilet in front of me.

"Did you say something?" comes Jasper's voice from the other side of the bathroom door, which surprises me. I've been in here throwing up my guts for at least an hour. I thought he would've left by now, gone back to his side of the suite.

"No," I moan miserably. Even to my ears, it sounds more like *Nuhhh* rather than an actual word.

"Muse?"

I don't answer. I lie perfectly still, hoping he'll think I passed out and then go away.

"Muse?" he calls again, louder. I don't make a peep.

The door handle rattles threateningly. "Can I come in?"

"No!" I say with a little more vigor, but it's too late. Before I even get the word out, I see black shoes stop a few inches from my nose.

I don't bother moving. I just squeeze my eyes shut and pray he goes away. I'm in no shape to see Jasper. Or for Jasper to see me. I'm sure I smell like hell and look twice as bad.

When the nausea (and the countless shots of rum I had at that tavern) caught up to me, I was just stepping off the elevator. In my efforts not to soil the elevator car or the carpeting in the hallway, I tried to stop my regurgitation and ended up puking all down the front of my shirt. I ran in here and thanked the porcelain gods about six times before collapsing on the floor in front of the toilet. I haven't moved since.

"So sexy," I mutter to myself as I think of what kind of picture I painted for Jasper. *Humiliating.*

"What was that?" Jasper asks, his voice nearer my ear. I crack one eye and see his face. He's squatting beside me, his expression curiously blank. As always.

"Nuthin," I mutter as intelligibly as I can. "Goway."

Just before I close my eyes again, I see his face disappear. I'm filled with relief that he's listening. But then I hear the hiss of the shower spray coming on.

"Take a shur. Doh mine me," I babble, shifting my head slightly to find a cool spot of tile again. But then I feel gentle hands slide under my chest and hips, lifting and rolling at the same time until I'm cradled against a hard chest. I tuck my face into the curve of his neck as the room spins uncontrollably. "No! Dohn moo me!" I squeeze my eyes shut.

I feel a slight jostle and then a floating sensation followed by the shock of lukewarm water hitting me in the side of the face. "Noooo!" I sputter.

Jasper never responds, he just slowly lowers my legs until I'm standing in the shower, facing him, still plastered to his front. Neither of us moves for a long time. Eventually, the room stops spinning and the water, neither cold nor hot, begins to soothe me.

I relax and Jasper, seemingly aware of the smallest details, senses it immediately. He nudges me backward, farther into the spray, and lifts his hands to push the hair away from my face. Tepid water spills onto my forehead, running over my eyes and mouth. I tip my chin up a little to increase the flow so that it trickles down my neck and chest, cooling my hot skin.

I stand like this for countless seconds until I feel hands at my waist. Jasper's fingers curl into the hem of my T-shirt and start to pull it upward. My head levels and my eyes snap open, colliding with dark amber ones. "What are you doing?"

"Cleaning you up. You smell like vomit. Stand still."

My pulse trips up a notch, but I don't argue. I'm too tired and too sick to care that much.

With a sigh, I gingerly raise my arms so as not to move too much as he tugs the soaked cotton over my head. I hear the wet slap of it hit the ceramic of the tub behind me. I keep my eyes closed as I lower my arms. Jasper's movements are efficient yet surprisingly unobtrusive. I stand still, almost in a daze, as he tugs my yoga pants down my legs. I hold on to his shoulder as I step out of them, feeling better than I have since I left the tavern. The coolish shower was a good idea.

I smell a familiar scent seconds before big, warm hands materialize at my neck. Jasper rubs small, soothing soapy circles over my skin, working his way down over my collarbones and onto my chest. His fingers slip under my bra straps to rub my shoulders and upper arms, his palms grazing my breasts. I let my head fall back, losing myself to the sensation of being cared for like this, of being touched like this—so innocently, yet so erotically. It's like I'm doing something I shouldn't, enjoying something I shouldn't, all under the guise of something purely functional.

Jasper's movements slow even more as he works his hands back toward my center. I feel his thumbs dip into the cups of lace covering my breasts, coming dangerously close to nipples that are now tingling with awareness. In the quiet, I hear his breathing, heavy and steady. I listen to it, letting it lull me as he cleans my chest. Mesmerized, I follow his every stroke with anticipation of what he might touch next.

A tiny whimper escapes my lips when he moves away from my aching breasts to wash my ribs. I crack my lids just enough to see Jasper. His eyes are trained on my face, his lips parted slightly. His expression is still the blank mask that I've become accustomed to, but it's his eyes that seem different. They're sleepy and dark and even more intense than usual. The change, although slight, is potent enough to turn the cool water to steam.

I watch the whiskey-colored orbs follow his hands as they work their way over my ribs and down to my waist. I sway gently, back and forth, with each languorous circle he makes.

He reaches for the soap and rolls it between his fingers again before attacking my stomach. At the first touch of his palm to my navel, I gasp. It scorches my cool skin and sends a gush of heat into my core. The muscles between my legs throb painfully and I let my head fall back on my neck again.

The water sluices down my face and throat, pouring into my bra to tickle my prickly nipples. Jasper's hands are tantalizing my skin with slippery caresses that draw ever closer to my core. With every pass of his hands on my belly, he dives a bit more under the elastic of my panties.

My breath is coming faster and faster, my concentration fully focused on his touch. The water coursing down my stomach trickles under the raised band to bathe my sex in cool liquid, a sharp contrast to the hot touch of his hands.

I sway again, unsteadily this time and I reach for Jasper. I grip his granite waist as I widen my stance to keep my balance, still absorbed by his sweet torture.

Jasper moves his sensual assault from my belly to my hips. He bends to stroke me in long ovals that trail down to the tops of my thighs. Then he moves both hands to my left leg, one broad palm splayed over the outside, one on the inside. As his slick hands move over my skin, one slips in and out between my legs, his wrist grazing me as it passes. I feel my muscles clench, every nerve and thought I have concentrated on the stimulation of his caress. Back and forth his hands glide around the top of my thigh, his right thumb slipping under the edge of my panties to tease my heated flesh as it passes.

I'm panting by the time Jasper moves to treat my other leg to the same kind of unnerving attention. My insides are already on fire and I'm so aroused that I moan at the first pass of his wide wrist against my sex.

Jasper resumes his rhythm, back and forth, slow and steady, rubbing between my legs with every gentle stroke. I reach for his thick biceps, a silent plea for him to keep doing what he's doing, as I poise on the precipice of an unexpected orgasm. It's the pinch of Jasper's teeth at my left nipple, nibbling at it through the wet lace, that pushes me right over the edge.

I dig my fingernails into the smooth skin of his arms as I grind against his wrist. He presses up, increasing the friction of my soaked panties against my aching flesh and helping me to ride out the wave.

Heat spears through me almost violently and my breath comes in harsh bursts. Pleasure. So much pleasure!

After the first few seconds, my knees threaten to give out beneath me. Jasper wraps one arm around me, cupping his hand between my legs and stroking me until the very last spasm tightens and releases.

I'm limp and exhausted when Jasper scoops me up into his arms and steps out of the shower. He sets me on my feet and turns off the water before wrapping me in a towel. I can barely stand as he rubs my skin dry.

It's when the euphoria of my climax completely abates that embarrassment slips in to take its place. I drop my face into my hands as Jasper dries my legs. "Oh God!"

When I'm dry except for my underwear, Jasper tugs my hands away and forces me to look at him. "Stop it," he says in his no-nonsense way with his no-nonsense expression.

"Why did you do that?" I ask, my residual intoxication making me blunt.

"Because you needed it," he replies, matter of fact.

"Oh God!" I moan louder, covering my face again.

But again, Jasper pulls my hands away. His eyes are on mine, sparkling like two warm topazes. "But I also did it because I wanted to. I wanted to see you. I wanted to touch you. I wanted to put my hands and my mouth on you. And I wanted to watch your face when you weren't thinking of anything more than what I was doing to you."

My heart is pounding so hard I'm sure he can hear it. I'm caught between humiliation and the desire to throw myself against Jasper and beg him to make love to me.

"I took advantage of you. If anything, you should be angry, not embarrassed."

Maybe he's right. Maybe I should be.

Only I'm not.

"I knew you were upset about your ex. I knew you needed to work through it. I should've left you alone."

Jasper. Always so controlled, so logical, so . . . cool. "Then why didn't you?"

"Because I can't stop thinking about that damn kiss. And even though I know you've got other things on your mind, I wanted to feel you again." He pauses and I say nothing. I'm surprised that he's telling me this much, my quiet, reserved Jasper. "I've never had to take advantage of a woman before. I've never wanted to. I left it up

to you to decide if you wanted to come to me, left it up to you to
decide when you're ready. I know the time will come. I can feel it like
static between us. But I was getting tired of waiting. So I took advantage of your weakness. I took advantage of your heartbreak over
another man. And I'm more than a little disgusted with myself."

Jasper's lip curls up into a sneer at the last and I can practically
feel the self-loathing radiating from him. I don't doubt he's never
had to take advantage of a woman before. I imagine that anyone he
looks twice at just gets naked and throws herself at his feet. Hell,
under different circumstances, I might've done the same thing.

It's this uncharacteristic glimpse into his emotion, into *any*
emotion from this man, that draws me closer to him.

I reach up to touch his cheek. "Please don't feel like that. I've
wanted you from the second I saw you. Yes, it is a bad time, but if
I hadn't been ready to be taken advantage of, I'd have told you to
stop. And you would've."

Jasper winds his long fingers around my wrist. "I don't know if
I would've or not."

A thrill chases its way down my spine at the thought of being
taken by Jasper, at the thought of him roughly pinning me to the
bed, holding me down with his delicious body and taking what he
wants. I'm not a fan of forced *anything*, but I know that Jasper
would never have to force me. If anything, I'm a *too*-willing par-
ticipant. So willing, in fact, that I'm having trouble keeping my
mind focused on my priorities lately.

With his eyes on mine, Jasper reaches behind me and unsnaps
my bra, pulling it from me so slowly that I hold my breath until my
nipples spring free of the material. His eyes descend for just a second.
I see them rove my naked breasts. I hear the hiss of his breath. I feel
the heat of his want.

Neither of us speaks as he hooks his fingers in the band of my panties and drags them down my legs. On his way back up, I feel the soft brush of his lips over the skin of my inner thigh. But then he's standing before me again, a tower of control and restraint.

Once more, he sweeps me up, never taking his eyes off mine as he carries me to the bed and tucks me under the covers. He stares down at me for several long, silent minutes. I don't want him to go, although I know he's going to. But I won't ask him to stay. I can't.

I'm learning quickly, though, that Jasper is extremely intuitive. He seems to notice the smallest things, appears to be able to read my mind almost. Or at the very least my slightest body language. Just like he does now. It's as if he knows I don't want him to leave me.

I watch with eyes I can't tear away as he strips off his wet shirt and pants, climbs in behind me on top of the covers and pulls me into the curve of his body, resting his chin on top of my head.

I'm hyper-aware for the first couple of minutes. Jasper just holds me in silence, as though he's letting me get used to the feel of his body against mine. And I do. Quickly.

His warmth coupled with the fatigue from the stress and worry of the last week work to relax me, and I find my chaotic thoughts settling onto Matt. And what Jasper must think of it all.

"I went to the bar because of Matt, but probably not for the reason you think," I blurt into the quiet. I don't want Jasper to misunderstand.

"And what reason did I think?" His voice is low and hypnotic, as soothing as the soft cotton sheets.

"You probably think that I was so heartbroken over seeing that he's living with Megan that I ran off. Couldn't take it."

"But that's not right?"

I think about my reaction, about what I was feeling then and what I'm feeling now. "Maybe a little, but it was more . . . residual. It was like the loss of *what was*. But it was also about what *never was*." I stop, my eyelids drifting shut as I think.

"Explain," he urges gently, his chin moving atop my head.

"I tend to fall for men with a fatal flaw. When I didn't find Matt's, I thought he might be the one. But I'm beginning to think that *I'm the one* with the fatal flaw. The fatal flaw of falling for men who don't love me."

"What makes you think he didn't love you?"

"He let me go. If he loved me, he didn't love me *enough*."

"What constitutes enough?"

"It's enough when you can't bear the thought of life without that person. It's enough when you can't let them go, or when you'd cross an ocean just to be with them. Anything less than that is just . . . less. It isn't enough."

"But he *did* let you go."

"Yes."

"And then he moved on."

"Yes."

"Which means he didn't love you enough."

"Yes." After a few seconds, I add, "But that wasn't *all* that was making me upset tonight."

"What else?"

"I . . . I felt selfish and stupid for wanting him to love me like that when I didn't love him enough either."

"Explain," he says again.

"If I'd loved him as much as I thought I had, I wouldn't have kissed you like I did. I wouldn't have had any trouble putting you out of my mind and staying focused on Dad. If I'd loved him enough, I—I wouldn't want you."

"And that makes you feel guilty?"

Perceptive as ever. "Yes."

I feel Jasper lean up. I feel the scruff on his chin at my temple. It softly abrades my skin when he speaks. "Don't. If he'd loved enough, you wouldn't be here. Alone. With me. He'd be with you."

I sigh. What he says is true. "I know, but—"

"No buts. Be glad that he didn't chase you. I am."

The next words I say are the absolute truth. "Right now, I am, too."

That's the last thing I remember.

TWELVE

Jasper

I hear Muse stir. I hear her groan and I have to smile.

I don't try to be quiet as I roll the room service cart into her bedroom. I wasn't trying to be quiet when I answered the knock, spoke to the waiter and let the door slam shut either.

"Time for some breakfast. We need to get on the road."

Muse raises her head and glances at the cart, frowns and then lays it back on her pillow. "Not hungry," she mutters.

"You need to eat. You'll feel better."

She opens one eye and glares at me. Pretty effectively, too, I might add. "Why the hell are you so chipper?"

"I'm not chipper. You're just hungover."

I take the silver covers off the two plates of food.

"You didn't order eggs, did you?" she asks, her words garbled like she might be getting sick.

"No. Lots of bacon. And water. And coffee. Some fruit, too. Now sit up."

Reluctantly, she pushes back the covers, kicking at them with her legs when they tangle around her feet. I watch her naked breasts bounce, the nipples puckering against the cool air. Blood rushes to my cock. Evidently, I've found the one thing I can't completely control myself against.

Muse Harper.

A woman, for God's sake. But not just any woman. She's a woman who makes my blood blaze and my body ache. She's a woman who has enough fire to thaw a small piece of what's been frozen for a long time.

In a different situation, that might be cause for concern, but right now it's not. She's got a father to find. I've got answers to obtain. And then, *we* will come to an end. An unfortunate end. She deserves better, but it is what it is. I have a job to do and it has to come first. Always first.

Muse finally sits up and rubs her hands over her face. Her hair is dried in thick clumps that fall down over her shoulders like flames, licking at her pale flesh. My mouth goes dry as I watch her unabashedly. It's her gasp that brings my eyes back up to hers. They're wide and round, and her lips are parted like they were last night. Last night when she came in my arms. Her cheeks flood with color and she crosses her arms over her chest to cover her nudity. The action only makes her look sexier. More forbidden.

I've never wanted her more.

"A little late for that, don't you think?"

More color rushes into her face. More blood rushes to my cock.

"Oh God," she whispers, closing her eyes as though the memory is painful.

I step around the cart and take one of her hands from where it's nestled in her armpit. I press her palm to the bulge that strains toward her from behind my zipper.

"This is what you do to me. Don't be embarrassed. Be proud." Her eyes are fixed on mine now, the pupils eclipsing almost every speck of her green irises. "Now eat before I change my mind about being a nice guy."

I release her hand and she lets it fall slowly into her lap. She glances away as she drags the sheet around her where she sits, covering up what I'd much rather look at. Disappointing, but probably for the best.

She clears her throat before grabbing a fork.

I move back around to the other side of the cart, taking a strip of bacon from the second plate and downing it in one bite.

"Since when are you a nice guy?" Muse asks, peeking up at me from beneath her lashes as she stabs a grape with her fork. Her lips are curved into the hint of a smile. It does nothing for my raging hard-on. Then again, it seems that my body is determined to react to nearly everything she does with a massive erection.

I sigh.

Until I get inside her, I don't suppose that's going to change.

"Good point." We eat the rest of our breakfast in silence. When Muse finishes, wiping her mouth on her linen napkin, I ask, "Feel better?"

She nods. "Actually, I do. Thank you. I've never had a hangover like that before."

"Are you a good girl, Muse Harper?"

She shrugs. "No, not really. I just usually stick to wine."

"Red or white?"

"Red. Why?"

"Just curious. When this is over and I come to collect, I wanted to know what kind of wine to bring."

"You bring wine when you collect your money?"

"I wasn't talking about collecting *money*."

The bloom of pink in her cheeks assures me that she knows *exactly* what I *was* talking about.

THIRTEEN

Muse

I'm a bundle of nerves by the time we reach Treeborn early the next afternoon. Being back on the familiar streets is both comforting and unnerving. As we near my father's house, I reach into my purse for my sunglasses and the hat I brought. The sun is setting, but I still can't risk being seen.

"If you're going for incognito, you might want to pull all that red hair through the hole in your hat. It draws attention."

When I was younger, I used to be very sensitive about my locks. Gingers don't exactly have it easy, but I grew into being okay with it. "Are you making fun of my hair?" I ask teasingly.

Jasper glances over at me as I grab handfuls of red and wind it into a tail that I can pull through my cap. His eyes, as always, are unfathomable. "Not at all. I love your hair."

I stop what I'm doing and stare. "You do?"

His comment is matter of fact. His expression is as unreadable as ever. But something about his words, words that he chooses carefully and doles out sparingly, pleases me right down to my toes.

"Very much," is his short answer. Although it's given when he's already looking back at the road, that doesn't lessen the impact. I tuck the compliment away into a pocket somewhere on the side of my heart, where it can warm me right on and on.

I try to act casual as I finish my disguise, but for some reason my fingers are shaking. This man . . . *God!* He just does something to me.

Jasper parks across the street from the Colonel's brick ranch. We sit in the quiet as he looks around. What he's searching for, I don't know.

I slump down in the seat and angle my body toward Jasper when I see Millie, my father's nosey neighbor, come out the front door with Eli, her springer spaniel. She usually walks him just before dark, which makes me think she must've noticed us parked here because it's far too early for her to be out.

"Oh shit! Here comes the neighborhood watch committee," I whisper.

"Does she have super powers?" Jasper asks in a hushed voice.

"Of course not. Why?"

"Then why are you whispering?"

"Because I'm scared. Why are *you* whispering?"

Jasper doesn't respond because his eyes are focused on something just behind my head. I can almost picture Millie making her way across the street to us in her comfortable shoes and blindingly floral blouse, nose wrinkled in that annoying way she has.

"Here she comes," he warns in his scratchy voice. For about ten seconds, my mind spins with what we could do other than just drive away, which would defeat the purpose of coming here in the first place. That's as far as I get before my brain is scrambled, though. All thoughts flee my mind when Jasper reaches behind my head, grabs my ponytail and pulls me to him.

Our lips meet just before there's a sharp knock on the passenger-side window right behind me. Jasper holds me still as he peers around at what I can only imagine is Millie's disapproving face.

"Get lost, lady!" he calls without rolling down the glass.

"You can't park here," she declares in a voice that's as pinched as her features.

"You don't own the street," he rebuts just before returning his attention to me, effectively dismissing Millie.

"I'll call the police!"

Jasper ignores her and bends his head to mine again. Slowly this time, with our eyes locked until the moment our lips touch. This kiss is different from his first. That one said wanting me was an inconvenient truth. This one says having me is an inevitability.

His mouth is soft and coaxing, yet firm and demanding. It seduces. It devours. It tells me that he will not stop until I'm all his, until he is all that I can think about. He wants to consume me. And he'll settle for nothing less.

When he releases me, he still holds my head, our faces only centimeters apart. His breathing is as heavy as mine, and his eyes are that dark whiskey color.

"I'm one sick bastard," he mutters. Of all the things I might've expected him to say, that was nowhere close to any of them. His voice is both self-deprecating and remorseful. Before I can ask for an explanation (one he would undoubtedly refuse to give me) he's pulling away.

He glances over my shoulder. "Okay, she just went in to call the cops. Give me ten minutes and pick me up on the street behind this one."

He's out the door and across the street before I can even process what he just said and act accordingly. Finally, once I collect myself a little, I climb across the console and into the driver's seat.

I can barely reach the pedals, as Jasper is probably a foot taller than me, and it takes me a few seconds to find the controls that will move the seat closer. When I finally shift into gear, I make a mental note of the time, subtracting a minute just to be on the safe side.

I drive around Dad's neighborhood, grateful for the deeply tinted windows of Jasper's car. They give me some amount of anonymity. As I inspect the passing scenery, I wonder vaguely what my highly educated, quietly competent, probably dangerous bounty hunter is looking for at the house. I also wonder what he might find. I don't get far with either line of thought, so I abandon them both.

I'm in so far over my head that I have nothing except a whole slew of unanswered questions. At this point, I don't even have any theories as to what might be going on. But maybe Jasper will return with something useful.

When the ten-minute mark is nearly upon me, I head back toward Alton Street, the one directly behind my father's. I cruise slowly past each of the modest homes, noting toys in yards and dogs in driveways. I smile when I see Jasper pop out onto the sidewalk a few houses down. He's walking casually, hands stuffed in his pockets like he might be going to the neighbors' for a barbecue. All that's missing is pursed lips as though he's whistling. But on Jasper that would be overkill. He doesn't have to say a word for it to be clear that he's not the carefree whistling type. He's too intense for that. Too alert and guarded and . . . dark. It's something he exudes like Marilyn Monroe exuded sex appeal. It's not something he works at. It's just something he *is*.

I slow as I approach. He smiles the polite smile I've seen him give others, the one that says I'm pleasant, but I don't want to be bothered. It's very effective. And it's very intriguing. I'm sure that nearly everyone who sees it wants to know more about the man who wears it. I'm equally sure that not one of them dares to ask.

He slides into the passenger seat and I accelerate down the road.

At the stop sign, I make a right, turning away from my father's street. I pause at the yield sign and bear left. It's then that I see a police cruiser heading *toward* my father's place. Jasper timed it perfectly. Not that I'm surprised.

"What did you find out?"

Eyes locked on the road, Jasper points to a gas station up ahead. "Pull in there. We need gas."

I swallow my sigh and do as he asks. While he's pumping the gas, I push his seat back to its previous position and walk around the front of the car to climb into my side. I wait patiently as he goes into the convenience store and I wait patiently as he unpacks a small plastic bag of snacks upon his return.

"I got you a bag of those chips you like. And the water you drink."

I ignore his thoughtfulness. I overlook how observant he's been. I have one thing on my mind.

"Thanks," I say, biding my time until we are back on the highway and he can't put me off any longer. And as soon as we are, I find that I can hold my tongue no longer. "Tell me, Jasper."

As the seconds stretch between us, thin and fragile, I feel my throat constrict and tears burn the backs of my eyes. He's stalling. And the only reason he'd stall is because he has bad news.

My chest feels like it might collapse, crushing every vital organ behind it. I press the heel of my hand into the center to ease the panicky discomfort.

"Are you okay?" Jasper asks, a frown on his face and a small thread of concern in his voice.

"Not really. Just tell me. Don't sugarcoat it or beat around the bush. I have to know and I have to know *right now*."

"Your father is fine," he says, unscrewing the cap of his own water and taking a long sip like we're discussing nothing more important than the weather.

My heart stutters for a few beats before it picks back up at a rapid pace. I'm almost afraid to get too excited, certain that I must've misunderstood him.

"Wh-what?"

"I said I'm sure he's fine."

"How do you know?"

"Well, to most people, it looks like he's just out for the day. Working, running errands, whatever he does. Bed's made, toothbrush is in its holder, mail's on the counter, coffee cup's in the sink. But to someone who looks more closely, it seems like he left with no intention of coming back right away. Yes, his toothbrush is there, but his razor is gone. Men can use any kind of toothbrush, but a good razor is hard to find. There's a gun safe on the top shelf of his closet that still has a revolver in it, locked up tight. But there's another one behind a box of pictures in the back corner that's empty. He left the obvious one and took the hidden one. As for how he left, the vehicle's gone, but the automatic garage door opener cable has been disabled. There are no signs of him being forcibly taken from there either. So I'd say he left for good reason and that he's holed up somewhere."

"You don't sound surprised."

Jasper shrugs. "I'm not. There's a reason he's juicing up that apartment in Atlanta."

I feel overwhelming relief. That would explain why he wasn't there when I called. And maybe why he hasn't called me either. If he's hiding out, he'd want to keep me out of danger. A giddy laugh bubbles up in my throat like a Halloween concoction might bubble in a witch's cauldron. I'm afraid to get *too* excited, though, to let my guard all the way down. "And you're *sure*?"

"Well *obviously* I can't be one hundred percent certain until I knock on the door of that apartment and he answers the door, but I'm reasonably sure."

I digest his words. I consider them carefully. I consider the source, too. His expertise, his confidence, his calm demeanor. And without really making a conscious decision to do it, I take the leap and I trust Jasper. Trust his judgment, trust his words. Trust *him*.

It's not until later that I realize just exactly what I've done. And how much it would hurt me.

FOURTEEN

Jasper

Muse is quiet on the drive to Atlanta. Her nervous energy, however, fills the cabin with so much silent noise it's hard for me to think. She's tapped her foot, twirled her hair, clicked her fingernails and probably rubbed a raw spot on her palm with the thumb of her other hand. She hasn't made much actual sound, but I can hear her nonetheless.

If I could ignore her, I'd be much better off. I could think. And plan. But I can't. Somehow, she got under my skin and that's screwing up everything. I have a job to do. Right after I get some answers that I need. And for the first time in my adult life, I find myself putting off the inevitable rather than just embracing it.

I've always put duty above all else. Some people are just built that way. I'm one of those people. You can imagine that the first time I'm tempted to veer from the straight and narrow path I follow comes as somewhat of a surprise. And very little surprises me.

Three and a half hours later, I'm pulling into the gravel lot of a club named Dual. I left a message on Gavin Gibson's cell phone.

There's a possibility that I might need some help and I wanted to talk to him. He's a good resource and I trust him to some degree. More than I trust most people, I guess. We have an . . . understanding. The kind of understanding few people would comprehend or approve of. We lend a hand in certain types of situations. The next time he needs a favor, he'll call and I'll do my best to help. It's sort of like an unspoken pact.

Usually I find that making final plans for one of my jobs gives me a peaceful edge, a clinical nonchalance about death that keeps me calm and rational and quick. Deadly quick. I'm making them early this time. Why? Because for the first time that I can ever remember, I'm thinking of stalling, so I'm making it harder. For me. Harder for me to stall, to reconsider following through. I've never had to thwart myself before, never had to tie my own hands. But I can't trust my own intentions anymore. They're too wrapped up in a fiery redhead that I can't stop thinking about.

Maybe it's because of who she is. Maybe it's because of the way I'm having to go about this. Maybe it's because she's actually a decent person. Or maybe it's something I haven't even thought of. I don't have an answer. I only have a potential problem. And problems of any kind are never a good thing. Not in my line of work. I make sure to deal with them decisively and immediately. It's just one more thing that makes me the best at what I do.

When I cut the engine, Muse finally tears her eyes away from the passing landscape and glances straight ahead. "Where are we?" Her puckered brow shows her confusion.

"Atlanta."

"But why are we at a club?"

"I need to speak to someone here. I won't be long. Stay put. Keep the door locked."

I get out and slam the door shut before she can ask any more questions. Not that she'd really expect an answer at this point. I just feel like her inquisitiveness would only aggravate the way I'm feeling. And that's a liability I can't afford.

Once inside, I glance around the interior of the club. A few dozen people are crammed onto a dance floor, rubbing against one another. I've never understood their desire to do that. I'm more of a loner, a "let me take you into a dark corner" kind of man. Plus, I don't like crowds. I'd never work in a place like this, but I can see how Gavin does. He's a congenial kind of guy. You'd never know by talking to him that if you cross him or someone he loves, he can be one sadistic son of a bitch. I guess we all hide our *real* selves behind some kind of mask. Mine is one of indifference.

I make my way toward the back-lit bar that stretches out to the left. Doesn't look like much has changed. There were two hot bartenders back there the last time I was here. There are three tonight, which makes sense for a weekend. I remember two of them. I never forget a face, especially dangerous ones and beautiful ones. And this one is beautiful.

A pale oval face smiles out from a long, straight sheet of dark hair. Olivia. She's petite in a voluptuous way, a lot like Muse. But while this girl is beautiful, she has zero effect on me. The only thing that's making my dick hard lately is a talkative redhead with jewel-green eyes and a body that begs a man to tear it apart with lips and tongue, piece by delicious piece.

Dark eyes meet mine and she smiles. I nod at her and she looks away, tipping her head in the direction of the back of the club. I follow her gesture and see her husband standing in the doorway of his office. His name is Cash Davenport. Gavin's boss and the owner of this place. I make my way through the crush of bodies, aiming for him.

I glance back at Olivia to nod my thanks. She winks at me and then slides her eyes back to her husband as she deftly mixes a drink in a silver shaker.

As I approach Cash, I can see that he's still looking at his wife. The expression on his face reminds me of the way a man might look at the sun when he sees it for the first time, when he's spent his whole life in the dark. They're that kind of couple, the kind that nothing comes between. The kind that lasts forever. The kind that survives anything. And they've had their fair share of obstacles to overcome. The thing is, they're tighter than ever, it seems. More in love than ever.

When I stop to his left, Cash finally tears his eyes away from his wife to smile and offer his hand. "Jason! Good to see you, man."

I nod, taking his hand for a quick shake. "Thanks. I hate to drop in on you like this, but I'm looking for Gavin. Have you seen him?"

I can tell by the way his sharp brown eyes narrow momentarily that he knows I'm here for work that he probably doesn't want to know too much about. He knows more than most already, I think. And he knows that people who know too much usually end up in danger. And Cash Davenport isn't the kind to take that kind of thing lightly.

FIFTEEN

Muse

Jasper hasn't been inside the club for even five minutes when my bladder reminds me that I haven't used the bathroom since we left. And after coffee and water this morning, then water on the trip, I feel like I might float away any minute. And it's only worsened by the fact that I have nothing but darkness and quiet to distract me from it.

Taking the keys from the ignition, I get out, touch the handle to lock the doors and head for the front of the club. A big, 'roided-out giant greets me when I poke my head through the door. His smile is warm in a gentle way, making me think that it's mainly his size that's intimidating. I return his smile and step up to him.

"I'm waiting for a friend, but I really need directions to your ladies' room."

He winks at me and nods to the back corner of the club. There are lighted red male and female signs on the wall. I thank him and start off in that direction.

A dance floor full of people stands between me and the oasis for my bladder, so I take a minute to determine the best route and the path of least resistance, which appears to be skirting the crowd by way of the bar to my left.

Just as I'm deciding on my course, a deep, attractively accented voice sounds from very near my right ear. "Something I can help you find, miss?"

I clutch my racing heart. I didn't even know someone was standing behind me. I whirl to find a tall, incredibly handsome man looming over me. "Oh God! You scared the bejesus out of me!"

"That wasn't my intention, but I'm glad I did. Damn me, but you're beautiful!" he says with a rakish grin that has probably wrestled thousands of uteruses into submission. Mine is *aware*, but not as affected as most, I'm sure. My female body parts are securely under the influence of a drug called Jasper. "Please say you're here to see me."

"Who's 'me'?"

"Gavin Gibson. At your service."

"Sorry, Gavin, but I'm just here to avail myself of your . . . facilities."

In the landscape of his tanned face and beneath his crop of short black hair, his eyes are startlingly blue. They twinkle with mischief and pure masculine confidence. And charm. Loads of charm. "Can I pick the facility?"

On any other man, suggestive lines like these might seem cheesy, but not this guy. They just seem flirtatious, genuine and highly complimentary.

"Afraid not, but I appreciate your willingness to accommodate me."

"I'd be willing to accommodate you in any way you could dream up in that pretty little head of yours."

The Australian lilt to his words gives them an innocence that precludes that sleazy vibe most Americans would emanate at this point. I can't help smiling back at his unflappable determination.

"As much as I—"

My words are interrupted by a heavy-cream voice and a tingle of recognition.

"Do you mind?"

Gavin's merry blue eyes flit to a position just above my head. They would tell me Jasper's position if I didn't already know, if I couldn't already feel him with every dancing red blood cell. I don't know how he does this to me—makes me forget everything except for him, makes me feel nothing except for him—but he does it. Consistently. Effortlessly. Thoughtlessly.

He's so close at my back that I can feel his body heat. For a second, I feel like closing my eyes and sinking into it. Into him. He's like a talented hypnotist who has somehow managed to invade my every thought, my every emotion, my every jangling nerve.

"Jason!" the man in front of me exclaims happily.

Jasper leans into me, his chest brushing my back as his long arm shoots out from behind my shoulder to accept the handshake of the Aussie. When they finish, Jasper withdraws his arm, but I feel his other hand come to rest at the curve of my waist, the fingers tensing, urging me to step back.

I don't resist. The action brings me against his side, our bodies in full contact from shoulder to thigh. My skin tingles with awareness and I fight the desire to lean farther into him, to be absorbed.

Jasper doesn't glance down at me, but he doesn't have to for me to see the dark and dangerous expression on his face. The normally blank mask that rests over his features like a veil is gone, revealing a fierceness that takes me aback. It's as though he's mentally ripping the other man to shreds.

What the hell?

"Gavin," Jasper responds quietly, his low voice filling the space with an intimidating rumble.

Gavin's eyes flicker to me and back up to Jasper. One black brow rises and he asks simply, "Yours?"

I feel Jasper stiffen against me before he replies. "Certainly not *yours*."

His fingers flex against my side again, like a reactive twitch, and I wonder to myself if this could possibly be about *me*.

The mere suggestion warms me like hot chocolate—from the inside out. It's not an overtly possessive gesture, but for someone as cool and aloof as Jasper, it's enough to melt my heart and curl by toes. I glance at his face once more and when he quickly flicks his gaze to me, I see that my suspicion is correct. He looks ready to kill.

And I couldn't be happier. My lips tremble with my suppressed smile that, if set free, would rival the sun in brightness.

Sensitive to the undercurrent, Gavin crosses his thick arms over his wide chest, his face adopting a friendly, non-threatening expression. "I got your message, mate. No worries." He nods, holding Jasper's eyes for a few seconds before he continues. "What brings you back into town?"

Jasper doesn't answer right away. Rather, he looks down at me again, this time the harsh lines of his face softening ever so slightly. "Did you need something?" he asks me.

"I came in to use the restroom. This is our first stop since we left. Remember?"

He has the good grace to at least look a little sheepish. "Oh. Sorry. They're back there," he points out, indicating the back corner. "I'll be waiting for you outside."

I nod and move to walk past him, but before I lose myself in the crowd surrounding the bar, I glance back at the duo. "Nice to meet you, Gavin."

His smile is wide and immediate, and every bit as flirtatious as it was a few minutes ago. "The pleasure was all mine, pet."

One quick peek at Jasper's face shows that stony, furious glint in his eyes again, his mouth a hard line, his brows pulled low. It's the most transparent I've ever seen him.

This time I do smile. I don't even try to hide my pleasure. I'm rewarded with a scowl and a growling sound that's so loud I can hear it over the music. I feel like giggling as I walk away. So I do.

As I'm weaving my way through the knot of people waiting for a drink from a couple of gorgeous bartenders, I see yet another handsome giant making his way through the throng. His dark blond head stands several inches above the tallest man in the crowd. He's big, easily big enough to be a bouncer, but still not quite as big as Jasper.

His nearly black eyes are focused behind me as I approach, giving me a chance to take in his authoritative presence. He seems in control, in command, like he's a master surveying all that is his. It makes me wonder if he owns the club.

When I get closer, his gaze flickers to me. He smiles and nods, to which I smile and nod in return. There's no attraction in his expression, just a polite curiosity.

I hear a feminine voice rise above the fray, calling, "Cash!" The guy's head whips around and I see his face soften the instant he finds the owner of the woman's voice. I glance back to see which one holds his heart, because it's easy to see that she does. He doesn't even try to hide it.

I'm not surprised when I see him leaning in to speak to the beautiful brunette behind the bar. She looks as love-struck as he does and I'm aware of a pang of envy that stabs me somewhere in the vicinity of my heart. I wonder if I'll ever find my happy ending, my *Dirty Dancing* Johnny, my *Sixteen Candles* moment. My *Officer and a Gentleman* exit.

I pause at the entrance to the hall that leads to the bathrooms and I glance back across the bar. I can easily make out Jasper's head as he follows Gavin to the door. Just before he disappears into the night, he turns. As though he could feel me watching him, his eyes find mine. Unerringly, across the top of a sea of people, they click to a stop on mine. His blank expression is back and I think with some amount of dismay that, as much as I'm beginning to wish he could, I doubt that Jasper will factor into my future at all, much less in a romantic-gesture kind of way.

I shake the thoughts from my head and turn to swing open the door to the ladies' room. I've got other things to worry about right now. I'll have Jasper to mourn another day.

SIXTEEN

Jasper

I'm optimistic that Muse will keep the questions to a minimum when we've gone thirty minutes without her opening her mouth. But I know better. That's why I'm not entirely surprised when I hear her tentative voice.

"Who was that guy—Gavin?"

"Somebody I work with from time to time."

"Is he a bounty hunter, too?"

"No."

"What does he do?"

I sigh. Loudly. "Among other things, he manages that club."

"Ah. And what do you two do together?" I throw her a look that, even in the dark, I'm sure tells her that I've reached an end to my loquaciousness. I see her lips thin and her brow furrow. "Time's up. Got it."

Her voice is sharp with an underlying note that sounds something like hurt. I feel another stab of an emotion dangerously close to guilt.

Even if I wanted to tell her everything, to answer all her questions, she'd then hate me for telling her. She'd wish she'd never asked. Then she'd wish she never met me.

She'd be better off, of course, if she hadn't. But she did. She's part of a world and a set of circumstances that are far beyond her control. She's an innocent in this game. Even without all the details, I know this to be true. I can feel it in my gut. And my gut is never wrong. I hope that holds true where her father is concerned. I'd hate for him to be the first time my gut is wrong.

As the GPS starts to take us off the main roads and into subdivisions and residential areas, Muse gets quieter. She could be asleep. But she's not. The only thing that gives her consciousness away is the way she's twisting the hem of her T-shirt between her fingers. Otherwise I might think she was dozing with her head leaned back against the rest, facing out the passenger window.

When I pull to a stop, she glances over at me. Her eyes are big and shiny and she looks near tears. Impulsively, I reach for the fingers of one busy hand. "Don't be afraid."

Muse gives me a weak smile that doesn't reach her eyes. Her fingers tremble inside mine. "I'm not afraid."

"Liar," I accuse softly.

Her expression doesn't change. She doesn't make a sound or make a move. She just stares at me, like she's willing me, *begging me*, maybe through the connection our hands make, to give her courage. Strength. To promise her everything will be all right.

"I know you're not going to like this, but I want you to stay here while I go check it out first." Before I can even get halfway through the sentence, she's shaking her head.

"No, I'm going."

I knew that's what she'd say.

"Fine. Just stay behind me, okay?"

"Why? What do you think is going to happen?"

I shrug. "Hard to tell. In my line of work, you learn to expect the unexpected."

"All right, I'll stay behind you. Let's just get this over with. I need to know he's okay."

I release her hand and we both get out, meeting at the front of the car. Muse trails behind me by a foot or so and stops on the top step while I approach the front door and use the clacker to knock.

The door swings open quickly, like someone was expecting us. A man fills the entrance. He's just over six feet tall, has salt-and-pepper hair and looks fit and trim in his Dockers and pressed white shirt.

"Jasper King," he says flatly, no surprise coloring his tone.

"Colonel Harper," I reply, addressing the man I used to work for, the man I used to respect. The man I used to trust.

SEVENTEEN

Muse

"Dad! Ohmigod! Thank you, thank you, thank you!" I cry, pushing past Jasper and throwing myself against my father's sturdy chest. He hugs me tightly and I let the sandpaper rasp of his cheek and the light scent of Old Spice soothe my nerves, nerves that have been frayed for eight long days.

"I knew you'd come," he says, his voice gruff in my ear. "And I knew he'd bring you."

I lean back to look questioningly into the familiar face. "What do you mean? How do you know Jasper?"

My father's shrewd, gray eyes leave mine to settle on Jasper where he stands behind me. I can feel his presence like a current of electricity tingling along my spine.

"We've worked together before."

I turn to glance back at Jasper. His blank expression, his tiger eyes are glued to my father's. They're unfathomable, as they so often are, but there's an animosity, a coldness pouring from him like an arctic breeze.

"How did you know I'd find him? I mean how . . ."

"He knew they'd send me. Because I'm the best one for the job," Jasper interjects. His voice is icy, his beautiful lips thin. Fingers of unease dance down my spine.

"Who's 'they'? And what do you mean 'send' you?" I ask.

When Jasper doesn't answer me, I look to my father. They're engaged in some kind of silent standoff, each man staring at the other, neither moving a muscle.

"Muse, honey, why don't you wait for me in the kitchen? I need to speak with Jasper."

"Dad, I think after all that's happened, after all I've done, that I at least deserve some answers."

Finally, he looks at me again. "You'll get them. I promise. Eventually, I'll tell you everything. In the meantime, you'll just have to trust me."

In his eyes I see the immovable force that I know my father to be. Some of the reasons that I love him—his protectiveness, his rock-solid reliability, his unconditional love of me—are also some of the things that frustrate me. When he gets it in his head that he's doing something to protect me, he's unshakable. Even by *me*. And this is one of those times. I can see it in everything from the firm set of his jaw to the stubborn angle of his chin.

As though sensing that I'm about to argue, he reaches out and cups the side of my head, right over my ear, like he's done for as long as I can remember. "Trust me, right, my Muse?"

I exhale. There's no use fighting. I'll never be able to change his mind. I know an unwinnable battle when I see one and anything involving my father when he gets like this gets that unique distinction.

"One of these days maybe you'll trust me as much as I trust you."

"I already do, sweetheart. It's not a matter of trust. It's a matter of love. I love you too much to risk you."

"I know, but—"

"No buts. Please, Muse."

I want to debate the issue. I want to argue until I'm blue in the face. I want to stomp my foot in a fit of temper. But I know there's no point. My father is a negotiating genius. At least with me he is. He has this way of making me feel like an ungrateful, difficult child for squabbling. I doubt *he* thinks that for one minute, but he can damn sure make me wonder about it.

I exhale loudly. "Fine, but, Dad, I'm a grown woman. I've made a lot of sacrifices because of secrets and I'm getting tired of being kept in the dark about things that somehow end up affecting me anyway. So I'll go wait for you while you talk in private with someone I evidently don't even know, but be prepared. I want answers and I don't want to wait too long for them."

With that, I pin Jasper with a glare thrown over my shoulder and I set out to find the kitchen, which is conveniently located about as far away from the entry as it's possible to get in this small place. Not that I'm surprised. Nor am I surprised when I hear the click of a door closing and go to find both Dad and Jasper no longer standing where I left them.

I have no choice except to wait. Not really, anyway. Jasper is about as close-mouthed as they come and my father . . . well, he won't tell me a thing until he's good and ready. So I'll wait, but I'll be damned if I'm going to wait in the kitchen, like a dog afraid to get up when my master told me to sit. I get up and go make myself comfortable on the worn couch in the living room. Although a tiny act of rebellion (which is admittedly ridiculous at twenty-four years old), I feel better for having moved to anywhere *but* the kitchen.

I pick up a magazine from the shelf under the coffee table. It's a medical journal dated three years ago. *Weird.* As I flip through it, something tickles my brain and I glance down at the couch cushion.

The faded plaid pattern is oddly familiar and I think this might be the couch we had in our living room in Treeborn when I was still in middle school. Has my father had this place since way back then? Some secret bat cave for whatever he does that I don't know about?

That thought bothers me. At times like this, I feel like I don't even know the man who raised me, just like I don't feel like I know the man who brought me here.

Jasper.

He was an enigma to begin with, but now? Now he's . . . I don't even know what he is. Or *who* he is. I have only questions, only curiosities. Questions and curiosities and a strange fascination that I worry could consume me.

My father is alive and well. Without that nugget of fear and doubt taking up space in my head, Jasper *could* take over. But now I have a different kind of unease to take its place, one also focused on Jasper.

Before, I didn't have to care that I knew so little about him. It didn't really matter because he was a means to an end. I didn't *need* to know. But now he's got history with my father. Dare I make the same mistake of getting involved with someone my father knows again? It didn't work out so well with Matt. And Jasper has the potential to hurt me far worse. I never found Matt's fatal flaw, but I feel sure he has one. All the men in my life do, it seems. But Jasper . . . I can't even imagine what his fatal flaw might be. I have a feeling that *he* could end up being *mine*, though—the thing that destroys me. Compared to Jasper, loving men who don't love me in return is child's play. Loving him could be the end of me, the end of the only Muse I've ever known.

But it doesn't look like that's going to be a problem. Our arrangement has come to an end. Once money changes hands, I won't ever have to see Jasper again. And if I can't see him, I can't love him. Right?

Can't see him. Won't ever see him. Never again.

Oh God!

The fact that thinking about that causes me great sadness is even more reason why I should be glad our association is over. I'm better off without Jasper in my life. That much I know.

Lost in thought, I jump when the door flies open and my father bellows, "Muse!"

"I'm right here, Dad," I respond, my heart pounding in my ears.

"I'm going to need you to go with Jasper."

And just like that, my plans—and likely my good, self-preserving intentions—go straight to hell.

"Don't you think you should at least tell me *why* instead of just telling me what I need to do and expecting me to comply like one of your soldiers?"

My father is sitting on the couch, facing me, one hand on my knee as if to keep me calm. Jasper is standing near the corner like a stoic, iron sentinel.

"I promised you I'd tell you everything, but sometimes it's better that you *not* know it all right away. It's safer."

Safer. Grrrr.

"How is it that I end up in the middle of such colossal messes when I have no freaking clue what's going on?"

At least Dad has the decency to look ashamed. "I would never want to be a liability to you, sweetheart, but unfortunately being my daughter comes with a risk. If anyone wanted to find a way to hurt me, to get me to do something against my will, all they'd have to do is use you." He starts to glance back, almost like he's going to look at Jasper behind him, but then he doesn't. His stormy eyes find mine again. "I'm sorry for that, Muse. I would never want you to get hurt because of me."

And now *I* feel ashamed. I know he's only doing what he thinks is best, what he thinks he needs to do to protect me. Being bitchy about it only makes it harder for both of us and makes him feel bad about being a good dad.

"I'm sorry, Dad. I know you're doing your best. It's just . . . I'm just frustrated. That's all."

"So you'll go, then?" he asks tentatively.

I slide my gaze up to Jasper. His expression is fierce yet unreadable. All he needs is a sword and chain mail to be a dark knight on a mission for his king. And if I'm not careful, he could slay my heart in the process.

"Yeah, I'll go, but how long is this gonna take? I can't leave Miran indefinitely, not with just Melanie for help. You know how—"

"Miran will be fine. I'll talk to her."

I should've expected that. Miran and my father obviously have a longstanding—and very trusting—relationship. It makes me wonder if I'm not the first person she's taken in like she did me. I mean, she owns the apartment that I live in, she deducts the rent from my pay and gives me the rest of the money under the table. She even gave me a burner cell phone the day that I arrived at her door. I more or less just stepped into a ready-made life, where I could be as anonymous as I needed to be. Heck, Miran and my friend Tracey are the only people in San Diego that even knew my last name. Yet Miran never asked one question.

"How will I know when . . . I mean, will you call me? Or . . . ?"

"I'll contact Jasper. He'll let me know where you are and then I'll come for you."

"You won't even know where I am?"

This puzzles me. And it obviously doesn't sit very well with my dad, judging by his expression.

"No, but you'll be safe with him. He's the best." Dad *does* throw a look back at Jasper this time. I'm still clueless, though. I can't see my father's face, and Jasper's shows nothing. As usual. He just nods at Dad. But I'm assuming that's enough communication because when my father turns back around, he looks somewhat satisfied. Even if *I* am not.

"Will I be able to reach you? Just to know you're safe?"

"It's better if there's no contact until this is all over."

Suddenly I feel desperate, panicky. I reach for my father's hand. "Dad, please tell me what's going on. You're worrying me."

His smile is stilted. "Don't you worry about me. This is about *you* and keeping you safe. I'll be fine. I promise."

Despite the ambiguous circumstances, his reassurance calms me. Colonel Denton Harper doesn't make promises he can't keep. And he doesn't placate. He might keep secrets, but what he *does* say is true.

"Okay," I say finally, tacking on no questions or complaints or conditions. The least I can do for this man is go along with what he's asking, give him peace of mind. *That* will have to be enough for me, too. I have a feeling that peace of mind will be nonexistent for me in the coming days. Not only will I be waiting for my father to come for me, but I'll be trapped with a man I already find intriguing and irresistible beyond that with which I'm comfortable. And he gives me the feels. All of them. What will become of me when I can't escape him, when I can't slip away into my own troubles?

I'll succumb.

And we'll share.

Then he'll destroy.

I know it. I know it like I know the triangle of freckles that dot my left shoulder. And I know myself well enough to know that this forced seclusion will seal my fate with him. Part of me looks forward to it—to his kiss, to his touch, to having time to delve as far into his life as he'll let me—but part of me dreads the end. Because it *will* come. And it will be brutal.

Dad cups my cheeks and leans forward to kiss my forehead. He lingers for a few seconds too long, causing me to wonder if he's more afraid than he's letting on. And, if so, what he's afraid of.

EIGHTEEN

Jasper

I've had to do a lot of unsavory things in my life. I was in the military for years, working missions that required some . . . questionable things. I never got into the morality of it. I never trusted my moral compass, not when I grew up the way I did, with a monster for a father. No, I always trusted the judgment of those I work for, those who gave me orders. I trusted that the missions were justified and that they're what kept people safe in the long run. When I took this job, I had my own reasons for wanting to find the Colonel. I don't particularly like that there was the collateral damage of a woman—his daughter—but those are details that I can't afford to get too hung up on. I need answers.

But this . . . this takes it to a whole new level. What kind of person would agree to something like this? What kind of person would use a woman to find her father, knowing what I have to do, and then agree to *this*? I'm keeping her safe until the Colonel gets me the proof I need, but even then, my orders won't change.

I know what's going to happen. We *will* end up sleeping together.

I can practically smell the want on her. Don't get me wrong, I want it, too. I want it bad. I want *her* bad. But even when that happens, it will be with the knowledge of what's to come, of how I'll betray her. What kind of person could do that?

A monster, that's who.

And *I'm* that monster.

I came to terms with it a long time ago. My father was a monster. According to him, my brother was a monster. I guess I always knew I had it in me, too. It's why I did what I did, so that my mother wouldn't have to suffer through knowing how I turned out. It's just never felt quite like this, though. This . . . bitter. This sick. This dirty.

But will that stop me? Will that stop me from sinking into her delicious, willing body?

No.

Because I'm the monster.

Muse hasn't said a single word since we left. I could understand her reticence on the trip here, but now . . . I assumed she'd pommel me with questions. Yet she hasn't opened her mouth. She's just stared out the window, into the night.

"My mother used to do that when she was worrying about something," I tell Muse when I see her playing with the charm of a necklace I've noticed she keeps hidden under her shirt.

Muse glances down at the small, silver disk she's been rubbing against her lip for the last hour.

"This was my mother's. I found it under the edge of her bed after she left."

"What is it?"

She shrugs. "I don't know. Some sort of charm. The back side is missing, so I can't really tell what it's supposed to be."

"I'm surprised you kept it."

At this she turns to look questioningly at me. "Why wouldn't I?"

"You said you wouldn't look for her because she didn't want you and your dad. I just assumed . . ."

"What? That I didn't love her? That I haven't missed her every day for the last twenty years?"

"I guess."

She turns away. From the corner of my eye, I see her chest rise and fall with her sigh. "Unfortunately, that's not how love works. No matter what she did, she was my mother. Nothing will change that."

"How do you think love is *supposed* to work? How does it work for you?"

"It holds you captive, whether you want it to or not. It never lets you go, no matter how much you want to be set free."

"Yet you were upset because Matt didn't love you like you wanted to be loved. Is that what you'd want for him?"

Glassy emerald eyes slide onto mine and stop. "Yes. But I want love to be *wanted*. *I* want to be wanted."

"I feel sure that wasn't the problem between you two."

"And why is that?"

"I can't imagine a man *not* wanting you."

At this, she turns in her seat to face me. She looks all too eager to talk now. Maybe I shouldn't have tried to pull her out of her shell. *Damn guilt.*

"Do *you* want me?"

"I haven't tried to hide that I do."

"Exactly *what* do you want from me?"

I glance in her direction. Even in the flash of oncoming head-lights, I see the intensity of her expression. She's got some anger to get out and she's looking for a fight.

Anger I can deal with. It's the other things she makes me feel that concern me.

"I think you know."

"Maybe, but tell me anyway."

There's tension in everything from her voice to the stiff set of her shoulders. Angry tension. And sexual tension. "What do I want from you?" I ask softly, glancing over her face, her shining eyes and pouty lips. "I want your moans in my mouth. I want your fingernails on my skin. I want your naked body against mine."

Her lips part and I see the tip of her tongue wet them. For a few seconds the sexual wins out over the angry. It breaks through the haze like a plea and it pulls me in so much that I don't want to look away. *God, just to think of the moment when she gives in, when she lets go and throws herself into feeling, like she wants so desperately to do.*

But then, as though she makes a conscious determination to hold on to the anger, she pulls away from me and crosses her arms over her chest. "How very gallant! Just what every girl wants to hear."

I turn my attention back to the road. "It should be because it's honest."

"Still, you could've said something else."

"Would you rather I lie? Would you rather me say that you make me feel things I don't want to feel? Would you rather I have said that I can picture myself spending nights inside you and mornings watching you sleep? Would you rather that I mislead you to get what we both want, just so you can feel better about wanting it?"

As I watch her, I'm pissed by how true those words felt. The worst thing I could do is fall for this woman.

Anger battles with hurt. Or maybe disappointment. It's there on her face. I just can't be sure which. Her mouth works itself open and closed a few times before she replies with a soft, "No."

"Then why don't we just stick with what we know? I want you.

You want me. We have some time to burn. Why not spend it as pleasantly as possible?"

"Maybe I'm not like that. Maybe I'm not that kind of a girl."

"Maybe you're not. But maybe you could be. Just for a little while."

"You could really be happy with that?"

"Yes. Very. And so could you if you'd give it a chance." To this, she says nothing, just stares at my profile so hard I can feel her eyes like a touch. "What if I promise not to tell that you're 'that kind of girl'?"

"Is that what you'd promise me?"

"I could. Why? What kind of promise do you need?"

"A promise not to hurt me, but I bet you'd never give me that one," she says quietly, her eyes cast down at hands that now move restlessly in her lap.

More guilt.

Guilt. Damn it.

But why? Why now? Why her?

"I don't make promises I can't keep."

"Can't or won't?"

"Does it matter?"

"Of course it matters." When I say nothing else, she prompts, "So, which is it? Can't or won't?"

I look over at her one more time and I tell her the truth. "Honestly, I don't know."

I don't have to tell her to stop asking me questions this time. She falls quiet all on her own.

NINETEEN

Muse

Jasper steers the car competently, carefully, quietly. I can't really be mad at him for being honest. It's not his fault that I didn't like his answers. I guess no man has *ever* been quite so honest with me, not even my own father. I guess I should be thankful that *someone* will tell me the truth. Now if I could just get Jasper to tell me the truth about other things.

By this point, however, I know him well enough to know that asking him outright won't do me any good. He's shown me that time and time again. But I *do* wonder, though, if he'll be more forthcoming and trusting when we start a physical relationship.

I know it's coming. Trying to resist him would be as silly and futile as trying to resist the rising of the sun or the rotation of the earth. And, truthfully, I don't really want to resist. Not really. I want him. More than I've ever wanted anyone. He makes me *feel* on a level that I've never felt before. Maybe it's his secrecy. Or maybe it's the air of danger that surrounds him. Or maybe it's this sense that I've not met the *real* Jasper yet. I've been getting this feeling that he's wounded so deeply that he doesn't let people in anymore. If he ever did.

The thought of that brings an ache to my chest. Who or what could hurt a person to that degree? And why would I be so drawn to that?

Probably because I embrace feelings, all of them, and I suspect that he is a well of feelings. Raw and untapped feelings. The kind that could flatten a girl like a category-five hurricane. But also the kind that could make survival the most rewarding thing in all of life.

I don't know. Maybe I'm wrong. Maybe this guy is just a cold, sneaky womanizer, albeit a fairly honest one. Maybe I'll regret getting involved with him. Maybe. But there's a small yet powerful part of me that says maybe I won't. And would I really want to risk missing out on something amazing, if that's what it turned out to be?

No, I wouldn't. Because *feelings* are what happen when you're alive. They're what make life worth living, good or bad. It's pain that makes pleasure so poignant. It's tears that make laughter so valuable. It's hate that makes love so important. And for this man, this gorgeous, strong, enigmatic man, maybe I could be the difference between them all. And maybe, in the meantime, he'll trust me enough to tell me some of his secrets.

"Where are we going?" I ask when the tires drop off the paved road onto a narrow gravel path that leads through increasingly dense forest.

"Some place safe."

"How much longer?"

"Not far."

I sigh. He's so damn vague sometimes that I wanna stab myself in the eye. At least it's not as frustrating as it *has been*. I guess I'm starting to expect it.

He meant it when he said not far. Less than ten minutes later, the road ends in a driveway that pulls up to a smallish A-frame cabin with what looks like a wraparound porch. A stone chimney splits the side facing us, softly illuminated by a tall, fading dusk-to-dawn light that looks like it belongs on a wharf.

"Where are we?" Before Jasper can answer, I preempt him. "And don't say 'someplace safe.'"

"Isn't that the most important thing?"

I glance over at him, his face brightly lit by the interior light that popped on when I opened my door. My heart stutters for a second, as though it might never get used to the handsome perfection of his honey eyes and bronze skin. He's beautiful. Beautiful and powerful and dangerous.

"Safety?" I ask. Something about his expression, about what happened at Dad's, about everything that's happened with him thus far, tells me that he's asking so much more than the obvious. "Not always."

"No?" One dark brow shoots up, making him look daringly sexy, like in a James Bond kind of way. The kind of way that says he'll crush me, but I'll never be able to fully regret such an amazing ride, no matter how many things get broken. Yes, it makes me a little nervous. Yes, I dread the fallout, but I'm also looking forward to knowing him. At all. In any way, physical or otherwise. Something inside me wants desperately to be close to him, to touch him and soothe him, to be touched *by* him. Maybe I'm crazy, but if I am, there's not a damn thing I can do about it. "What's more important than safety?"

"Making a life, making the choices, having the things that are worth keeping safe. *Those things* are more important. If not for them, what would be worth saving?"

He studies me in that way he has, that way that makes me think he's mentally stripping me down to nothing, able to hide not even the tiniest secret from his knowing eyes. "I've never thought of it that way."

I tilt my head to the side and consider him right back. "That might be the saddest thing I've ever heard, Jasper King."

"Then maybe I can cheer you up. And you can show me the important things."

Something about this moment, this place, this dark, quiet night, makes me feel like the world is a lifetime away, and that it's just us up here. Alone. No troubles. No appointments. Nothing but each other and what could be.

If only . . .

"I'd like that very much."

I can't hide the smile that curves my lips. It comes from too deep inside me.

Enchantment, Georgia. This is what Jasper calls "safe" and I'm inclined to agree with him. It feels remote here, secluded. Intimate. It also feels enchanting, making the name seem apropos. But that might just be me and my attitude.

I'm unpacked in my room. I have no idea how long I'll be here, so I just took out what things I brought and put them into the cedar drawers of the neat, rustic chest that's in my room. When I'm done, I know I'm too restless to sleep, so I set off to explore. And maybe find Jasper. It seems that no matter what else is going on, what else I'm thinking of, he's there. There in the back of my mind, seeping into the front. Drawing me to him . . . always drawing me to him.

My little cubby empties out into the main room, which is a combined living and dining room. One wall is the same stone as the chimney outside and boasts a fireplace so big I could almost stand inside it. There's already a fire crackling in its belly. I stand for a few seconds staring at it, letting both the literal heat and the charm of a cozy fire warm me.

Although it's not cold, there's a nip in the air, probably from the nearby mountains, that could probably turn very quickly into a damp chill. I'll probably be grateful for the warmth of the flames come morning.

I turn from the orange glow and take in the rest of the room. Comfy olive green furniture is angled to perfectly enjoy the logs or the view that I imagine rests beyond the floor-to-ceiling windows during the day. A chunky wooden table and six matching chairs sit against the opposite wall and, behind that, a doorway that I guess leads to the kitchen.

I walk that way, leaning around the corner to peek in at the stainless appliances and surprising accoutrements of the room. The space is laid out and accessorized like someone who uses it lives here, making me all the more curious as to whether this place belongs to Jasper or a friend. I smile to myself as I try and picture my dark, brooding companion at the stove, wielding a spatula and wearing an apron that says *Kiss the Chef.* Yeah, not happening.

I make my way to the front door and out onto the porch. I walk to the railing and look over an open expanse of grass that gleams in the bright light of the moon overhead. As though a magical trail sprinkled with fairy dust, it leads down a gentle slope to a dock. The planks are wide and pale, and they seem to disappear into waters that are murky, lying far outside the wide beam of blue-white moonlight. And even more magical, more mesmerizing, is the man standing at the lake's edge, hands in his pockets, face downturned, staring into oblivion. He's so gorgeous, yet he seems so troubled sometimes. He's withdrawn and sullen, but I'm also beginning to see small indications of a heart inside that iron frame, tiny clues that say he might actually care. Why that should make

me feel like I've won a grand prize is beyond me. Maybe because I
get the sense that Jasper isn't close to anyone. Not really.

I descend the steps and pad quietly across the lush grass until
I'm standing beside Jasper. I glance once in his direction, staring
long enough to commit his strong profile to memory. His face is
bathed in a soft, silvery light that casts a shadow under his deep-set
eyes and beneath his cheekbones. He looks like a statue, carved out
of moonbeams and mercury. I say nothing for at least five minutes.
He seems okay with that, standing still and silent beside me.

"It's beautiful here," I observe. He nods once, but says nothing.
I stare a little longer, reluctant to take my eyes off the even more
stunning beauty beside me.

I notice a hint of sadness on his face, an emotion that I've never
seen there before. In the starkness of the night, I can almost imagine
that if his skin were laid open, revealing the well-hidden soul that
lies beneath, I would see scars, crisscrossing Jasper like the lashes of
a sword, standing thick and white in remembrance of his pain.

I cup my elbows against the chilly breeze blowing off the water.
From the corner of my eye, I see Jasper glance down at me.

"Cold?"

"Just a little."

"I thought you'd be asleep by now. You've had a big day."

I shrug. "That's probably why I *can't* sleep."

His sigh is so light it nearly blends in with the wind. "How
about a drink, then? I could use a drink."

"That sounds good." He sounds so . . . deflated, I feel the need to
lift his spirits, to give him back the smile that he's so stingy with. To
calm him, to ease his pain. It's stupid, I know, to want to help someone who could suck me into a black hole of emotional torment, but
I've never been one to refuse a challenge. Jasper turns back toward
the house. "And maybe some cards. Do you have any cards?"

"Cards?" he asks dubiously. "Seriously."

I tip my head. "Well it's not like we can talk or anything. We need *some way* to pass the time."

Jasper gives me a sidelong glance that's as hot as the fire burning inside that cabin. Even in the night, I can see it, bright as day. "I can think of several ways to pass the time that have nothing to do with talking. *Or* cards."

I feel breathless and giddy, but also a little bit nervous. He's so matter-of-fact about it that I feel a blush coming on.

"Let's start with cards," is all I say.

"Okay, then we'll *start* with cards. We've got all night."

And all day tomorrow. And the next day. And maybe even the next.

Suddenly, I actually look forward to my confinement. If no one will give me answers just yet, it will do me good to work off some of my frustration. And I get the feeling that there would be no better person to work it off with than Jasper.

He reaches for my hand, his long warm fingers wrapping around mine. It seems that my hand was designed to fit inside his, like my skin feels more alive against his than it's ever been before. I can only imagine what it will feel like when more of our skin touches. *All* of our skin.

Heat floods me and I shiver again.

"I thought you said you weren't cold," he says.

I glance up to meet his darkly glistening eyes. "I'm not."

He stops, turning to face me. The yellowish light from inside spills out across the porch and over one half of Jasper's face leaving him half in shadow. He's always half in shadow, difficult to see. Even more difficult to get to know.

His expression is intense, as always, but right now it's even more so. He looks determined. Fiercely so. And hungry. Very, very hungry.

With his tiger eyes on mine, he sweeps his thumb over my palm.

There's just enough pressure, just enough of a rasp of his lightly cal-
loused thumb to tear a small, breathy gasp from me. The sensation
flows through me like a languid ribbon of lava. It oozes from my belly
down into my core, heating me up and making my insides clench.

"We're going to go slow, beautiful Muse. Would you like to
know why?"

I can't breathe. Why can't I breathe? I'm outside in the cool,
crisp air.

"Why?"

"Because I'm going to enjoy every sound, every breath, every
squeeze that you make for me. I don't want to miss even one. Then,"
he says, bringing my fingers to his mouth, "I'm going to devour
you. Like an animal." As if to punctuate his words, he sinks his
teeth into the tip of my index finger in one sharp pinch. The sensation lands between my legs like a delicious stab.

"I thought you didn't bite," I say, nothing else able to surface in my
overcome mind.

"No, I said you'd have to ask nicely."

"But I didn't ask."

"Yes, you did. You just didn't use words."

I feel the hot flick of his tongue before he releases my finger and
pulls me up the steps behind him. I feel like a lamb being led to the
slaughter.

I've never wanted to be slain until now.

TWENTY

Jasper

Inside, I walk to the old cabinet that sits in the corner of the living room. It's hip-high and has three doors along the front. It's the only furniture I kept from the house that I grew up in. My mother loved the cabinet because she said my brother and I used to like to play in it when we were little. It was also my father's favorite since he kept his liquor in it.

For me, the distressed piece of history holds memories that I can't let myself forget. The happiness that my mother brought me. The pain that my father did. Now it holds a quilt that she made from pieces of T-shirts that Jeremy and I had outgrown, along with what remains of my dad's alcohol stash.

Like the cabinet, I carry both of them around in me every day. Good and bad. Light and dark. Laughter and pure evil. I can't escape either. But maybe one even more than the other.

I take out the bottle of vodka that's been behind the creaky wooden door since I brought the cabinet here. I blow off the thin layer of dust coating the top.

"Wow, you must be a big drinker," Muse says from behind me.

I'm studying the bottle as I turn toward her. "I can't remember the last time I had a drink. In my profession, it's important to be alert."

"But not tonight?"

I raise my eyes to hers. "Oh no. I want to be alert tonight."

"Then why are you getting that out?"

"For you. I'm hoping to loosen up your delicate sensibilities."

"Ummm, I don't really want to drink alone."

"I'll have a couple of drinks. Just enough to relax, but nowhere near enough to dull what comes next."

I see her cheeks stain with pink. She's a walking, talking contradiction, this one. Maybe that's what I like most about her. I can't always anticipate what she'll say or how she's going to act.

I grab two tumblers from behind another door in the cabinet and take them to the coffee table in front of the fireplace. I reach in the drawer of one of the end tables and pull out a deck of cards.

I pour an inch of vodka in each glass before I sit down on the floor and lean up against the couch. Muse kneels in front of the table across from me. The firelight flickers against the smooth cream of her skin and I commend myself on picking this spot. She'll look incredible lying on the rug, spread out beneath me, wearing nothing except that soft, orange glow.

"What?" she asks, nervously tucking a stray flame of hair behind her ear.

"Nothing. I was just imagining what your skin will look like with only the light from the fire covering it."

Her pupils dilate and she licks her lips, dropping her gaze from mine and attacking the deck of cards that rests between us.

"I love that you're nervous."

"I'm not nervous," she defends.

Liar.

"Good. There's no reason to be. It's not like I haven't already seen you naked."

Cheeks turn redder, bottom lips gets bitten. "I know," she replies, trying to sound nonchalant.

"Then you won't mind making this interesting." Emerald eyes fly up to mine again.

"What do you mean?"

"Strip poker. What do you say?"

She clears her throat and begins shuffling the deck. "Fine. Strip poker it is. Five-card draw. Jokers are wild."

As she deals the cards, I notice the tremble of her fingers. Before I pick up my hand, I pick up my tumbler and hold it out toward her. "To animals and delicate sensibilities."

"To poker and vodka."

"To teeth prints and claw marks."

At her third blush, I toss back my drink and pick up my cards.

TWENTY-ONE

Muse

I sputter at the burn of vodka searing its way down my throat. Within seconds, a pleasantly warm sensation erupts in my stomach. It's no match for the heat coming from Jasper's eyes, though. I doubt even the open flames that flicker in the fireplace just a few feet away could match the scorching intensity of his gaze.

I examine my cards, trying hard to concentrate on what I'm doing rather than the man sitting across from me. It's incredibly difficult, though. I'm hyper aware of every glance in my direction, every movement, every sound. It all works together to tease my taut nerves, like fingers plucking the strings of a harp.

"So what's going in the pot, kitten?"

"Kitten?" I ask.

"Yes, kitten."

"Why kitten?"

"Because sometimes you're a kitten. Like now."

"And other times?"

The flames are perfectly reflected in the golden sparkle of Jasper's eyes when he looks at me. They're every bit as intoxicating as the vodka I just drank.

"Other times you're a wild cat."

"And how do you know that?"

"I've tasted it. And I'm dying to taste it again."

My pulse is thrumming in my neck like the tick of an anxious finger, tapping against my skin.

"I guess I bet my shirt," I say, disconcerted by this side of Jasper. He's as unrelenting as the one I've spent the last few days with, only in a totally different way. A delicious way that makes my blood sing with anticipation. Anticipation and a little bit of fear. Not the kind that says he might hurt me. The kind that says he might hurt me in the best sort of way. The sort of way that will make my knees weak for the rest of my life.

"Brave little kitten, then," he remarks. "I figured you'd go with shoes or socks first."

I could kick myself. Why the hell didn't I think of that? "Wait! I—"

"Ah-ah-ah. No changes. I'm in with my shirt, too."

I clamp my mouth shut and glance back down at my cards. "How many do you want?" I ask Jasper.

"I'll take two."

I deal him two new cards.

I look back to my semi-pathetic hand and announce that I'll take three, so I slide three from the top of the deck. The three new cards dramatically helped my chances of winning. I smother a smile, my heart pounding at the thought of Jasper stripping off his clothes in front of me.

"I'm in for my socks," I say, upping the ante.

Jasper cocks one raven brow at me, amusement shining in his

eyes. God, if he's gorgeous in his dark, brooding state, he's flat-out incredible in this one. "Then I'll give you my pants."

Hot flash!

I resist the urge to fan my face.

"Call," I say.

I spread out my cards on the smooth wooden top of the table.

"Full house," I announce with a smile.

"Damn," Jasper whispers. Then with a wink that could melt the panties off a nun, he splays out his cards and mutters, "Four of a kind."

My mouth drops open, whether because he just won and I have to strip or because I've never wanted to strip for someone so much in my life, I don't know. All of a sudden, I can't wait for him to touch me, for him to look at me with a passion in his eyes that blots out everything else in the world. I need that. I need *him*.

"Oh," I say breathlessly. "I, uh, I guess I owe you some clothes, then, don't I?"

I reach for the laces of one shoe, ready to give up my socks, but Jasper's voice stops me.

"Wait. What are you doing?" he asks.

"You won. I'm paying up. Isn't that how this works?"

"Not in *my* game," he replies. His voice is a low growl, his eyes never more tigerlike. Stalking. Predatory. Ravenous.

I watch as Jasper rolls forward onto his hands and knees and crawls around the front of the table toward me. I don't speak. I don't move. I just take him in, frozen in place by the sheer want I see on his face.

"In my game, the winner gets to *take* his winnings. Like any *real* winner would."

Take his winnings. Sweet God, he's going to strip me!

Long, strong fingers wind around my ankle and tug. In one slow, smooth motion, he drags me toward him, his eyes never leaving mine.

Nimbly, he unties my right shoe and pulls it from my foot. Then, with deliberate movements, he slides his fingers under the elastic of my sock and slips it down my foot, easing it over the tips of my toes. The material softly scrapes my skin, the friction resounding in my belly like a caress.

He treats the other foot to the same kind of methodical attention, leaving enough moisture between my legs to douse the fire. But not nearly enough to douse *my* fire. It's just beginning to rage out of control. This time there will be no stopping. This time I will feel all of Jasper and he will feel all of me.

When he's discarded my socks, Jasper grabs me behind the bend of each knee and pulls me toward him again, guiding my legs to either side of his. I'm resting on my elbows, my sex throbbing like native drums, when Jasper reaches for the hem of my shirt. Rather than curling his fingers into it, however, he lays his hands flat against my stomach and starts to push the material up.

His palms are broad, hot torture to the bare skin of my midriff. I suck in a breath and his lips turn up at the corners.

"Easy, kitten," he murmurs. "Don't scratch me yet."

At a pace that has me nearly writhing against him, Jasper raises my shirt, his rough hands a tantalizing scrape of skin on skin, a promise of wicked delight to come.

When he reaches my breasts, he moves up and over them, cupping them for just a second before continuing on. He turns his hands just enough that his thumbs graze my nipples with enough pressure to make me arch my back. And then they're gone and his fingers are on my chest. At my throat.

"Lie back," he instructs quietly, his voice as hypnotic as his eyes.

I do as he asks. He scoots up between my legs and leans over me, easing first one arm then the other out of their sleeves so he can pull my shirt over my head. With every movement, he rocks ever so slightly against me, the hardness of his erection straining against his pants, straining against me.

When my shirt is gone and I'm lying with my arms by my sides and my legs practically around his hips, Jasper rests his weight on one forearm and bends to speak into my ear.

"I can feel how hot you are all the way through my jeans." A tiny bit of blood rushes to my face. The rest pools at the very point where his body touches mine. "Tell me, kitten, can I take the rest of what I won?"

"You haven't won yet," I respond breathily.

"But it's just a matter of time."

"How can you possibly know that?"

"I'll make sure I win. Even if I have to cheat."

"That's hardly fair."

Jasper flexes his hips, pressing into me in a painfully slow rhythm that makes my whole body tighten. "It's hardly fair that the only taste I crave is the inside of your mouth. It's hardly fair that I go to bed thinking about you or that I wake up aching for you. It's hardly fair that I want you so bad my cock feels like it's going to explode. But, then again, whoever said life was fair?"

"I guess you have a point," I manage past the moan that's bubbling in my throat.

"Is that a yes?" he asks, the fingers of his free hand sliding under the waist band of my yoga pants to grip my hip.

"That's a hell yes."

The last thing I hear before his lips meet mine is a throaty laugh that makes the hair on my arms stand up. And then I'm lost, lost in a sea of sensation and desire.

Jasper's tongue slides effortlessly past my lips just as his hand turns and slides down the front of my panties. My spread legs leave me open for him. There's nothing between him and the emptiness that only he can fill.

He moves into my panties and I hold my breath, anticipating the first electric touch of his fingers. He eases one fingertip between my folds, unerringly finding my nub. He rubs over it in one soft sweep, bringing my hips up off the floor before he moves down to my entrance, circling it as his palm cups the rest of me. "Holy Jesus, you're wet. So wet," he moans against my mouth, teasing me with several more circles before pushing one long finger inside me.

I groan into his mouth and he flexes his finger within me, rubbing me from the inside as his rough hand massages me from the outside. His lips fall gently away from mine, like a leaf might fall away from a branch and drift slowly to the ground. They descend in a sensual exploration that leaves me with boiling blood, blazing skin and, somehow, no clothes left on my body. His mouth hovers over my belly, his breath hot against my sensitive skin.

"The night you came for me, right there in the shower, with my eyes on your face and my hands on your body, I don't think I've ever wanted something as bad as I wanted to be inside you. To feel that warm gush, that hot squeeze. God, you were amazing to watch."

Trying to focus on his words, trying to think past what his lips and his fingers are doing only seems to heighten the sensation that I'm spinning out of control. Is this part of his game? Is he doing it on purpose? Could he possibly know what he's making me feel? Or is it simply Jasper, the man who does crazy things to me without even trying?

"Jasper, please," I beg when his mouth is inches from his hand. His lips brush slowly back and forth between my legs, his moist breath more a tantalizing promise than a concrete touch.

"Please what?" When I don't answer, when I can't find the air or the energy to form words, he fills in the blanks for me. "Please lick me?" he asks, pressing his tongue into my crease and sweeping me from top to bottom in the most delicious lick I've ever experienced. "Please suck me?" He draws my clit into his mouth, flicking it with the tip of his tongue before sucking on it until my back arches off the floor. "Please put your cock in me?" He leaves me for what seems like only a few seconds—the rustle of clothes, the rattle of a wrapper—before I feel him again, burning skin to burning skin. "Or please do anything you want to my body as long as you make me come?"

"Yes! Yes to all of it!"

"Then come for me, kitten. Give me everything you've got." He groans the last just as he pushes his body into mine.

"Unh," I half grunt, half gasp as he stretches me painfully. He's so big. Almost too big.

Just before the pleasure-pain becomes too much, he withdraws, but not completely. With his broad tip still resting within me, Jasper reaches between us to rub me as he sucks on one nipple and makes shallow thrusts into me, giving me time to accommodate him. When I relax again, my body clutching for more of his thick length, he eases in farther, biting down on my nipple at the same time, creating a sensual overload. I dig my fingernails into the smooth skin of his back.

"Oh God! Jasper!"

"Mmmm, that's right. Give me your claws."

With that, he pulls out and then slams back into me, hard and deep. My body stretches around him and then squeezes in that divine way that I feel in my every bone and muscle. When he withdraws again, he pounds back in deeper still, but not completely. I know the moment he's fully seated within me. He flexes his hips in one last thrust, one more delicious push that sends me falling over the edge. I'm thrown onto a wave of ecstasy and then carried out to sea by a million more.

I'm so enraptured that I hardly hear his feral grunt when he stiffens against me, but I feel it when he lets go. I couldn't *not* feel it. He pulses within me, each throb so strong it tosses me right back into the fray of my orgasm. And this one, we ride out together.

TWENTY-TWO

Jasper

I carried Muse's limp, naked body from the living room floor to her bed. She asked me to lay with her. For some reason I agreed. Now she's resting quietly against me. Her head is on my outstretched upper arm and she's facing me, her fingers drawing lazy circles on the cool sheets between us.

I don't open my eyes. I don't look at her. I'm sure she knows I'm not asleep. Even if I could sleep in the room with another person, I couldn't do it right now anyway. I can almost feel her mind spinning, like vibrations of unrest in the air around me. Stirring. Churning.

I smile into the dark when I hear her voice. I knew she wouldn't be able to stand the silence for very long.

"Jasper, where are we? Whose cabin is this?"

I sigh. *Always with the questions.*

"It's mine."

"Is this your house? I mean, where you live all the time?"

"I don't live anywhere all the time."

"But do you live here *some of the time*?"

"What if I do?"

I feel her shrug. Even with my eyes closed, I can picture it in my head. The way the corners of her mouth dip in. The way her eyebrows rise just a little. The way her hair moves against her shoulders. I can recall with absolute clarity nearly every small detail about her. Just like I've never really felt much guilt, I've never really been haunted by someone I've met on one of my missions before either. But Muse . . . she is one who will haunt me, I think. Forever.

"It's fine if you do. I just . . . It seems . . ."

"It seems what?" I prod gently, enjoying the residue of pleasure that's still softening my muscles.

"It doesn't seem to reflect *you*. Like, I don't see things that make me think of you, ya know? Is that weird?"

It's my turn to shrug. "I don't know. I guess I don't really pay much attention to décor."

She turns the nervous attention of her fingers to my ribs, tracing each one, starting from just beneath my arm. "What about this place or what piece of furniture or what knickknack says something about you? About the *real* Jasper?"

She's clever, trying to get to know me this way. As someone who most often employs deceptive, devious or covert means to get information that people wouldn't normally divulge, I can appreciate it. Her method doesn't surprise me. She's an intelligent woman with a curious mind. I like that about her. What *does* surprise me is the ease with which I decide to tell her what she wants to know. It comes with a pang of guilt and melancholy, though. I know why I'm going to take advantage of the first person I've felt close to in a long time and tell her some personal things about myself. It's because she won't be a threat to me. She can't be.

"There's a white china dish in the master bathroom. Right beside the sink. I see it every time I wash my hands, brush my teeth, whatever. It was my mother's. Since I was a little kid, she kept her hair ties in it. When I take the lid off, it makes the whole room smell like her."

Muse's voice is hushed, tentative when she asks, "Is she . . . is she gone?"

"She might as well be."

I don't know why I even give her that answer. I know she won't be satisfied with it. Muse is the type of person who wants to know everything about the people in her life. What they love and hate, why they do the things they do. What makes them tick. She's that much like her father.

"So she's not dead?"

For about a tenth of a second, I ask myself if I really want to do this. Let someone in. Take the risk. But then I remind myself that there's no risk at all. And for whatever reason, that bothers me more than if there was.

"No, she's very much alive."

"But you don't see her?"

"No."

"Why not?"

"She thinks I'm dead."

Muse lifts her head off my arm and her hand stills. "Dead? Why?"

"Because I wanted her to think I'm dead."

"But why on earth would you do that to her? To yourself?"

"Because she's better off not knowing what I am. This way, she got to mourn the boy I used to be. That's better than hating the man I've become."

Muse's gasp is soft, but I still hear it. It's like a slap in the dark. "But why? What's so wrong with the man you've become?"

"He's too much like my father."

"In what way?"

"In every way. He's cold and heartless. Ruthless. He destroys everything he touches. She wouldn't be proud of what I've become, so I let her keep the boy she loved. Besides, it's safer for her this way. To the world, her son is dead. There would be nothing for anyone to gain by hurting her."

"I don't . . . I don't understand. You're a bounty hunter. Why would people be after your mother?"

I open my eyes and roll my head to face Muse. Her eyes are dark in the low light, dark and confused. "The people I hunt don't want to be found. And they certainly don't want to be found *by me*."

I see the wheels turning behind her narrowed gaze. I see the exact moment she begins to process what I might mean. Her eyes go from slim slits to wide, stunned orbs. "What are you saying, Jasper?"

"Probably just what you think I'm saying. I'm saying that I do the things few other people have the stomach for."

She sits up straighter, pulling the sheet over her naked torso, like she's suddenly uncomfortable. But not with her nudity. More with our intimacy. And I can see why. Most people abhor what I am when they get an inkling of it.

"Wait. Dad said that he knew you'd bring me, that he knew they'd send *you*. What does that mean? That meeting you was no accident? That you were sent to . . . to . . ."

I shouldn't hedge. I should lay out the cold, hard truth for her, but something in me can't stand seeing the look of hurt and disgust on her face.

"I knew him. Quite well, actually. They knew if anyone could find him, it would be me."

"So you weren't going to—"

I interrupt her. "Your father knows that he needs to get me some information and that he needs to do it fast. He knows that as long as I have you, he's under no threat from me. I have no reason to hurt him because he has *every* reason to comply. *You* are his reason to get me what I need."

"So I'm like insurance?"

I seesaw my head. "Sort of, if that's how you want to look at it."

"You keep me until he delivers?"

"Yes."

Her brows knit together. "Why would he keep that from me? Why wouldn't he just tell me? He has to know that I'd go along with it if it meant keeping him out of danger, out of trouble. I mean, hell, I left South Carolina and moved across the country to keep him safe."

"At least that's what he wanted you to think," I add. I probably shouldn't get involved in their arrangements, but she might as well know that he did it all for her.

"What's that supposed to mean?"

"Think about it. Is the Colonel *really* the type to let his daughter uproot her entire life and move away from him just to keep him safe?"

She pauses to think. "I knew it didn't really seem like him, like something he'd do, but . . ."

"But you trust him. I get it. And that's good. He'd never do anything to hurt you, so your trust isn't misplaced."

"No, but he obviously thinks nothing of lying to protect me." There's an angry set to her jaw, an aggravated angle to the tilt of her chin.

"People do that for the ones they love."

As she looks at me with those big, exotic eyes, I see the anger fade into a curious sadness and I know before she speaks that she's turning her attention back to me. I admire that she's always ready to throw herself so completely into the life and trust of another person. It's inadvisable as hell, but I love the haphazardness with which she lives. It's the absolute antithesis of everything about my life.

"Like you did for your mother."

Leave it to Muse to go there, to take what I've told her and paint me as some sort of martyr. But she's wrong and I can't let her think otherwise.

I meet her eyes, baring all the coldness my soul possesses for her to see, driving home my point before I even open my mouth. "Don't mistake me for a good guy, Muse. My motives were purely selfish. I didn't want the pain of my mother's disgust. I didn't want the heartache of her being captured or tortured because of me. Letting her believe me to be dead was anything *but* a selfless act."

"Maybe those were the main reasons, but still, you loved her enough to spare her that pain, too. Has it ever occurred to you that you might be selling yourself short, Jasper?"

"No, it hasn't," I reply, deadpan. "If I stand in a room full of people anywhere in the world, I know who the monster is."

She tips her head to one side to consider me, a sweetly pained expression on her face. I recognize it for what it is. And I hate seeing it.

Pity.

"Is that what you think? That you're a monster?" I don't answer her. I hold my tongue, gritting my teeth against all the uncharacteristic emotions swirling through me right now. Anger, disbelief, bitterness. Hope. Cruel desire. "Let me tell you something, Jasper," she says, dropping the sheet and moving to straddle me.

Despite the fact that I just slaked my hunger for her, despite the fact that I hate this subject and my obvious weakness in telling her so much about myself, I feel my cock stir instantly to life, rising toward her warm moisture.

She does things to me, things no other person has ever done. She makes me feel . . . Hell, I don't know. She just makes me *feel*. And that's dangerous. For both of us. But will it stop me? No. Because I'm a cold, calculating man who puts feeling and consideration aside for what must be done. It's who I have to be in order to be able to do what I have to do. So whether she believes it or not, I *am* the monster.

"You're a foolish woman if you believe otherwise," I bite, holding on to my anger like a kid refusing to give up his candy. After so long of never letting emotion in, letting some of my fury take hold is darkly invigorating.

"Maybe I am, but monsters don't love, Jasper. And whether you see it that way or not, you love your mother. You love her enough to never see her again just to spare her pain and suffering."

"My father loved her, too, but he made her more miserable than anyone on the planet. It *is* possible to love someone so much that it hurts them. Or love them and *still* hurt them."

"I'm sure it probably is, but that's not what you do. I can't believe that."

"Then you're a fool. Just like I said."

She is unflappable, a smile curving her lips as she leans toward me. "You're not a monster. I couldn't do this to a monster," she says in a husky voice, brushing her silky lips over mine. I hold perfectly still, fighting with the anger that's roiling within me. I want to believe her, but I know better. It's the reality of that disparity— what I am versus what *she thinks* I am—that keeps some softer emotion from overtaking that anger. So I let it flow. To protect her from me, I let it flow so that she can *see*. So that she can *know*.

"You're making a mistake, Muse. I'm not playing around."

"I'm not either," she continues, tracing my lower lip with the tip of her tongue. "Unless this feels like play." She lightly scrapes her fingernails down my stomach, reaching between us to cup my tightening balls.

I'm balanced on a pinhead, teetering between violence and something I can't identify. I give her one last chance to come to her senses before I go with what I know, with what I'm good at.

"Do you really want to know what it feels like to play with a monster?"

"Yes," she breathes into my mouth.

"Then I'll show you how a monster plays," I hiss against her lips.

She gasps in surprise when I roll her over, pinning her to the mattress. "One last chance," I tell her, restraining both wrists above her head with one of my hands, leaving her open and vulnerable beneath me. I bite down on her bottom lip, hard enough to draw a single drop of blood. I taste the coppery liquid on my tongue. It's like high octane in the jet engine of a raging machine.

"Show me," she pants, a miniscule trace of fear in her voice. That's good, though. She needs to know who she's dealing with and how disgusted she should be by him. Scaring her is the best thing I can do for her.

I lick the blood from her lip as the last of my control slips through my fingers. "I will destroy you, too," I confess, guilt and desire and reluctance fueling me.

As if to prove my point, my sick, twisted point, I crush my mouth to hers, grinding our lips together, forcing her to open for me. When I taste the inside of her mouth, the submission there, my blood ignites. Suddenly, I can't get enough of her, of her unconditional acceptance of the black beast that lives deep within me.

I push my knee between hers, parting her legs until I rest between them. I reach down to find her slippery core and I pinch the tiny muscle within her folds, rolling it between my fingers. She half cries, half moans against my mouth, her hips bucking against me. I look down into her wide, excited eyes and I feel moisture pour out onto my fingers as I thrust them into her.

"J-Jasper," she begs.

I revel in her response.

"Don't ask me for mercy. Monsters don't know mercy."

She gulps in air, her brilliant eyes fixed on mine as I spread her further. I wedge my hips between her legs and guide my cock to her entrance. We watch each other for three intense seconds—*one Mississippi, two Mississippi, three Mississippi*—recognizing each other for exactly what we are, and then I slam into her body with one brutal stroke. Her head knocks against the headboard, but that doesn't stop me. I withdraw and pound into her again, clamping my teeth down on one beaded nipple just as her body clamps down around mine.

I ride her silently, ruthlessly, aware only of her sounds of pained ecstasy and the heat that leeches from her body, from her soul into mine. I'm alive. Finally, after all this time, I'm alive.

Spiraling upward in my anger, in the simple emotion that I've fought for so long, I find that I can't stop. It's as though now that I've finally let feeling in, I gave up control over it. It was either or. Be dead or be alive. Not both. Never both.

With a feral noise that scares even the shadows in the room, I pull roughly out of Muse's warm body and drop down between her legs. I want only to consume, to take her in. All of her, leaving nothing behind but vapor.

Cupping her ass in my hands, I feast on her deliciously wet body. I bite and suck and nibble until she's begging me with incoherent moans and groans. But I'm already gone. My mission is to possess and I won't stop until I do.

When she's riding my face like I was riding her body, I eat her until the muscles in her lower body tense. In that moment, all I can think about is getting inside her. All the way inside her.

I thrust my tongue into her pussy. I thrust my finger into her ass. I penetrate her, body and soul, until she pours out for me like she's making a sacrifice to the god of war. And I drink her in. Her acquiescence, her surrender, her acceptance, I drink it all in.

And when she's lying limp beneath me, I grab her around the waist and flip her roughly onto her belly. When her face is turned into the pillow, I sink my fingers into the flesh of her hips and take her from behind. I drive my body viciously into hers over and over and over again, conscious only of the slap of skin against skin and the wet noises her slick body makes. But it's not enough. I want to see her face. I *need* to see her face.

Barely breaking rhythm, I pull out, roll her back over and thrust into her again, holding her legs wide and her gaze hostage. With our eyes locked together, black soul colliding with white, I pummel her willing body until I spill every ounce of feeling I have left within me deep inside her body.

TWENTY-THREE

Muse

My entire body tingles. My entire soul weeps. I want to take Jasper in my arms and soothe him, but I know that he wouldn't welcome it. I don't know how to comfort him, or even if that's possible. It seems he's spent so long convincing himself that he's a monster, he refuses to believe anything else.

I know that's what he was just now trying to prove to me. He was showing me what an awful person he is. But it didn't work. Despite his roughness, he never actually hurt me. What he doesn't know is that such raw emotion, especially coming from someone who rarely shows *any* emotion, turned an amazing sexual encounter into one of the most breathtaking, earth-shattering experiences of my life. My mind is reeling and my heart is opening like a blossoming flower. And my body . . . my body feels as though an entire symphony was played out on my every nerve by expert hands.

But those might not have been the best gifts of all. The best gift might be when Jasper raises his head and speaks to me, surprising me yet again.

"I'm sorry," he says flatly. The remorse isn't evident in his voice, but I can see enough of his face and his eyes to read it as plain as day.

I reach up to touch his cheek. "Don't be."

"I didn't use protection. I could've . . ."

He drops his forehead onto the pillow at the curve of my neck, so he doesn't see the mild alarm that crosses my face.

Honestly, I hadn't even thought about that. I was so caught up in my feelings and what just happened between us, the consequences of it hadn't even sunk in yet. But they're sinking in now.

I swallow hard. "I'm clean. I haven't had sex since Matt and we were both tested, so . . ."

"I am, too. I've been tested, even though I don't usually have unprotected sex."

I nod, letting that bit calm half of my fears. The other half . . . only time will tell, but I try to focus on the positive. On what's *likely* to happen. Or, rather, what's likely *not to* happen.

"Good, so we're clear there. As for the . . . other concern, I just got off my period a few days ago, so I think we'll be okay."

I send up a quick prayer that I don't get pregnant, although, perversely, the thought of having Jasper's child—a beautiful dark-haired girl or a handsome amber-eyed boy—gives me a warm, contented feeling in my chest.

Maybe you're finally losing it, Muse. Maybe you finally cracked under the pressure.

"Okay," he replies, the word muffled. "I don't . . ." He raises his head and meets my eyes again. "I don't usually lose control like that. In fact, I never do. Not. Ever. I just . . . I just don't." His expression is one of stilted disappointment. In himself, it seems.

"Jasper, it's okay to have a feeling every once in a while."

His expression is unyielding. "Feelings lead to weakness, to uncalculated actions and reactions."

I smile, undeterred by his surliness. I'm beginning to think that's just the way he *tries* to be. It makes it easier to not feel, makes it easier to keep people out. But that's not going to work with me. I don't know why I'm so determined to figure him out, to know him, to *rescue* him, but I am. I think Jasper needs me, whether he knows it or not. And I might need him, too.

"Ummm, I'm pretty sure there was *nothing* weak about what just happened." A blush of sudden shyness stings my cheeks as I think about all the details of the past few minutes. "If that's the monster you're hiding, I think I'll keep him around for a while."

Even as I speak, I feel Jasper hardening where he still rests inside me. A thread of excitement is just working its way through me when he surprises me by taking my wrists again, this time in each of his hands and pinning them out to the sides. "Don't you get it? You shouldn't like this. You shouldn't like *me*. I'm not a good person. I'm not someone you can just happily toy with and then go on about your life unscathed. Knowing me, spending time with me, will only end in unimaginable pain for you."

His teeth are gritted. His eyes are fierce. His tone is venomous. I have to admit that it does give me pause. But not for long. What I *do* realize, however, is that it might be best not to make light of this. He obviously takes it very seriously.

"Look, you're not going to scare me off, so stop trying. If you're uncomfortable with this then we'll stop."

He squeezes my fingers so hard I fear the fragile bones might snap. I bite my lip to keep from yelping, determined not to back down from him in any way. I'm going to meet him head-on if it kills me.

"That's the problem, damn you! I don't want to stop!"

He flexes his hips and grinds into me as his mouth descends onto mine. He pumps his length into me in two short, savage bursts, as if he might be trying to punish me for wanting him. Or maybe punishing *himself* for wanting *me*. But it doesn't work. I meet him, thrust for thrust, raising my hips into his, opening my lips for his provocative tongue.

Finally, with a guttural sound that reminds me of the tiger that's in his eyes, he tears away from me and rolls off the bed, dragging me across the sheets and into his arms. Once his hungry mouth meets mine again, he doesn't stop kissing me. Not when he leans down to get a condom from the nightstand and not when my back is pressed to the shower wall and he drills his body into mine. Jasper never stops kissing me. And it occurs to me, somewhere deep down, that I never want him to.

I lie in bed thinking about last night. After Jasper finished trying *not* to want me, we bathed each other and then he stepped out to get dressed and leave me to my nightly preparations. Nearly half an hour later, I exited my bedroom to find him gone, the house empty. I was too exhausted to go looking very far, but something told me before I even looked out the window that I'd find him at the water's edge. And I did. I left him to his thoughts in favor of falling onto the tangled sheets of my bed and drifting straight into a dreamless sleep.

My first thought upon waking was of Jasper, of this complicated, broken, multi-faceted man who shows so little yet feels so much. I've always had a weakness for flawed men. It seems that I gravitate toward the ones who are emotionally unavailable for some reason. Ambitious, womanizing, cheating men who clean up pretty, but never really change. But Jasper . . . he's a different animal.

An animal.

A tiger.

I wouldn't even know where to begin to describe him. I've never met a man less emotionally available, but at the same time, I've never met someone who's more brutally honest about who and what he is.

From what I can tell, his flaws are so inextricably interwoven with loyalty and dedication, it's hard to see where good stops and bad begins. Or even if there *is* such a clear, black-and-white way to view him. All in all, he's probably the strongest, most determined person I've ever known, but I don't think I've ever met someone more in need of saving. It's that paradox, that strength overlying a shattered soul, that draws me. Maybe even more than the magnetism with which he has held me since the second I met him.

I roll out from beneath the covers and head for the bathroom. After splashing water on my face and brushing my teeth, I wander to the kitchen where I find an empty mug on the counter and a fresh pot of coffee on the brewer. I pour a cup and go in search of the man who dominates my every waking thought.

I'm not surprised when I find him standing at the lake's edge again. Something about his expression last night made me think he'd be here. Something about his expression *this morning* makes me think this place haunts him.

I walk up to stand beside him, cupping my hands around the steaming mug rather than touching him like I want to. I'm still not always sure how to proceed with him, how much of me he'll welcome. Unless we're in bed. It's easy to see that he wants all of me when it comes to sex. He doesn't want to leave any part of me untouched, unscathed. He wants it all. And I want to give it to him.

"Thanks for the coffee," I say into the quiet morning.

He grunts. I sigh, ready for another battle of pulling teeth to try and get him to open up. Slipping on my thick skin, I step over in front of him, putting myself between him and the lake. That's when I see his face, full-on. I see the pale complexion, the dark circles, the drawn mouth. "Jasper, are you okay?"

His dull eyes flicker down to mine. "I'm fine. Why?"

I reach up to brush the smudge under one eye, like it might rub off, like it might be made of something other than misery. "Did you sleep? You look awful."

"Thanks," he says snidely, one side of his mouth twisting up into a humorless grin.

"I'm serious. Did you sleep at all?"

"No."

"Why? Did something happen?"

He holds my eyes. He looks into them so intensely that I wonder if he's trying to read my mind. When he finally answers, it's not an answer at all, but merely something that gives rise to more questions.

"You. *You* happened."

My mouth drops open. "Me? What did I do?"

"You dug too deep. You gave too much. Now there's no going back, whether you want to or not. It's too late. You'd have to leave here to escape me."

A chill chases its way down my spine despite the balmy morning temperature. "I don't want to escape you."

He threads his fingers into the bound hair at my nape, working the strands free from the confines of the knot I tied them into. "Good. Because I'd find you. No one can hide from me."

With a mixture of last night's fierceness and this morning's odd desperation, Jasper strips me of every piece of clothing, lays me down on the soft grass and makes love to me with the murky waters of the lake lapping just behind my head.

"So what's the deal with this tattoo?" I ask Jasper as I trace each sadistic-looking thorn that makes up the tangled bramble inked across his right chest and shoulder.

"You don't want to know," he says in his guarded way.

"I wouldn't have asked if I didn't want to know," I reply with some amount of exasperation. Trying to ferret information from him is exhausting.

"There's a thorn for every person I've found, every assignment I've completed."

My heart trips over itself. Maybe I thought I'd misunderstood what he was getting at last night. Maybe I just refused to believe it. Maybe it's just easier *not to*. But now, here, in the bright light of day, it's unavoidable.

I gulp, but keep my voice as steady and unaffected as possible. "So these are all for people you've k-killed?"

Saying the word, even pushing it past my lips, is like giving birth to something I don't want to acknowledge. I say a silent prayer that he'll tell me I'm wrong. That he'll tell me I misunderstood.

But he doesn't. Because I didn't misunderstand.

This man is a killer.

His head bounces in one short, sharp nod. "I told you."

"You told me what?"

"I'm a monster."

When panic threatens to pull me away from him, I reach for the things that I know about Jasper, for the things that I *feel* about him, and I cling to them with a desperation that's almost dizzying.

The emotional side of me wants to run. In disappointment, in disgust. In confusion. People like this exist only in the movies.

What am I to do with a *real* killer? How can people interact with them like they're normal?

My breath freezes and my heart stutters as icy fingers claw and grip, pulling me deeper into fear. I shiver in response.

That's when the rational part of me steps in, the part that comes from my father. It's the side of me that doesn't get much love or attention. It's the side that thinks with a level head and straightforward thought processes, devoid of emotion and weakness. It's this part that saves me from falling apart, that keeps me from running away. It walks me through this in even, logical steps, each one a checkmark in the column of reasonable explanations.

Jasper knows my dad. My dad is a good man.

Check.

Jasper worked with my dad in the military. Our military isn't comprised of monsters. It's comprised of heroes who sacrifice for the safety of others.

Check.

Jasper takes lives for the greater good, probably the lives of war criminals and terrorists. My father, although he never gave me details, has alluded to having to do some very difficult things over the years, having to make some very tough choices. This makes them good men, not bad ones.

Check.

My father trusted Jasper, not only to find him and then *not* kill him, but he trusted Jasper with *me*. And *I* trust my father. Ergo, I can trust Jasper. Whatever his deeds, he's done them for the right reasons.

Check, check.

Once my mind has calmed, I reiterate my rationale aloud, almost like saying the words will cement them, make them so. Make them true.

"You worked with my father in the military. Doing what you're called upon to do for our country is something to be proud of, not something you should be ashamed of or something you should feel the need to hide from people. You're a national hero, Jasper."

As I work to convince him, I'm still convincing myself, too. I become aware of the slight tremor that's shaking every muscle in my upper body and I will myself to quiet.

"Does that make it more palatable for you?"

Yes, it does. But I don't tell him that, I just persevere.

"Government operatives aren't monsters. They're men and women who are trained in certain areas to do certain things."

Jasper glances down at me, his eyes unreadable. "It's still based on aptitude. Predisposition. They don't pick undamaged people for black ops, Muse. They pick ones who are already broken enough to make it in this kind of life. They pick the ones with no ties, no future. No conscience. No soul." His pause is long and fraught with dark tension. "So they picked me."

"Just because you're strong enough and capable enough to do the things . . . to do what has to be done doesn't make you damaged or broken or soulless."

He sits up so suddenly I nearly roll into the water. He grabs me with one big, sure hand, the fingers gripping my upper arm so tightly I know I'll be bruised tomorrow. The thing is, I can almost feel that same kind of pressure digging into my heart, too. Making a place for Jasper that will always be shaped like him, one that no one else will ever be able to fill. Only my wildly different Jasper. The man who thrills me as much as he scares me, the man who only draws me closer the more he tries to push me away.

Once more, I feel my determination spike.

"They picked me because they knew about my father. They picked me because they knew about the blood that was flowing through my veins."

"Your father? Why would he matter?"

"Because he was in federal prison."

"How could they possibly know about him?"

"Because they were looking into me. And it was my testimony that put him there."

Jasper is a trained killer who put his own father in prison?

Oh God!

Another bomb. Another left turn in the convoluted maze that is Jasper.

I want to curl up in a ball and cry for him, but I also want to throw my arms around Jasper and shield him from the pain that he can't escape, the agonizing memories that obviously haunt him. But I don't do either. I simply bow my head, dropping it on my bent knees, and close my eyes until I can regain some equilibrium. "I'm so sorry," I whisper.

"Don't be. He was a black-hearted bastard who deserved to be buried *under* the prison, not drawing breath with the rest of the lowlife criminals."

In the lag that follows his venomous proclamation, I'm almost afraid to ask the question that's circling my mind. But I'm even more afraid *not to.*

"Wh-what did he do?"

I don't glance up when Jasper doesn't answer me.

"He drowned my older brother. In this very lake. Behind a little white house not far from here."

Sweet Jesus!

I keep my eyes closed and my head down, trying to weather this as gracefully as I can. Falling apart won't do either of us any favors.

My stomach lurches, overtaken by a tidal wave of nausea. I want to ask why. I feel the word form on my lips, but the ringing in my ears prevents me from hearing whether it makes it out into the air or dies on the tip of my tongue.

But it must've, it must've floated out. That or Jasper intuited it, because he answers.

"He'd hated Jeremy for as long as I could remember. I don't know why. Maybe it was because Jeremy was sick. Oppositional-defiant disorder and conduct disorder is what the doctor said. He told Mom that my brother was exhibiting early signs and strong traits of antisocial behavior. He needed medication and therapy, but my father wouldn't hear of it. The worse Jeremy got, the worse my father treated him. When my brother would misbehave, Dad would take him out back, to a stump in the yard, and whip him until his belt broke. I never once saw Jeremy cry. It infuriated Dad that he didn't. Maybe he'd have stopped if he'd seen tears, but I don't think Jeremy was capable of crying." Jasper's voice is cool and robotic, like he's numb. "The last time he got sent home from school, my father dragged him right out into the water and held him under until he stopped struggling." Jasper's voice drops into a low rumble, as ominous as thunder. "That day he killed one replica of himself. But he left the other one alive."

I don't even know what to say. My heart is breaking. The agony in his voice, a voice that normally shows so little, is enough to rip through me like a scalpel.

There are so many things I could say, and maybe *should* say, but what comes out is a question instead. "Why do you come here? Why did you buy a cabin here, where you can never escape what happened?"

"I could never escape it anyway. This way, I'm in control of it. I come here to remind myself of who and what I am, of what I came from, and what I'll always be."

"A monster," I finish flatly. *That's* what he feels like he can't escape. His father, his brother, his blood. His perceived destiny.

Jasper rolls smoothly to his feet and steps to the very edge of the yard, where ground meets water. The gentle current sends slender green blades of grass waving in front of his toes.

I let my eyes wander his nude form—the wide, wide shoulders, the trim, trim waist, the absolutely perfect butt, the long, thick legs. He's magnificent and I don't think I could ever tire of just watching him. Even with his head bowed and his muscles tense with his hellish memories, he's the most beautiful thing I've ever seen, monster or not.

"I've tried to make myself get back in this water, to kill that fear like my father killed Jeremy. But I can't. I can't make myself get in. All I see is my brother, floating away, and me watching him. Helpless. I'll never know if I could've saved him if I'd gone out sooner, if I'd had the courage to face my father. I only know that I *didn't*. That I survived and my brother didn't."

Once again, I feel the urge to go to him, but I'm fairly certain my comfort would be more of an annoyance to a man like him. Such a loner, such a silent sufferer. It's heartbreaking, but it's also amazing to watch. I can almost *see* the strength coursing through the veins beneath his smooth, golden skin. Even at his worst, even when he feels defeated by a past he can't control and thwarted by genetics he can't escape, he's ready to take on the world. And win.

I see his upper torso expand and contract. A sigh.

When he turns to me, his eyes are clear again, as though the haunted man of moments before was more a ghost of *mine* rather than *his*. "Let's get you dressed so I can show you around. It's that or spend the day like this," he says, pointing down at his erection. It has already filled the condom we just used and is threatening to burst from the tip.

"Where the hell did you get your stamina?" I ask, trying to just go with his mood swing rather than continuing to delve into something I'm not sure can be fixed.

"Costco," he replies, deadpan.

I can't help laughing, especially when I see the slight twitch of his lips. Maybe this is how he heals. Maybe this is how he keeps moving on. He embraces who and what he is and pushes the rest down, shoves it so deep he can ignore it for a while.

The only problem with that tactic is that one day, it won't be pushed down. It will refuse to go and he'll be forced to deal with it or suffer the consequences.

But that day is not today. Today can be whatever we want it to be, whatever he *needs* for it to be. And I'll be that for him, *with* him. Because I care. Probably more than I should.

Definitely more than I should, I correct in my mind. I think I've already done something stupid like fall in love.

TWENTY-FOUR

Jasper

For reasons I'm more comfortable *not* exploring too deeply, I was already looking forward to spending the day with Muse. Even before she walked out onto the front porch with her flaming hair in a loose knot and her long, curvy legs squeezed into form-fitting pants. But now, seeing her, I'm even more enthused.

She stops suddenly and my eyes drift up to hers. They're twinkling with mischief. They tell all, which is something I love about her. She's transparent and doesn't try to be anything more than that.

"Have you changed your mind about how you want to spend the day?"

"Yes, but I think it's important that you're able to *walk*."

Her laugh is a tinkle. That's the best way I can describe it. It's light and happy and carefree, three things I never attribute to myself or my life. It resonates within me, like something comforting and highly desirable might.

Maybe comforting isn't the right word. I don't feel comfortable, necessarily, when I look at Muse, when I hear her laugh. I feel all sorts of other things, though—desire, possessiveness, ferocity. A trace of anger that confuses me. Guilt. Protectiveness. In truth, I have no idea what she makes me feel or why. I only know I shouldn't want this. But I do.

Spontaneously, she launches herself at me where I'm standing on the second step. I catch her easily and she winds her arms and legs around me. "You're a tease, Mr. King," she says in a throaty voice, her eyes locked on mine. There's heat in the emeralds and I think for a second about carrying her right back inside and losing myself in them, in *her* until neither of us can think. Or walk.

But to do that would be even more heartless than what I've already done. She thinks she knows the worst about me now that I've shared some of myself, some of my history with her. But she doesn't. And she won't. Not until it's too late.

Another surge of guilt. And dread. And something worse, something I don't think I've ever felt, therefore can't identify. But I don't like it. It makes me feel agitated and angry.

Feel, feel, feel. I've got to get away from all these feelings.

I kiss Muse's shiny pink lips before I ease my hold, which encourages her to let me go. I don't maintain contact with her very long. At this point, it's counterproductive.

"Maybe a hike will work off some hormones," I say absently as I take her hand and pull her down the steps behind me.

"Hormones? Is that what you call this?" she asks.

I look back at her. There's disappointment where the heat was, dulling the green rather than lighting it up.

"Honestly, I don't know what I'd call this. I've never been here before."

I don't elaborate on where "here" is and she doesn't ask. I'm sure she knows that I mean us, *this*. Because I haven't. For years, the only women I've gotten involved with are useful to me in one way or another. They give me an in. Or an out. They give me pleasure. They give me information. They give me *something*.

Muse started out that way. Not only was she a way in with the Colonel, she was also a means of exerting pressure on him. She was part of my assignment. Period. Beyond that is where the trouble starts. Since meeting her, since traveling with her, since getting to know her (even though I had no desire to know her at first), she's become something more. I don't know exactly what, but what I *do know* is that waters that have always been clear for me are now muddy. She and she alone muddied them.

We walk in silence toward the woods. I notice her doing some of the same things I do when I'm here—stopping to look around, taking deep breaths, touching trees as we pass. Only she smiles when she does it. She's enjoying the view, letting the fresh air invigorate her, savoring the feel of rough bark. I can't remember the last time I smiled as I walked these woods. They're therapy for me, but therapy of a different kind.

"I can see why you come out here," she says when we enter a pine stand. She stops in a ray of sunlight that's filtering down through the canopy and turns her face up to it.

"Why is that?"

"It's so quiet and peaceful, like we're the only people in the world. I could set up an easel here and paint for hours."

I study her as she spins in a slow circle, taking it all in. "I'm glad you like it. Maybe it will inspire your next canvas." Uncharacteristically, I get the urge to share something with her again. Also uncharacteristically, I do. "My mom used to bring my brother and me here for walks in the woods. No matter what kind of game we played, how much noise we made, it never seemed to affect that peaceful look she had on her face. It showed up the minute we stepped into the trees and didn't leave until we did. It's probably the only time she was ever really happy. Or felt carefree."

"So you love it here."

"As much as I love any place, I suppose." The memories are good ones, but they only remind me of all the bad ones, too.

When Muse stops, facing me, she levels a look in my direction. It's inscrutable, which is unusual for her. "So this is a special place for you."

"I guess."

She purses her lips. "Do you, um, bring many people here?"

"No."

"Hmmm," she mumbles noncommittally, casting her eyes down as she digs at the ground with the toe of her shoe. "Have you ever brought a *woman* here before?"

I need no other information than what she's giving me to know that she's feeling a little insecure, possessive. Maybe a touch jealous. I find the sentiment both odd and strangely flattering. I've never given a woman enough of my time, enough of myself for her to *become* jealous. Or if one ever has, I've never noticed. That might well be the case. For some reason, I notice all sorts of things about Muse that I normally pay little attention to.

I wait until she picks up her dazzling green eyes before I answer. "No. Never."

She simply nods. Says nothing. But her expression, as always, is a different story. It shows pleasure and relief, which in turn pleases *me*.

I'm not sure why, but seeing her react gives me a charge that nothing else—not even the adrenaline-filled tasks often associated with my job—ever has. There's a sense of power in being the person who brings an end to a life, but I've never fallen victim to it. I've always felt that I was just doing my job, not playing God or anything of the sort. But this . . . being with Muse, seeing her react to me the way she does, *feeling* her react to me . . . it's very seductive. To know that with the simplest of words or actions I can bring her such pleasure—or such pain—is intoxicating. Addictive.

I duly note the warning alarm that's going off inside my head when I acknowledge that I much prefer bringing her pleasure than the idea of bringing her pain. Even the anger that I let her see, even the rough, thoughtless ways I've treated her body have not been cruel or abusive. She has derived great pleasure from it all and has made no secret of that fact. Even *that* makes my cock hard with a rush of exhilaration.

"What are you thinking about?" she asks when we are back on the move, weaving our way through trees along the thin trail.

"Power," I tell her bluntly.

"Power," she repeats, shaking her head. "I imagine you're a man used to power."

I can't argue that. "I'm powerful by virtue of physical strength, mental acuity, by the mere reality of my occupation—finding people who hide, taking care of problems that others can't deal with—but there are other kinds of power, too."

"Is that what you're thinking of, then? Some other kind of power?"

"Yes."

"And what is this other kind you speak of?"

There's a twinkle to her eyes—the light of mischief. She's teasing. She thinks *I'm* teasing.

"The power of giving pleasure. And pain. The power of having such a profound effect on another person."

I know by the way she glances down again that she knows what I'm referring to.

"I'd say taking someone's life is pretty much the ultimate profound effect."

"That's not what I mean and you know it."

"I know," she concedes.

"I know that I'm powerful. I know what I do is definite, irreversible. I know the difference between *being* powerful and *feeling* powerful. In my line of work, *being* powerful is necessary. Like a job requirement. *Feeling* powerful is a hazard. If I began to think about it as having the power to take a life, or to dispense death, that would make me a psychopath, don't you think?"

She shrugs. "I guess. I didn't really think of it that way. But obviously you've thought about it quite a bit."

I lift *my* shoulder this time. "I have to think of it that way. It keeps it all in perspective. To some degree anyway."

"Well, at least you found a kind of power that you can enjoy," she offers with a titillating peek of her tongue at the corner of her mouth.

"Oh, I like that kind of power very much. I'm so tempted to abuse it that I'll have to watch that it doesn't go to my head. Become a problem for me."

"And how could *that* become a problem for you?"

"I'm not sure *the power* could, but I think there's another component that could be quite problematic."

She raises one smoothly arched brow, one of the sexiest things I've seen her do. Or maybe it's just that everything she does is starting to seem sexy now. "Are you saying that *I* have some power, too?"

Her smile is bright and pleased. No doubt she likes knowing that she holds some sway over me as well. "I'm just saying that a woman like you could make a man start thinking that things could be different, that *life* could be different. He could find himself in trouble if he's not careful."

"And are you always careful?"

I pause. "Always."

Not the answer she wanted, but it's the truth nonetheless. I'll give her as much of the truth as I can.

"What makes you think things *couldn't be* different, Jasper?"

When I glance back, Muse's eyes are on me, her fingers dancing over some lacy spikes of tall fern undergrowth.

Her question pricks my anger, probably because it serves only to remind me that things can *never* be different. Not for a guy like me. "You mean why couldn't I have a family, have a normal life? Grow old and live happily ever after?" She nods. "Wake up, Muse!" I bark. "What kind of life could I offer a woman? A child? Fear? Stigma? Danger? I would never do that to an innocent. Never!"

I regret my vehemence. Muse looks taken aback.

"Is that how you really feel? Like you've got nothing more to offer than that?"

"It's not how I feel. It's what I know."

She starts to say something else, but my expression stops her. I turn and walk on ahead, annoyed with this conversation and the things it's making me feel.

We walk in silence for another half hour or so, until the trail turns to go up a fairly steep incline. I start up it, pausing to reach back and offer Muse my hand, thinking she might need the help. She looks at it with disdain, waves me off and then climbs up and around me, turning only to give me a sassy wink before she continues following the path up the hill. Now I'm stuck watching the muscles in her legs and ass clench and shift as she picks her way upward.

She's only slightly out of breath when we reach the top.

"It's so beautiful here," she says quietly, reverently as we stand on the small peak overlooking the lake. She holds her hand over her forehead to shield her eyes from the sun as she glances off into the distance. "Looks like there are more houses down that way, but this end . . . it's practically deserted."

I nod. "That's the way I like it."

She turns to me and smiles. "I guess I should've been more concerned about that this morning when *somebody* was stripping me out of my clothes in broad daylight."

"Why? You have a beautiful body." Pink stains appear on either of her cheeks. It charms me this morning just like it has every other time it's happened. I reach out and touch one satin-covered cheekbone. "You have nothing to be ashamed of."

"Thank you, but I . . . I don't know, I'd just be embarrassed for anyone to see us . . ."

Suddenly shy, she glances quickly away and then down at her feet as she shrugs, trailing off. When I hook a finger under her chin and lift her face back up to mine, I find her more breathtaking than the view.

"For anyone to see me sucking your perfect nipples?" Her pupils dilate, black nearly eclipsing green. Blood rushes to my cock. My pulse speeds up. My chest feels tight, like I've been running rather than walking. My reaction to her is *that* immediate, *that* profound.

"That and . . ."

"And me putting my hands on you?" I ask, easing her tank top strap off one shoulder and down beneath one plump breast. I tug the lacy cup of her bra until one pink, pebbled nipple is exposed. "My lips on you?"

I bend to draw the button into my mouth, running my tongue around it and then sucking it gently between my teeth.

"Or was it the rest you were worried about?" I ask around her flesh as I ease my hand down the back of her pants to squeeze her firm ass. "Like when I put my fingers inside you?" From behind, I spread her until I can feel the warm wetness of her core. It's like a siren calling to my fingers, to my tongue, to my dick. Every part of me wants to taste her, to be inside her, to feel her and consume her.

She arches her back, pressing her breast into my mouth and her ass into my hand, giving me deeper penetration into her. She takes a fistful of my hair and holds me to her, her shallow breathing a ragged rasp in the stillness.

I lean back, releasing her nipple to look into her face, the sensual expression nearly my undoing. Her eyes are at half-mast and her lips are parted on a silent moan as I probe her with my finger.

"I think that's the first selfish thing I've heard you say."

Her gaze is cloudy, foggy with the haze of what I'm doing to her, making her mind slow to grasp.

"Wh-what do you mean?"

"I think the world would be a better place if everyone in it could see your face when you come. If they could watch your beautiful body move against my hand, against my mouth, against my cock like the graceful motions of a ballerina. I think they would all love me and hate me at the same time if they could see it." Her breaths are growing louder, her hips working rhythmically with thrust of my fingers, trying to ride them to her orgasm. With our eyes locked, I slide my other hand down the front of her pants, slipping a single finger between her slick folds until I feel the tight little muscle that I want. I press in and rub, matching the cadence of my fingers, and I watch the few seconds that it takes her to come apart in my hands. "But they'd never forget it," I tell her when her mouth drops open and her knees buckle, when her face flushes and her eyes nearly close. "Just like I won't. *Sarò sempre pensare a te.*"

Watching Muse's face is fascinating. It's so expressive, so open. So soft and real. Each time she comes is slightly different, like the location and intensity plays out on her features. This slow, unexpected build took her by surprise and it shows. But her genuine pleasure and awe are also there, as plain as the trees at her back.

I capture, catalog and file away a thousand minute details every day. I already know that these are some that I will pull out and examine often. And when I do, I'll be able to conjure the warmth of the sun on my face, the scent of the fresh air mixed with her lilac skin, the way she melts in my hands. And her face. Her beautiful, angelic face.

TWENTY-FIVE

Muse

The sun seems brighter, warmer. So do Jasper's eyes. Maybe it's just my imagination, which is admittedly overactive, or maybe we've reached some sort of milestone where he silently agrees to let me in, to let me *see* him. It could be that, or it could be that I'm seeing what's not there simply because I so desperately want it to be.

"What was that?" I ask, even my lips languorously relaxed.

In one of the few actual grins I've seen from him, Jasper's perfectly masculine mouth curves up at the corners, his face easing into a less intense version of its normal state. "You need me to explain that to you?"

I would probably be blushing if all the blood in my body weren't still pounding between my legs. Instead, I laugh, a soft breathless sound. "Not *that*. I know precisely what *that* was. You've made sure I'm quite familiar with it." A dimple appears right below his left cheekbone. I've never seen a man as sexy as this one. Not once. Not ever. "I meant the last words you said. What language were they in?"

"Italian," he responds, helping my fumbling fingers to straighten my clothes. I feel like I could fall over at a moment's notice. And not care at all. I might just lie on the ground, smiling.

"What does it mean?"

"It means 'I will always think of you.'"

"Not just like *this*, I hope."

He reaches up to pull a stray strand of hair from my cheek and tuck it behind my ear. "Not just like this. In *every* way."

Little by little, his barely-there grin dies. He looks unbelievably bothered, which in turn bothers *me*.

"You don't have to make it seem like such a bad thing," I half tease.

"For the most part it won't be."

I don't really know what to say to that. I only know that my chest feels uncomfortably tight, like he just told me that we are doomed never to be anything more than what we are right now. And while, going into this, I had no such expectation, I'd be lying if I said that *now* I wouldn't love to have something more with Jasper. More time, more days, more emotion. Just more. More, more, more.

I try to gloss over it the best I can. "So why Italian? You know so many languages, why does that one come out unexpectedly?"

"One of my first assignments was in Italy. I stayed in a little town east of Rome. I met a woman there. She taught me quite a bit about the culture, some of the subtleties of the language. It was hard not to see the beauty that she found in it. I guess it just rubbed off."

A spike of jealousy stabs me right through the sternum. This was obviously a long time ago, but that makes no difference to my wild emotions. It doesn't stop me from wanting to scratch out the eyes of the woman I picture to be a dark, voluptuous, exotic Italian.

"You were happy then?"

"I suppose I was. Happier than I'd been in a long time."

It's hard for me to ask questions without letting some of my resentment seep into the words, but I try. "Why didn't you stay?"

"I told you. It's just not practical in my line of work. I pose more of a danger to people I'm close to."

"But you're a big, strong, capable guy. You can surely protect those you love."

Jasper's eyes settle on mine. They're fierce once more, fierce and intense. "I'm not unique, Muse. There are others like me. Not many, but there are some who are as good at what they do as I am. If I wanted to get to someone, I could. Nothing could stop me. I would never take that chance with someone else's life."

"Not even if they chose it? I mean, what if she loved you enough to risk it?"

"It wouldn't have mattered. *I* wouldn't have risked it. But that wasn't the case anyway. She knew exactly what we had. And what we didn't."

As though that ends the conversation, Jasper turns and starts back down the path, the way we came.

"So you haven't seen her since you left?"

"No."

"D-do you still think of her?"

"Not until today." My heart sinks. I should be glad he hasn't thought of that woman again, but for some reason the fact that he hasn't dashes a few unrealistic hopes I was beginning to harbor. When Jasper stops suddenly, I run right into his back. With a muffled yelp, I take a step back and stare up into his dark gold eyes. "Would you like to know one of my favorite Italian sayings?"

I gulp, thinking to myself that I probably really *don't*. But curiosity (and pride) gets the better of me. "Sure."

"*Non potrò mai pensare a te*. It means 'I will *never* think of you.'

Muse, you have to understand what my job is like, what my *life* is like. I can't have attachments. I can't look back. I can't think of the people I've met, the ones I've found. If I do, it'll eat me alive. The things I've done, the things I've seen . . . I couldn't live with them any other way."

"But you just told me—"

He takes a step closer. "I know what I just told you. And it's the truth. I *will* always think of you. God help me, but I will."

After a long, unnerving stare down into my face, Jasper turns on his heel and walks off gracefully down the path, like he didn't just tell me that he basically hates that he won't be able to forget me.

On the walk down, I'm more confused and discouraged and *hopeless* than I've been since I left Treeborn all those months ago.

Jasper's mood shifts into a darkly brooding state. When we arrive back at the cabin, he announces that he has a few things to take care of and then closes himself in a room behind the kitchen I hadn't noticed before. Must be an office.

Or an armory, I think, picturing the dozen or so spy films I've seen over the years and how they all seem to have a hidden armory somewhere.

I flit aimlessly through the house for the first hour, lounging in the living room and then making my way out onto the porch. When my stomach starts to growl, I go into the kitchen and rummage for something to eat. A peanut butter sandwich is the best thing I can come up with because I refuse, *refuse* to eat sardines, which is the only other thing in the pantry.

I take my lunch down to the dock, walking all the way to the end to sit on the edge and let my feet dangle in the water. As I stare into the dingy gray depths, I think of the pain Jasper has seen at the hands of this lake. I ponder the strength of character, the sheer will that it takes for him to come back here time and time again, torturing himself until he can get back into the water. And for what? To prove to himself that he can, that it hasn't conquered him. The thing is, I have no doubts that he will eventually do it. Jasper isn't the kind to let anything get the better of him. He'll overcome it with logic and perseverance.

Just like he'll overcome me.

My lip curls into an outward pout at the inner thought. Why can't Jasper have just been a regular guy? Why couldn't he have just been the bounty hunter I thought I was hiring? Things would be so much easier.

I correct myself. I doubt anything would ever be easy with a man like Jasper, no matter what his profession. It's his fatal flaw. And I'm becoming more convinced every day that *he* is mine.

When my sandwich is nothing but a few white crumbs floating on the placid surface of the lake, I climb to my feet and backtrack a few steps to where a small boat is tied off. I glance back at the house. Still no sign of Jasper. I figure a leisurely row around the cove will be a nice way to pass the time until he's finished. So, with only the briefest of hesitations, I untie the dock line, hop in the boat and grab the oars in both hands.

The whole trip probably takes no more than thirty or forty minutes, and only that because I stop several times to just sit in the quiet cove. On the still waters, I find that if I tip my face up to the sun, it feels as though I'm almost drinking in the warmth and serenity, sucking it in through my pores. The brevity of my trip is why I'm surprised when I start back and find Jasper's tall form standing on the grassy shore, arms crossed over his chest and what looks like a thundercloud on his face.

My first thought is that something has happened. Has he heard from Dad? Is something wrong?

My heart speeds up and so do my strokes. I hurriedly propel the boat through the water, anxious to get back to the dock now. When I do, Jasper makes no move to come closer. He just watches me coast in on the boat, tie it off, leap out and run down the old wooden walkway.

"What's wrong?" I ask, frantic by the time I get to Jasper.

Big hands shoot out to grab my upper arms, startling me. "What were you thinking?"

"What do you mean?" I ask, confounded by his reaction.

"If something were to happen out there, who the hell do you think would save you? I just told you a few hours ago that I can't get in that water!"

I frown. "Why would you need to? I was in a boat. And it doesn't look like there's another person around for miles. Why would I be in any kind of danger?"

"What if that boat had a hole in it?"

"Then it wouldn't have been floating by the dock."

Sparks fly from Jasper's amber eyes. "What if you'd hit something and *knocked* a hole in the boat?"

"Then I'd have swam back to the dock and let it sink."

For some reason, my response only seems to further agitate him. His fingers dig into the backs of my arms and I try to shirk away from him. "Jasper, you're hurting me."

"Good! Maybe you'll *think* before you do something so stupid next time."

"That wasn't stupid. I didn't take any unnecessary risks. I don't know why you're so angry with me."

His teeth are gritted so hard, I'm surprised he can push air through them, much less whole words. "Because I can't lose another person to this lake. I can't stand by and watch it swallow up someone else that matters to me."

I go completely still. I think even my heart has stopped beating for a second. "I matter to you?"

"Yes! Is that what you want to hear? Would that make you happy?" He's nearly yelling now. Bellowing. This calm, cool, unaffected man is showing me another little piece of himself, only this display is very much against his will.

"As a matter of fact it would, but I'm sure that's not what you want to hear."

"No, that's *not* what I want to hear!"

"Then why did you ask?"

He growls in frustration and lets me go, turning away from me and running a hand through his hair. When he pivots back to me several seconds later, he's calmly livid, but livid nonetheless.

"You're dismantling everything I've worked for. You're ripping open old wounds, making me feel things I don't want to feel. Making me think things I've got no business thinking."

I don't know whether to be insulted or flattered. I'm uncertain, unsteady as always. With Jasper, there is no steady ground. There is no predictability. Just when I think I've got him figured out, he throws me a curve ball.

"What the hell is going on, Jasper?"

"I didn't want you. I didn't ask for you." Bitterness. I can almost taste it. I wish that it didn't hurt me to hear it.

"I know you didn't."

"Then why the hell couldn't you just leave me alone?"

"If that's what you want, I'm sure I could find a way back to Atlanta." My heart is aching.

His eyes search mine, furiously, frantically. "No! Absolutely not! Don't you see?"

"Jasper, I don't understand. What do you want me to do?"

"I want you to stay. I want you to stay and never leave."

My shivering heart warms, heating the blood in every artery and vein throughout my body. "You do?"

"Yes, damn you! You're the only thing I've wanted for as long as I can remember. And the one thing I can't have."

"But you *can*, Jasper," I say, moving closer to him and setting my hands at his firm waist. "You *can* have me. I'm right here."

The fire dies in his eyes, leaving them cool and defeated. His voice is low, sullen. "But you shouldn't be. And you won't be for long."

There's no talking him out of this, obviously, so the only thing I know to do is work around it. "Then love me while I'm here. Love me for all the tomorrows that we won't have."

Jasper raises his hands, running his fingers around my neck and into the hair at my nape. "I'll love you for today. That's all I can give you."

"Then love me for today."

When his lips take mine, they're gentler than they've ever been, but also more fierce. The rage, the roughness is still there, but it's tightly controlled. Like he doesn't want to hurt me.

It only makes me wonder if he's certain that he's going to. And what that might mean for me.

The phone ringing stirs me from my drowsy rest on Jasper's chest. We are in the spacious master bedroom, in a bed that's hard as a rock, but I couldn't care less. My bones are like butter and my brain like mush.

Jasper shifts me enough that he can stretch for his phone. I can tell by the muffled chirp that it's probably still in the pocket of his pants, which are now in a heap on the floor. Where he left them when he tore out of them to get to me.

I smile just thinking about it. He's as fierce in his lovemaking as he is in every other area of life. I didn't see it before. I saw this calm, cool, collected, even aloof man who showed no emotion. He still doesn't show very much, but I've learned where to look for it. It's there. He burns as hot on the inside as I do, just in a different way.

"What is it?" he says as he rolls back into bed.

I watch his face as he listens. It shows nothing. But I notice that when I scrape my fingernails up his stomach, his nipples pucker and chills spread over his chest. When I bend to lave one with my tongue, I feel his hand at the back of my head, urging my face up to his. His pupils are so big his eyes look black. He's turned on, but he doesn't want to be right now, hence the single shake of his dark head.

I stick my tongue out at him pluckily and I squeak when he grabs it between his thumb and forefinger.

"Uh-huh," he says into the phone, still holding my tongue. Just to be obtuse, rather than trying to free it, I move toward him, taking his fingers into my mouth and sucking on them. His eyes are locked on my lips, ever darkening in his increasing desire. I love that look. I love his chameleon eyes that tell me so much of what he's feeling even when he doesn't want me to know.

Finally he releases my tongue and slowly withdraws his fingers. His gaze is still on my mouth as he rubs his thumb back and forth over my wet bottom lip, slowly, sweetly. Almost sadly, I see, when his eyes flip up to mine.

What is he hearing that would make him sad all of a sudden?

"Fine. I'll be in touch. Give me until tomorrow."

When Jasper hangs up, he tosses the phone aside, but remains stretched slightly away from me.

"Who was that?" I ask, only half expecting an answer.

"The Colonel."

I lever myself up off his chest. "What did he say?"

"He got what I needed."

"So what does that mean?"

He doesn't really have to answer me. I can see it all over his face that it's nothing I want to hear.

"It means that I'll take you to him tomorrow. It means that this will all be over soon."

TWENTY-SIX

Jasper

I left Muse to shower. I wanted to be in there with her, but I can't think as clearly when she's around, much less when she's wet and naked. That's why I'm in the front yard, keeping a distance from her.

The time is at hand and for the first time since I left home all those years ago, I'm pausing. Hesitating. Considering not doing my job, not doing what I'm told. I let someone get too close. *I* got too close. Too familiar. I let myself feel and now it's come to this. She doesn't know it yet, but the day I walked into the little shop where she works, Muse's life changed forever. It was never going to be the same from that day on. She just didn't know it.

In my gut . . . even though my head is still trying to work out options and plans . . . I know I can't complete my assignment. I could never hurt her that way. For *any* job or assignment or greater good. But if I don't, someone will. I'm not so worried about the Colonel. He can take care of himself, but Muse . . . she's a different story.

It will be up to me to make sure she's safe. To hide her well enough that no one will ever be able to find her. Maybe not even me.

It's that thought that's bouncing around in my head when I hear the explosion. Reflexively, I duck, reaching for the gun that isn't at the back of my waistband. I curse under my breath, curse how lax I've become in such a short period of time.

The ground beneath my feet trembles with the impact and a bright flash of yellow-orange lightens the sky to the west, over the treetops. That's when my heart comes to a complete stop in my chest. I know what lies in that direction. *Who* lies in that direction. She's the only thing on my mind as I race toward the house, my heart now pounding at a speed that's almost painful.

I jerk open the screen door and nearly topple a partially dressed Muse as she heads for the porch.

"What the hell was that?" she asks, her eyes round and frightened.

"I have a feeling it was somebody's death wish," I respond grimly, moving past her to grab my keys. "Stay here. Lock yourself in the bedroom. There's a sawed-off shotgun under the bed. It's loaded. Keep that in there with you. If anyone other than me comes through that door, aim and fire."

"What? You're crazy! I'm coming with you," she says frantically, pulling the shirt she's carrying over her wet head.

"No, you're not. It's hard to tell what I could be walking into and I don't want you—"

"Where *you are* is the safest place I could be. I'm not letting you go without me."

I don't even stop to ask her what she thinks she could do to stop me. I just move toward the door. "Fine, but you'll do exactly as I say. No questions asked. Even if I tell you to get in the car and drive away, you do it. Got it?"

I know my tone and my expression are harsh, but she needs to know how serious I am. I don't have time to argue with her and I don't want to have to worry about her doing something stupid.

"Okay, okay. I will."

Together, we hurry out to the car. Once inside, I fire up the engine and tear out of the driveway, flying off down the gravel road. I know the path well. I grew up on these roads. I just never thought I'd be traveling them again like this. I thought I'd done everything I could to keep her safe.

My fingers ache from gripping the steering wheel so tightly. I'm already thinking through possible scenarios and possible outcomes, preparing myself, expecting the unexpected.

"Reach in the glove box and hand me the gun in there," I bite off to Muse. She quickly and quietly does as I ask.

"Jasper, what's going on? What do you think has happened?"

I grind my back teeth together, praying that I'm wrong about what my gut is telling me, what my *heart* is telling me. The thing is, neither one has ever been wrong before.

I take a deep breath, reaching for the level head, the eerie calm that has helped make me so good at what I do. I need my skill. I need my sharp senses.

"There was an explosion to the west. My childhood home . . . *my mother* is still there. A little house, west of my cabin."

I hear her gasp. I smell the fear. I suck it in like cocaine. It burns through my blood, triggers a rush of adrenaline that pushes me into a razor-sharp focus.

Minutes tick by like centuries, but I finally turn onto the old, dusty road that leads to the place I grew up, the place I spent a thousand sleepless nights and cried what few tears I've ever shed.

The glow is getting brighter. The acrid tang of smoke and things burning that shouldn't be burning fills the interior of the car. I steel myself for what I know I'll find, for what I did everything in my power to prevent. I faked my death so my mother would be safe, so she could finally live a happy life. Free. But someone knows. Someone found her. Like someone found one of my friends.

Before the familiar busted-cement driveway appears, I see bits of smoldering debris littering the street. Some shingles scattered across the drive, a piece of guttering, a couple of smoking two-by-fours, still nailed together and now lying in the middle of the road in the shape of a cross. I weave around it all.

And then I see the flames.

They lick up at the trees like the tongues of a dozen snakes, flickering sharply against the night sky. It's when I make the turn that I finally see it—the house. I see the house that I was born in, the house that my brother died behind, the house that held so much good and bad, all but destroyed. Half of it has been blown out and the other half is engulfed in a writhing blaze.

I ease to a stop, taking in the dead space that was once the living room and, beyond it, the master bedroom. They're gone now and the emptiness inside me tells me that the woman who lived there is gone, too. A strange numbness emanates from my chest.

I look into the darkness where my mother used to park her car at the back edge of the house, nearest the kitchen door. I see one taillight and the corner of a pale blue hatchback peeking out from behind the ruin.

She was here.

Was.

A piece of wood burns on the trunk lid of Mom's car. It makes the whole scene even more surreal, unbelievable.

I shift into park and get out to walk slowly across the yard, picking through small fires scattered around the grass as I approach the front door. I feel the heat of the flames, but it doesn't penetrate the cold that's seeped into my skin. I feel it burn my eyes and throat and nostrils, but I don't veer from my path. It never occurs to me that I should. I'm not afraid of dying.

As I take in the wreckage, I feel detached, robotic, like I'm watching a bad movie through a crystal-clear camera lens. It isn't until I stop at the closed front door that I start to feel the cold recede, and then I almost wish it hadn't.

I reach for the knob, wrapping my fingers around the scorching metal to test it. It's locked.

Pain threatens to explode from my chest, to shred muscle and bone. If my mother had been able to escape, she wouldn't have turned and locked the door behind her. She'd have run. But this door is locked. That means my mother is dead.

My boot against the front door is like a shotgun blast in the night. It gives easily and I walk over it as though a violent fire isn't raging all around me. I scan the mostly intact dining room. Empty. I walk toward what's left of the kitchen. Empty. No sign of my mother, dead or alive. She must've been in one of the obliterated rooms. And now she's obliterated, too.

With the crackle of support beams giving way overhead, I head toward the bedroom I slept in as a child. Even filled with smoke I can see that she hadn't changed a thing since I was here last. She preserved it for her dead youngest son just like she'd done for her dead oldest.

Despite the suffocating air, it still feels like home, like all the memories I left behind are housed in the wood and the plaster, in the grass and the leaves and the trees outside. They were all I had left. Them and the tiny woman who lived here.

I feel all the angst I lived with as a child. I feel all the desperation and anger. But I also feel a bone-deep sadness, a sense of loss that comes from the death of the only person on the planet I've ever loved.

Like battery acid leaking out of a weakness in the casing, barely controlled fury starts to eat away at the sadness. It gnaws at my gut, burns through my insides until soon it's a raging inferno that threatens a far worse destruction than the explosive that went off in my mother's home.

I fist and unfist my fingers. Fist and unfist. Like a pump, each squeeze seems to force more pressure into my chest, into the space where a primal growl, where the pained yet vengeful howl of a wolf grows. I push it down, keep it locked behind clenched teeth and tight lips, promising myself that I will make this right. That I will find the person responsible for this.

When I walk back out to the hole that used to be the other end of the house, I realize with an unbearable anguish that my mother died with a hole something like this inside her. The explosion of my father had ripped Jeremy from her. Years later, an explosion of mercy and protectiveness had ripped me from her life. I thought I was doing what was best for her, but a monster has no control over things like that. The shadows follow a monster and no one he loves is safe. No one.

Not even Muse.

As I look out into the dark ring that stretches beyond the light of the fire, I see a white sliver. My guts clench. It's a leg.

I take off in a haphazard path through the wreckage until my foot hits solid ground then I run. It takes me seconds to reach her. It'll take me a lifetime to forget what I find.

My mother. Bloody, burned. Gone. One arm juts out at an unnatural angle and her dark eyes are open and staring off into nothingness. The vision of her lifeless form collides with memories of her from my childhood. Her sweet words. Her gentle soul. Too good for this world. Too good for our family.

My eyes sting as I kneel beside her and pull her limp body into my arms. Beyond the scent of burned flesh and smoke, I smell her, my mother. The only person I've cared enough to leave. And even then she couldn't escape what I've become. She couldn't escape whoever is hunting our crew. She's dead because of me.

With a hollowness in my chest that hurts like a gunshot, I curl her toward me and I bury my nose in her hair. I inhale, drawing in one last breath of the woman who gave me life, who patched the wounds she could see and loved me for the ones she couldn't. Part of me hoped that one day I'd be able to see her again, both of us alive. The past behind us, unable to hurt us. But that was stupid. Unrealistic. This is who I am and this is what happens to people I care about. This is what will happen to Muse if I'm with her long enough.

As though my thoughts alone summoned her, I hear Muse's muffled voice, yelling for me from somewhere in the distance. A pang of alarm shoots through me. Reluctantly, I return my mother to the cold ground. It kills me to think of leaving her this way, but I have no choice. Someone did this to her. And that someone is still out there. And Muse might be next.

I turn and run back through the house, leaping over debris as I make my way toward her trembling voice. When I find Muse, she's standing near the open front door, tears streaming down her face, streaks of soot marring the cream of her cheeks.

"What's wrong?" I ask when I stop in front of her. Instantly on high alert, I scan the tree line at the front of the house, my eyes digging into that place between fire-bright and pitch-black, looking for the nameless, faceless enemy that always lies in wait for me.

Muse throws her arms around my neck, smashing her body to mine, and she squeezes me until her shoulders tremble.

"Muse, what is it? What's wrong?"

"Oh God, Jasper, I'm so sorry," she wails.

"Sorry for what?" I ask, my concern growing by the second. I'm running through scenarios again. What has she done? Who did she call? What did she see?

She leans away long enough to look up into my eyes. The bright orange flames all around us are reflected in the glistening green pools and I think for a tenth of a second that I'd like nothing more than to lose myself in there, to just turn my back on the world and hide away with Muse somewhere. Somewhere safe.

"Your m-mother. I'm so sorry!" Tears stream down her cheeks and her expression is one of intense agony, like it's *she* who just lost a parent rather than me. Her empathy flows over me like cool, soothing water.

"It's okay, baby," I tell her softly, quieting her the best that I can. "It was fast. She didn't suffer." She buries her face in my neck and I brush my hand over her hair, eyes trained on the darkness at her back. "Her pain is over. She's free now. She's finally free."

She's finally free. Truly free. Free of every monster that my father created.

The notion brings me some small bit of comfort. Muse brings me more. With her in my arms, I'm reminded that I *do* have something left to lose. I can grieve later if I must, but right now, I need to focus on the living, focus on getting Muse to safety before I seek my vengeance.

"We need to go," I whisper near her ear as I loosen her hold on me.

She pulls her hands around to cup my face. "Are you okay, Jasper?"

"I'm fine," I assure her.

Her brows knit together. I know what she's thinking. She's thinking that a decent person would be devastated right now. "But . . ."

"But nothing. She's gone. She's dead. Nothing I do will bring her back. This part is over. Someone will pay a price for her death, but that has to wait. Right now, you're more important. I need to get you out of here."

She nods. "Okay." She reaches for my hand, curling her fingers tightly around mine. This is who she is. She is the kind who gives comfort, the kind who shares in grief, the kind who gives of herself. The kind who will only be hurt by getting involved with someone like me. The best thing I can do for her once I get her to safety is to let her go. Because once I do, she'll never be able to find me. I'll be in the wind. A ghost. A nightmare best forgotten.

TWENTY-SEVEN

Muse

I catch myself glancing repeatedly at Jasper as he steers the car back to his cabin. He's stoic. Calm. *Eerily* calm. He just saw his childhood home in fiery pieces scattered all over the place, probably along with his mother's remains, and he's acting as though everything is fine.

Well not *fine*, really. He seems in a hurry to get me away, but other than that, he's quiet. No tears. No roaring like a lion, no howling like a coyote. No nothing. Just . . . calm.

When he rolls into his driveway, he slams the gearshift into park and turns to me, fierceness on his face. "Lock the doors. Stay put. I'll be right back."

It's not a request, nor does he pause to see if I agree to comply. He simply turns and crawls out of the car, knowing that I surely can't be crazy enough *not to do* what he says.

And he's right. I'm not. I'm just not as quick as he is.

I'm watching Jasper mount the steps in two long leaps when my door is wrenched open and a hand covers my mouth. I start to scream when something is jammed into my ribs. It's cold and unyielding. Instinctively I know it's a gun.

My heart is slamming around inside my chest, but I remain absolutely still.

"Scream and I'll shoot you. Try to get away and I'll shoot you."

I listen to the words, which are alarming in and of themselves, but it's the voice with which they're spoken that I find most disturbing of all.

I roll my eyes to the right and get a glimpse of Matt's face in the glow of the headlights reflecting off the side of the cabin.

He catches my wide eyes staring and grins in that half-cocked way that used to melt my heart. Right now it merely freezes it.

"Matt?" I mutter against his hand.

"It's good to see you, too, little girl," he says, using his old pet name for me. I'm sure it's supposed to put me at ease, but it doesn't. If anything, it puts me on guard.

"What the hell are you doing here?"

"Shhh," he says, clamping his hand over my mouth again. "Come on. I'll take you to your dad."

"Dad's here?"

"Yeah. We came for you. Now come on. And be quiet about it unless you want your bodyguard to get shot."

My lungs tighten at just the suggestion of Jasper getting hurt. I don't understand what's going on, but I'm sure my father will explain it. And in the meantime, there's no reason to risk Jasper getting shot over a misunderstanding just because he's on high alert.

"Where is he?" I ask in a hushed voice.

"This way. Come on."

Matt takes my hand and tugs me from the car. He doesn't let go as he starts off around the front of the cabin, sticking to the edge of the trees where the darkness creeps in. He leads me down to the lake and to the dock, but I pull back before stepping on the first plank.

Matt tugs, but I resist. "Where *is he*, Matt?" I'm digging in my heels.

"We came by boat so no one would see us. Now shut up before you get somebody killed." With a sharp jerk, he pulls me forward again, and this time I let him.

We walk all the way to the end of the dock and Matt urges me into Jasper's little flat-bottom boat. He hops in after me and unties us. Tucking his gun into his waistband, my ex begins to row us away from the dock. When he gets to the middle of the cove, he stops.

My eyes have adjusted to the moonlight, which is full and bright tonight, allowing me to see the lake and Matt quite clearly. It's the smile Matt is wearing that sends a shiver of apprehension skittering down my spine.

"Why did you stop?"

"I'm waiting."

"For what? I thought you were taking me to Dad? Is he coming to get me *here*?"

Matt turns a dubious look on me. "God, you really *are* stupid, aren't you?"

I stare at him for a few seconds, mouth agape, before anger kicks in. "What the hell is that supposed to mean?"

"Your father isn't *here*. And he isn't coming. But don't worry. I'll be sure to pay him a visit later."

My blood runs cold, colder still when Matt produces his gun and aims it at me. "Matt, what are you doing?"

"I'm paying for my future, that's what I'm doing."

"And just how are you doing that by holding me at gunpoint in the middle of a lake? No one will *pay you* for me, if that's what you're thinking."

"Oh, this is nothing as pedestrian as a kidnapping. God, Muse! Give me a little credit. Actually, this really has little to do with you at all. You're more like a . . . a . . . bonus. Collateral damage, even. But no, this isn't about you. It's about Jasper King. He's the one I'm after."

My temper boils and I lash out with venom. "If Jasper is who you're here for, you're a bigger idiot than I thought, *Matt.*"

"We'll see, but I think you've underestimated me. This is how I see it going down. When your daring rescuer realizes that you're gone, he'll come to find you. At that point, one of two things will happen. He will either stop there on the dock like the pussy that he is and I'll shoot him where he stands *or* he'll actually nut up and try to swim to you, in which case I'll shoot him when he surfaces. Either way, his time is up. Tonight."

My heart is beating so fast I feel nauseous. My chest burns with panic and my eyeballs feel as though they're throbbing with a pulse all their own.

"But why? Why would you want to kill Jasper?"

"Money, Muse. It's what makes the world go 'round."

"Bu-but why would anyone want Jasper dead?"

I can only imagine that there are possibly hundreds of people who might want Jasper dead, but I'd rather keep Matt talking so I can think, think of a way to help Jasper. I cannot, *simply cannot* sit here and do nothing while he walks into a trap. If I have to watch him die . . .

My guts—my stomach, my intestines, all the muscles in my middle—squeeze painfully at the thought. I can't let that happen. I can't even begin to think of what the world would feel like now without Jasper in it. I don't think I could bear to see the sun rise if I had to live with the knowledge (much less the image) of his death. I'd have no reason to get up, no reason to *live.*

I don't even hesitate to confess in the privacy of my mind that I love Jasper. I think I fell for him when I first collided with those tiger eyes of his, shining so brightly down at me. Something in my soul knew I'd met the other part of me, the part I wouldn't want to live without.

"I'd say there are a lot of people who would want him dead. And for a lot of reasons. Lucky for me, I don't give a damn about any of that shit. I don't really care who wants him and his cohorts dead. I just want the money that his death will bring me."

"His cohorts?"

"Yes, his *cohorts*. Some special ops team your father commanded. Seems they've made some enemies on their own side. Guess that's the risk you take when you do black ops for the government."

"Black ops? Are you saying my father . . ."

"Killed people? Taught other men to kill people? Yes, Muse, that's what I'm saying." His sigh is exasperated, like he's talking to a child. "Ahhhh, sweet Muse. So clueless."

Although it's shocking to have it *confirmed*, I can't say that I'm entirely surprised to hear this. My father has said some odd things over the years, and since meeting Jasper . . . well, I'm just not really surprised. If they knew each other in a work capacity and Jasper is a killer . . .

But I still believe they're the good guys. It's people like Matt and the traitor he's working for who are a danger to the world, to the greater good.

"Does this have anything to do with the information Jasper wanted from my father?"

"How the hell should I know what that sadistic son of a bitch wants with the Colonel? Maybe he knows his team is being targeted. Maybe he thinks the Colonel is involved. Who knows? When I was approached about taking this once in a lifetime assignment, I didn't ask many questions. These people aren't big on divulging more than what's absolutely necessary. I just took the assignment, hacked into the network the government uses to establish these kinds of covert missions for its operatives and then set up the hit. Jasper was going to help me with my job. He'd kill the Colonel and then I'd kill him."

"How did you know Jasper would take it?"

"I know all about him. I'm in IT, remember? Information is my specialty, Muse. And Jasper King has a file a mile long. I know how good he is at his job, how seriously he takes his assignments. No matter what his feelings are for the Colonel, I knew he'd come for him. I *am* a little surprised that he's let you live this long, though."

Let me live? This long?

Thud, thud, thud. The beat of my heart is so heavy, I can't be sure that Matt doesn't hear it.

"Wh-what do you mean?"

"Don't tell me you haven't figured that out yet." Matt clucks his tongue and shakes his head in pity. "Poor Muse. Didn't even know the man she's been screwing plans to kill her. Wow, that's gotta suck. But the hit was on you, too. I couldn't be sure how much you knew, how much your father might've told you about what he was discovering. So I included you in the mission. Jasper was sent to kill you, too."

He's lying! He's lying, he's lying, he's lying! I chant to myself, closing my eyes against the smug smirk on his face. I wish now that the moon wasn't shining so brightly, that I couldn't see so clearly. Without *or* within.

But that's not the case. There's no more hiding or pretending or *not seeing* anymore. All sorts of little things about Jasper are coming together to make perfect sense now—the reticence, the subtle sadness, the odd comments. The guilt—it all paints a perfect picture. I just couldn't see it until now. I didn't want to.

"Of course, I guess I shouldn't be surprised that you didn't catch on to King. I mean, damn! You haven't even caught on to who your mom was and what dear old Dad did to her, and you've had *years* to figure that shit out." While my brain is whirling and my heart is withering, I open my eyes and fix them on Matt, who shakes his head woefully. "You sure didn't inherit the Colonel's brains, did you?"

I feel like the boat is rocking, even though my eyes assure me that it's not. My insides pitch and sway, rebelling in a visceral way against what Matt is insinuating. I want to ask questions, but part of me is stuck firmly in denial of what he's saying, of *everything* he's saying.

"I gotta give you credit for using that sweet little body of yours to hold him off, though. Far as I know, the guy's never hesitated before."

Never hesitated.

I will always think of you.

I pray to God that means something, something good. Something different. I pray to God that means Jasper never really planned on killing me. Or my father.

In the midst of the panic that's threatening, in the midst of the devastation that's setting in, an odd sense of comfort assails me. It's sudden. And powerful. Like a hurricane force wind blowing through my insides. It's fierce. Fiercely reassuring.

Jasper.

I know it as certainly as I know I'm sitting here with my ex. He's close. He's coming.

A part of me is always attuned to him on some level. It's that part that draws my eye away from Matt and toward the dock. I see instantly that I wasn't wrong. There, standing on the end of the pier, is Jasper.

The silvery moonlight bathes his tense shoulders in an eerie glow that leaves his face in the deepest of shadow. I'm sure it's only my imagination, but I can almost see his eyes in the black of his face, a pale, haunting yellow in the darkness. He's absolutely still, as though he might not even be breathing. I wonder if he even is as he stares out across the unforgiving lake to where I sit, a million miles away. Or might as well be.

"Right on time," Matt mutters from beside me. "Come on out, King! I'll give you a front row seat to the job *you* should've done days ago," he yells.

Jasper says nothing. He doesn't move, doesn't acknowledge that he even heard Matt. He just stands there, head bowed. Now I wonder if he's even looking out at me. Or if he's staring into the water. And, if he is, what he's seeing.

TWENTY-EIGHT

Jasper

I'm frozen. Terrified. Torn. The water, the *lake* that has haunted me for seventeen years lies between me and the man who has Muse. I don't have to guess that he means to do her harm. I don't have to guess that he knows enough about me to know of my history with this place. I only have to act.

Therein lies the rub.

I'm calm. Surprisingly calm. My pulse is steady, my breathing is even. But those are just learned reactions. When real crisis strikes, I don't panic. Just like I'm not panicking now. But something else is happening. Like the reverse of panic. Like I can't process how to work this out and save Muse, so my body is just slowly giving up.

My heart is beating sluggishly, almost like it's running down, like it's forgetting how to work. My lungs are pulling in long, steady gulps of air. My eyes are clear and focused. So clear and focused, in fact, that it's as though they can see below the inky surface. On the water, I don't see a reflection of the moon above. I don't see my face or my surroundings. But I see into it, beneath it. And I see my brother there.

He looks just as he did the day he died. His face is a pale oval and his lips are cold blue. His brown hair, just a few shades lighter than mine, floats around his head like an unnatural halo and his eyes . . . God, his eyes! They're the only other reflection I see. But they don't reflect me or the moon or the lake. No, they reflect the emptiness, the *blackness* that resides where my soul should be. They accuse me of living when he didn't. They blame me for never fighting for him. They hate me escaping our childhood when he couldn't.

I try to lift one leaden arm, to reach out toward him even though some part of my mind knows he isn't there, but I can't. It weighs too much. Just like it did that day long ago when Jeremy drifted away. Away from shore, away from me, away from *life*. I couldn't move, couldn't go back in and drag him out again. I just . . . couldn't. Just like I can't now.

My feet are surely cemented to the dock, my legs made of iron. The only things that are working are my vital organs and my thoughts. And damn those thoughts!

I close the eyes that play tricks on me, but what I see is no different. Still, hanging there in the water, is my brother. The vision is seared into my mind. It's inescapable. My past, my life, who I am is inescapable. And if I can't overcome it, there will always be more casualties of it. Of me. Of the monster.

Casualties.

Muse.

I open my eyes to the small boat bobbing in the cove. I can barely make out Muse's face, but I can see enough of it to know something is wrong. Terribly, terribly wrong. And not just because her life is in danger. It's something else.

I see the flash of moonlight on a muzzle as her captor, a guy who looks a lot like the picture I saw of her ex, presses a pistol to her temple. Muse's eyes widen, but she shows no other reaction. She just looks . . . shocked.

But she'll soon look dead if I don't get to her. If I *can't* get to her.

My heart rate speeds. My breathing becomes labored. A twitch starts in the fingers of my left hand, the hand that held so tight to my brother's arm as I dragged him along behind me.

I have a choice to make, a choice with dire consequences one way or the other. I could drown trying to get to Muse. My muscles could seize, fall victim to the power of my mind. Or I could stand here and watch someone take her life. Take the life of the only person who's been able to penetrate the thick scar tissue that surrounds my cold heart.

Or I could swim out and get her. I could save her. Like she's been saving me, little by little, day by day.

"You're a coward, King. I had hoped for better," the guy calls across the lake to me. Then, before my sleeping limbs can wake, he turns his gun toward me and fires.

TWENTY-NINE

Muse

The gunshot is not what makes me scream. It's the violent jerk of Jasper's left shoulder followed by his headfirst tumble into the lake that rips the sound from my throat.

"Noooo!" I cry, standing up so quickly that the boat tips precariously toward the black water. "Jasperrrr!"

"Sit down!" Matt spits, yanking my arm and pulling me backward into the boat. "I'm not fishing your ass out of this lake in the middle of the night. I'd sooner leave you out here to drown, too."

Matt picks up the oars and starts to row toward shore. I stare at him for a few seconds, my mind spinning and my heart breaking, before a desperate rage overwhelms me.

With a growl that I don't even recognize as coming from me, I launch myself at him, fingers bent into claws that I plan to use to remove his eyes from their sockets.

"You bastard!"

I feel my nails sink deeply, satisfyingly into flesh when my fingers meet his face. I'm gratified by his yowl of pain, which acts as fuel to the wildfire burning in my gut. I lash and tear, scrape and scratch, kick and punch at every surface I can reach. Skin, clothing, hair. I'm a flurry of uncoordinated arms and legs, but all with the same goal—hurt, maim, cripple. Destroy Matt.

But all my adrenaline and fury is no match for Matt's superior size and strength. I hear the clatter of the gun on the bottom of the boat just before Matt uses his bulky arms and one leg to subdue me.

"You bitch!" he says, wiping at his left cheek. Streaks of blood mar his pale skin and bring a smile to my face.

"There's more where that came from, motherfu—"

Matt's long fingers wrap around my throat and squeeze, cutting off my rant. "Do you think I won't kill you and throw your whore's body into the lake?" he hisses.

I sputter ineffectively, trying to spit acid around his tight hold.

"But I can do worse. If you don't sit quietly while I row this shitty little boat to shore, I'll shoot you in both arms and both legs and then drag your ass down the road. You get me? I need you for a little while longer, to help me get your father out of the way, but I can make do without if you prove to be more trouble than you're worth."

A sob builds in my chest. Not because of his threat, but because I can't bear the thought of leaving the lake. Jasper's body is in the water. I can't leave him here. I can't leave him here all alone, to die with his brother in the water.

I nod since I can't speak and after another twenty seconds or so, Matt releases me. I pull in huge gulps of air, raising my hand to massage my neck. My head spins lightly as blood begins to flow to and from my brain again.

"Here," Matt says, pitching first one oar and then the other at me, the handle of the second hitting me just above my right eye. "You can row, little girl."

My eye tears and I blink rapidly so that I can see. As I'm winding my fingers around the oars, I imagine swinging one of the long pieces of wood and hitting Matt in the side of the head, as hard as I can. My grip tightens and loosens, tightens and loosens as I think, as I plan.

Just a few strokes to put him at ease and then I can stand and swing at the same time, catching him off guard. Maybe before he can get off a shot.

Or maybe he'll even drop his gun and I can get to it before he does.

Or maybe the blow will kill him and he'll fall into the water and I won't have to worry about him ever again.

I go through the motions as I think, lowering the oars into the water and adjusting my feet in the bottom of the boat. I glare at Matt as he uses his shirt to wipe more blood from what must be a deeper wound seeping at the corner of his mouth.

I hope it hurts like hell, you asshole!

I squeeze the handles as I pull back on the oars, sending us slicing through the water in a backward motion. *One,* I think to myself, deciding that lucky number three will be the upswing that I aim toward Matt's head.

I raise the oars and reset them in the water and pull again.

Two.

I don't take my eyes off Matt as he cleans and preens, the gun always aimed roughly at my chest. I raise the oars again, resetting them in the water, my muscles clenching for what comes after stroke number three, but it never happens.

The boat lurches sharply to the right and dips down at Matt's end as a dark, glistening shape arises from the water behind him. A thick arm wraps around Matt's upper body and, with a vicious twist, pulls him into the shiny blackness.

"Jasper!" I cry as I leap to my feet. But he's gone. They both are, disappeared into the liquid onyx below me.

I kneel and lean over the edge of the boat, watching, waiting. I hold my breath as I eye the glassy surface for any indication of struggle or movement. But it remains calm. So very calm.

I don't know how many seconds elapse before my anxiety rises to fever pitch and I bend down to slap my hand on the water. "Jaaasperrr!"

Oh God, oh God, oh God!

Nothing.

Then, like a bullet, Matt breaks the surface with a splash and a gasp, reaching for the edge of the boat. His fingers clamp down over my right hand and I screech, using the fingers of my left hand to pry open his grip.

Matt jeers up into my face. "Snuffed him just like I did his whore mother," he sputters, tightening his grip to lever himself up into the boat.

My muscles are preparing for another fight when I see Jasper surface silently behind him. I don't have to ask if he heard Matt's words. I can see that he did. His face is death and his eyes are murder. I see Matt's fate in the dark gold orbs. I see his end. Matt's life is over. He took something from Jasper that he shouldn't have. And now Jasper will take something from him in return.

Moments and movements tick by like days. Slow, frightening days. I see only the highlight of each, like a slideshow recap.

Long fingers move to Matt's chin.

They cup just before they close, like a lover might.

Matt's eyes widen.

Jasper's knuckles whiten.

Lips pull back from teeth in a sneer.

One loser.

One winner.

A sharp jerk.

A muted snap.

A pause.

My heart thunders as I watch, as I wait.

But then Matt's fingers slither off mine. Slowly, like five thin, cold snakes. I can't take my eyes off him as he slinks silently, bonelessly into the water, down, down, down, until he's out of sight.

Then it's over. As quickly and as unexpectedly as it began, it's over. Finished. Done. Forever.

I'm still staring at the place where my ex-boyfriend's face disappeared into the black lake when Jasper hoists himself into the boat. Tender yet urgent hands take me by the arms and turn me toward him, forcing my eyes away from the water.

"Are you okay?" he asks, his eyes dark and searching in the shadows of the moonlight. When I don't answer, he gives me a little shake. "Muse, did he hurt you?"

I shake my head negatively. Everything happened so fast. Nothing seems real. Like nothing up to this point has been real.

Cool fingers curl under my chin and Jasper tips my face up into the light. He examines it closely and then starts to gently touch and prod my head and neck, my chest and arms, and then down to my hips and legs. I sit quietly and let him check me out, my thoughts both chaotic and singular. It's like all the mess and drama of the last months have culminated in the one thought that nothing is as it seems. No one I thought I knew was even real.

When he's finished assessing me, Jasper threads his fingers into my hair and leans his forehead against mine. "Talk to me, Muse. Tell me what's wrong," he whispers.

So I do.

"Nothing is real."

"What?"

"Nothing that I've ever known is real, is it?"

Jasper leans back to look at me. I can see the crease between his eyes. A frown. "What do you mean?"

"My father, my boyfriend, my mother." I pin him with a hard stare. "You."

Slowly, like flower petals dying and falling from their stem, Jasper's hands slip away. Without the heat of his touch, my skin cools. Within seconds, my cheeks feel even colder than they did before. It's like Jasper's touch *took* something from me. Heat, vitality, some part of life itself. Soon, the coldness spreads and I'm filled with a damp emptiness that threatens to consume me.

I start to shiver.

"You're in shock," he says, moving over to insinuate himself behind me, wrapping his body around mine as much as he can as he takes up the oars.

"Are you just going to leave . . . I mean, what about the . . . the body?"

"I'll call a cleaner."

A cleaner.

"Like in the movies? Someone who works for the government and comes in to remove bodies and evidence?"

"Yes. Exactly like that."

So very cloak and dagger.

Jasper rows us the rest of the way to the dock in complete silence. When he ties off, I stand up and climb out, leaving him behind. I turn to watch him haul himself out of the boat. He moves with ease.

"He didn't hit you? When he fired at you, he didn't hit you?"

Jasper shakes his head. "No."

"You're a good actor," I observe with no small amount of bitterness. My heart nearly stopped I was so convinced Matt had shot Jasper, causing him to fall headfirst into the water.

"He thought I was too afraid to come after you. I let him think that."

"So you weren't afraid at all? Was anything you told me true?" My frozen blood starts to simmer with betrayal and humiliation. Anger eclipses fear. Bitterness swallows pain.

"It was all true. I've never lied to you."

"Well it sure is convenient that you were able to throw off that fear tonight, now, isn't it?" There's poison in my tone. I let the fury lick through me, like flames eating up all other emotion, devouring every soft thing. Anything less than rage is weakness. And I can't afford to be weak right now. Not when I'm dealing with Jasper.

"I suppose it was. It's hard to be thankful for that kind of motivation, though."

"Don't tell me you're afraid of a gun. You? An assassin? That's ridiculous."

An assassin. The word coats the inside of my mouth like sour chalk. My lips curl into a sneer.

"I wasn't afraid of the gun," he states flatly.

"Oh, then what was it that you feared more than you feared the water, pray tell?" I ask, crossing my arms over my chest. My every word, my every action is laced with disbelief and resentment. I can't seem to make myself behave civilly or rationally right now. This has all been just . . . too much.

"You."

"Me?" His answer surprises me. I was expecting some pat excuse.

"Yes, you. Well *the loss of* you."

My smile is as tart as my soul. "What a terrible bind that must've put you in! What happens if someone else kills one of your targets? Do you miss out on all that money, or do you share it, or . . . How does that work?"

"I could never hurt you."

"And yet you *have*. Isn't that a bitch?"

"Muse, I—"

"Save it!" I interrupt with a bark. "All I want from you right now is to borrow your car. I need to go to my father's."

"I can't let you do that." Before I can go completely off the deep end, he adds, "But I can take you."

My lips tighten. I want to refuse him. Out of spite. Right now, I don't want anything from Jasper, much less kindness. I'm clinging to the anger and the bitterness for dear life. The moment I let go of them, I feel I'll just fall apart. And I can't do that yet. I have too many questions. But I *do* need to get back to my father. And Jasper holds the only means by which to do so.

Swallowing a thick lump of resentment, I agree. I don't really have much choice. "Fine. Let me get my things." With that, I stalk off down the dock and across the yard to the cabin, flinging open the screen door and making my way toward the bedroom.

Angrily, I ball up my clothes, strewn here and there as Jasper and I left them after making love, and throw them into my suitcase. The ache in my chest as I think on those precious moments, moments that were nothing more than lies, goes deeper and deeper until I feel like it might gnaw right through my spine and leave nothing but a gaping hole in its wake.

I choke back a sob as I jerk the zipper closed and yank the case off the dresser. When I whirl around, Jasper is standing in the doorway, quiet and imposing. He's watching me with his turbulent gold eyes, his expression not much different than it ever is. But I've gotten to know him well enough that I can see the subtle differences. I've memorized every nuance of his face, his body, the heart of the man I thought I was getting to know. That's why I can see the tinge of regret crouching just beneath the surface.

A sob works its way up and out. I can't deal with his softness now, his sweetness. Not now. I just can't.

I stomp over to him, listing in one direction as I manage my luggage, and I throw my hand up between us. "Don't."

I hate that my voice breaks. Like a crack in a vase, I'm afraid that it will lead to total dissolution, so I grit my teeth against the surge of pain and I move past him.

Jasper catches my arm as I pass and he stops me. I don't bother looking up at him. I keep my eyes trained straight ahead.

He holds me like this for long, tense minutes. I don't know what he's waiting for, but I know that I can't stand it much longer.

One question pops out before I can stop it. "When?" Once it's free, every muscle in my body clenches as I await the answer.

He doesn't pretend *not to know* what I mean. As always, he's extremely intuitive. He knows the question that's eating a canker on my insides. Part of me *has to know* when he decided not to kill me. "I don't know. I just knew that I couldn't."

I slump in his hold and lean for a few seconds against the door-jamb. "I'm not afraid of you," I admit. And I'm not. "I'm only afraid of what knowing you and falling in love with you has done to me. I've never met someone who destroyed my hope. Until you. As much as I hate you right now, I know I'll never love someone this much again. But you warned me, didn't you?" I spit bitterly. "You told me you'd hurt me and you knew there wasn't a damn thing I could do about it. Not one damn thing."

I turn my hateful, disgusted glare up to him as I yank my arm free and walk proudly to the car. I open the back door and throw my suitcase in, completely disregarding the supple leather of the seats.

Everything beautiful is getting trashed tonight, I think harshly, blinking back a swell of tears. I refuse to crumble. I. Refuse.

I climb in the passenger side of the still-running car and I wait.

I see Jasper come through the door, turning to lock it behind him. He stands tall and imposing as ever, but something about his shoulders, the way they're set a little lower, assures me that this ordeal has left its mark on him as well.

Good. I hope you're hurting, too.

Although that should make me feel better, it actually makes me feel worse. Jasper has been hurt so much in life already, I only wanted to heal him, to love him. But that wasn't to be because he only wanted to *kill* me.

The reality of our circumstances hits home again, bursting through my anger with a sucker punch to the heart. I gasp in the quiet of the car and reach for my aching chest. But when Jasper opens the driver's side door and slides in behind the wheel, I let my hand fall away and turn to look out the window, into the inky blackness of the surrounding woods.

We ride in silence for miles and miles before Jasper speaks. I wonder that he didn't think I was asleep, but knowing him, he can probably hear my heartbeat or something.

"My father was the first person I killed," comes his hoarse voice in the dark.

Despite my upset, despite my disillusionment over him and what happened between us, my heart lurches behind my ribs. I say nothing, though. Just close my eyes and lean my forehead against the cool glass, willing myself to remain unaffected.

I listen as he continues, almost absently, as if he's merely thinking aloud. "I enlisted in the Army as soon as I graduated. I had to get away from him, even though he wasn't around anymore. I could feel him everywhere, everywhere I looked, everything I heard. Even *in me.* So I went through basic training, kept my nose clean, and stayed to myself. But it was during one of the aptitude tests that they picked up on what kind of person I really was. They could spot whatever's wrong with me. And they used it. Ruthlessly, they used it. When they showed me the X-ray reports from one of my mother's many trips to the hospital that I knew nothing about, they explained to me the years of abuse she'd suffered. They showed me the evidence of it. And then they told me that my father was going to be released, that his case had been overturned on a technicality. They knew how I'd react. They knew all they had to do was point me in the right direction, get me inside that prison, and I'd take him out. So that's what they did. They made sure I turned into the exact kind of machine they needed."

I steel myself against the rush of heartbreak for the young man that Jasper was, for all that he saw and experienced, for all the hurt that marked him so indelibly. Mercilessly, I remind myself that he was going to kill me. I can't afford to *feel* for him.

"Somehow my mother knew. When I went to tell her that he was gone, she cried. But not for him. She cried for *me.* That's when I knew that she couldn't survive what I had become. She couldn't watch me walk down the only road in front of me. Or at least that's how I saw it at the time. So when I was recruited into the Colonel's covert ops team, he, with all his connections and questionable associations, helped me fake my death. From that day forward, Jasper Lyons ceased to exist. I officially became Jasper King. Or Jason King. Or James King. Or whoever else I needed to be. But they were all men you never wanted to meet, guys you prayed never had reason to come to your door."

Jasper Lyons. How fun.

Lyons.

King.

Lion, king of the jungle. It's fitting and somehow acerbic that he'd choose the name.

Both names suit him. Lyons . . . it speaks to the man he was born into, his animal ways and instincts, his tiger eyes and bloodhound nose. But King . . . King speaks to what he has become. The cream of the killer crop, the top of the assassin list, better at what he does than anyone in his field. He wears the crown.

If that's anything to be proud of.

It's fitting for his personal life, too. For me, he's the king of heartache, something I can personally attest to. Even though I'm currently in a state of denial, refusing to deal with the havoc he's wreaked on me, I can feel the devastation, the utter destruction lurking right around the edges of my consciousness, lying in wait. It's biding its time, holding on for the moment when I lower my guard, my anger, my determination. Then I can be crushed, smashed, gutted like a bug on the windshield.

That's my future.

So much to look forward to, I think waspishly.

"The worst part is that I never really minded my job. I knew I was taking bad people out of the equation, wiping them out of existence and saving others from their particular brand of terrorism. Whatever that was. I never questioned it. Not once. Not until you."

Despite my resolve to remain detached, to listen with half an ear and keep my emotions out of it, I feel my chin tremble in response to his words.

Not until you.

"I don't know if there was any point, not from the second I met you, when I could've hurt you. Not like that anyway. I guess I knew all along that my attraction to you would end up hurting you one way or the other. But I couldn't resist you. Didn't really want to. Then again, monsters are selfish. I don't know why I'm even surprised."

I try to ignore the way his confession eases my soul, eases some of the pain that I'm trying so hard not to feel. I open my blurry eyes and trace a finger along the shiny wood inlay of the passenger-side door. I can't look at Jasper. I can't let myself see what expression he's wearing, see his eyes.

"And my father? You think killing him wouldn't have hurt me more than you taking *my life*?"

"Muse, you have to understand that I've never, *never* hesitated before. All the things you made me feel are new to me. I can't say for sure what I would've done, but I can tell you right now that even if he hadn't come through with the information I needed, I wouldn't have taken him from you. If he'd turned out to be a traitor, I don't know what I'd have done. I'd have hated whatever it was because he was my commander. Men like us, we live by a code. And if he'd violated that code, he'd have deserved death. But even so, I couldn't have killed him. I couldn't have done that to you."

I close my eyes again, battling over whether to believe him. He's never lied to me before. Left things out, yes. Vital things like being assigned to kill me and my father, but he's never *actually* lied.

"What did you want from him anyway?"

"I needed to know who he works for, who calls the shots for *him*. I knew if he wouldn't give up a name, he was dirty. That's how I would've known he was involved."

"Involved in what?"

He pauses. I hear him take a deep breath as though he's delving into something else that's unpleasant. "Killing the members of our team. Delta Five consisted of your father and four men. Rogan, Reid, Tag and me. We're being targeted. Now I know your father is, too. You'll meet the rest of them soon. Well, all but one. Reid. They got to him first. After I notified the cleaner, I called the others while you were packing, told them to get to Atlanta."

"For what?" I snap. I'm understandably alarmed. Four dangerous men, angry ones, at that, descending on my father. Who would be okay with that?

"They need to be warned. In person. Our trust needs to be reestablished. And they need to be able to take precautions. Obviously the people they care about could be in danger."

"So you all did the same kinds of . . . jobs?"

"We all had our specialties, but we all did whatever we had to do to get the job done. We worked as a team for three and a half years. The four of us practically lived together. And in situations like the ones we often found ourselves in, you quickly become like family. Tight. Trusted. Dependable. But when it came time to re-up, two of the four couldn't. Rogan had a brother who got hurt and needed him. Tag had a death in the family that required he take over the business back in the states. So it was just me and Reid left. Our assignments were solo after the group dissolved, but we kept in touch. We all have, actually. Until Reid got killed two months ago, that is." Another pause. When Jasper begins to speak again, his voice is taut with an underlying anger. "The thing about men like us is that it takes someone with a high level of clearance to even find out about our existence, much less to be able to find us on an op and take us out, like with Reid. Or to target the family of someone who took on a new identity like I did. There's a traitor somewhere in the mix. Someone who hired a low-level asshole like Matt. And I'm gonna find out who it is."

I finally turn to look at him. "And you think my father can help with that?"

"I know he can. Now that I know he's not involved."

"And then what? You find out who this person is and kill him? Is that your plan?"

"Yes." No wavering. No hesitation. No questions asked. "The penalty for treason is death."

"Wh-what about my father?"

"Your father can take care of himself. He's part of us. One of us."

"So you'll get your name, exact your pound of flesh and then disappear?"

"Yes. It's what I do."

"And if someone else is sent to finish the job you couldn't?"

"The only reason I even took the assignment to take care of the Colonel was so that no one else would get to him and kill him before I could get answers. He went underground because he knew what happened with Reid was foul play. He also knew that if anyone was sent after him, it'd be me. I'm the best at what I do. And I'm sure he knew once I found out about you, I'd use you to get to him. And that there would be no safer place for you than with me until I got my answers. He's always a step ahead. That's why he was chosen to lead a team like ours. As I said, your father can take care of himself. He has contacts. He knows things. He knew I was coming. Like me, he put it together about our team being sold out. Men like Reid don't just get killed on their way to an op that way. No one should've known where he was going. Except the very people who ordered him to go there."

"And me? What's to become of me?"

"I have a plan."

When he doesn't continue, I prompt, "Are you going to tell me what it is?"

"Not yet. But I'll do everything I can to make sure you're safe."

Jasper's face is somber. I don't ask why, though. I don't ask what he's feeling. I'm pretty sure that I don't want to know. This is already a disaster. I can't afford to get drawn in any further, can't risk a setback. And I'm smart enough to realize that I can't trust myself where Jasper is concerned. I'm in too deep. My heart is involved. Completely and irrevocably involved.

"And you couldn't have just trusted me with this? You couldn't have just told me? Did it never occur to you that maybe I could help? That maybe I could talk to my father, convince him—"

"It's too dangerous. I would never risk you like that."

"But you agreed to kill me," I spit.

"That was before I knew you, knew who you were. And unless I'd found out that you and your father were liabilities, I had no intentions of killing you."

"Why should that matter? If I'm a threat, I'm a threat."

"I didn't know for sure if you were. I came to find out if the Colonel was dirty. I knew I'd find out about you, too. But you're not. You never have been. Your father sent you away because you were in danger and he knew it. He must've suspected something all those months ago. But even if you had been a threat, I wouldn't have cared. I could never hurt you. Not now. Not after . . ."

I hate that my eyes sting. I hate that my feelings ache. I hate that my voice trembles. "And yet you've done just that."

"Not because I wanted to. I just didn't . . . I didn't know how to tell you. Or even if I should. You're only hurt because you know that there was a time, even though it was before I met you, when I might've done things to hurt you and the people you love."

For some reason, that makes me prickly and defensive, even though it's basically true. If I'd never found out, I'd have gone on blissfully ignorant, just as I'd been earlier today. And yesterday. And the day before that. Never knowing that Jasper came into my life with the intention of killing my father and me if he had to.

But I *did* find out.

And, as irrational as it might seem to him, I can't simply *pretend* that nothing has changed.

"Maybe that *is* part of it, Jasper, but that's not *all of it*. I think the worst part is that I trusted you. I believed you. And I fell—"

I won't tell him again that I fell in love with him. My pride had taken a back seat before, but now it's making itself known. And it's wounded.

Jasper's voice is low and defeated. "It doesn't matter anyway. I'm the worst thing in the world for you. But I promise that I'll do right by you and then you'll never have to see me again."

To this, I say nothing.

Why is it that his promise makes me feel worse rather than better?

THIRTY

Jasper

My antennae twitch when I pull up outside the Colonel's hideaway and find every light in the house on. Not very subtle for a man trying to fly under the radar.

I pull to a stop almost a block away and turn to wake Muse. She finally fell asleep almost an hour ago. I let her rest. She's been through a lot today. She's been through a lot the last several days, actually.

I don't blink at the pang of guilt that stabs at my insides. I deserve every bit of anger and disgust she's throwing my way. Probably more. If I'd been a halfway decent person, I'd have left her out of this after I met her, even though she was leverage for getting what I wanted from the Colonel. But even if I *had* made the same choice, I didn't have to compound things by sleeping with her. I didn't have to make things so much worse. But I did. Because I couldn't resist her. Because she awakened some part of my heart, of my soul that I wasn't sure I even had. She made me feel and, as much as I knew it was a bad idea, the lure of what she offered was just too much, too *good*. She was like fresh air to a man who has been locked in a basement his whole life. She was like the warm glow of a fire to a man whose heart turned cold a long time ago. She was like everything I never knew I wanted, served up with big green eyes and a sexy-as-hell smile.

I never knew I had an Achilles heel. Because I never knew Muse. Until now.

But now I know. And where do I go from here?

I cut the engine and wait to see if she wakes. She doesn't, so I speak her name softly, so as not to startle her. "Muse."

She makes a little mewing sound and turns her head in my direction, but her eyes are still closed. I reach out to brush a strand of hair from her cheek, the back of my finger grazing the silk of her skin. "Muse."

She leans into my touch, her subconscious not nearly as averse to me as she seems to be in her waking hours. Her lips curve the tiniest bit and she makes a sighing sound, like she did when she was open to me earlier today.

A lifetime ago.

Her response makes me hard and achy, and grumpy as shit.

Since my right hand is trapped between her cheek and her shoulder, I ease my other onto her neck on the other side, trailing my fingertips over the soft, warm skin. "Muse, wake up."

Sleepily, eyes still closed, she reaches for my hand, winding her fingers around my wrist and pulling it down to her breast. The air whizzes through my teeth with the hiss of my want. *God, how can she do this to me so easily?*

She arches her back, pressing the plump mound into my palm. Reflexively I squeeze and she moans.

I want to touch her. I want to slip my fingers into the neck of her shirt. I want to feel her nipple tighten, practically begging for my mouth. I want to crush her mouth under mine. I want to drag her warm body into my lap and ram my cock into her sweet heat.

But I can't.

I won't.

Because this is wrong. Messed up and wrong.

I jerk my hands away, bringing Muse fully alert.

Her doe eyes blink at me once, twice, and then she looks around. "Where are we?"

My breathing is harsh and fast, and I feel like I could bite through a steel I beam. "At your dad's."

She glances behind her and then back at me, her brow furrowing. "What's wrong? Why are you breathing so hard?"

"I was just . . . thinking."

"About what?" she asks, her eyes widening in alarm.

I could lie. I could spare her the discomfort of my truth. But I haven't lied to her yet. Why start now?

"About you. About us. About how much I miss touching you, kissing you. About how much I wish I could rewind. And how much I hate that I can't."

Her expression is sad and wary, but not openly hostile. "You and me both," she confesses quietly.

"Muse, if things were different . . . if *I* were different, I'd—"

"Don't," she interjects, turning away from me. "Please. Just don't."

It's my turn to sigh. "Will you stay here and let me go check things out first?"

"No."

I knew what her answer would be before she gave it. And the reason I don't argue with her is because things will end badly enough between us without me having to restrain her in the car because I'm overly cautious where she's concerned.

"Fine. Come on then," I tell her, unsnapping her seatbelt before I climb out from behind the wheel. While she's getting out, I grab her suitcase from the back seat and meet her at the rear of the car.

We walk in silence up the street. Muse is distracted, frowning as she stares off into the distance. I doubt she'd notice if an ambulance went by. I, on the other hand, am ever vigilant. I'm scanning the street and the dark spaces between houses, covertly glancing in the windows of parked cars and listening for any sounds that might seem out of place.

I notice that the license plate of a motorcycle parked along the street has a California tag. That's when I realize that at least one of my comrades is already here. This Ducati has Rogan written all over it. Another vehicle, a black Jeep parked up the street with a cluster of grapes on the license plate, makes me think the other might be here as well. Tag, my other brother-in-arms, grew up on a vineyard, one he's now running from what I understand. My guess is both of them are inside with the Colonel.

Muse and I mount the steps and ring the bell. There's no answer at first, but then I hear the raised voices. I try the knob and it opens easily.

"How the hell can something like this happen? All that shit's supposed to be classified. Which bureaucrat with a price tag has access?" I hear Rogan shout.

"I don't know all the players, but you can damn well be sure I'm going to find out," the Colonel replies.

I enter the kitchen with Muse trailing right behind me. All heads turn in our direction. The Colonel nods and then crosses the room to take his daughter into his arms.

"Boys, this is my daughter, Muse. Muse, this is Kiefer Rogan, goes by just Rogan, and Tag Barton. They were part of my team for a few years."

Rogan and Tag nod their greeting to Muse. Both men are openly appreciative of her beauty, which pisses me off. I grit my teeth against the urge to lash out at them. She's not mine. I don't have any right to be jealous. Of course, that doesn't make one damn bit of difference to my temper.

"Nice to meet you," Muse says with a polite smile. I'm glad when her father leads her out of the room, leaving me alone with Rogan and Tag.

After a short pause, Rogan smiles his typical devil-may-care grin and walks over to punch me in the arm. Even though he's horsing around, I feel the power he's holding back. It's no surprise that he dominates in the mixed-martial-arts championship ring.

"You dawg! Figures you'd be the first one to meet the Colonel's daughter. Man, she's hot as hell!"

Tag's approach is in line with his less cowboy nature. "Good to see you, man. Sorry to hear about your mom."

"Shit, dude. I'm an asshole. I'm sorry, too. I was thinking with my big head instead of my little head," Rogan chimes in. Although he adds the last in teasing, I can see by his expression that he's genuinely apologetic.

"Thanks. She's better off, I guess. Lost everyone she ever loved and was living all by herself."

"Yeah, but you were taking care of her, man. Sending her enough money to put her up for life. At least she never wanted for anything."

"For what that's worth."

"You did the best you could. We've all done the best we could."

"So you've talked to the Colonel?"

"Yeah," Rogan says, glancing at Tag. "Evidently, he has always answered to and received his orders from a committee. He's having trouble finding out who heads it up, though. I wouldn't be surprised if this went all the way to the top. Some sort of cover-up because a slimy politician wants a better seat at the table or some shit like that."

"I won't rest until I find out who's behind all this. Matt may have pulled the trigger on my mother, but someone pointed him in the right direction. I want to know who it is. Someone needs to pay."

THIRTY-ONE

Muse

I stand behind my father, surveying the room, taking in the power and adrenaline surging through the air. I tried to talk my father into leaving with me. Right now. Just picking up and moving to parts unknown, without looking back.

"Muse, honey, I can't do that. I *won't* do that. These boys trusted me. It's up to me to do everything I can to get to the bottom of this," he'd said. I should've known that's what he'd say. Running is not in my father's character.

I came with him to the kitchen. I'm tired of being left in the dark. This all very much affects me now and I dare even one of them to try and make me leave. They've never seen a hissy fit until they've seen *me* throw one.

"What's that supposed to mean?" It's Jasper who addresses my father's statement.

"A young man that I worked with put out the hit on Muse and me to draw you here. You and I were his real targets. He was going to have Muse killed to cover his own ass in case she'd overheard something that could prove detrimental to him. But he was working for someone, someone high up on the food chain. We just have to find out who that person is."

Rogan is the first to reply. "Well, shit! There could be a couple dozen people on that list. Damn bureaucrats."

His mouth is curved into a lopsided smile. He seems like the type who doesn't let much bother him, not even a Benedict Arnold. His disposition only adds to the laid-back appeal of his surfer good looks.

I've seen his incredibly handsome face before. Spiky blond hair, dreamy green eyes. He's not only a champion MMA fighter, but he's quite popular with the ladies, which lands him on tabloid covers fairly often. I guess I just never pictured him being a part of an elite black ops team. Of course, I can only imagine that those deadly fists were trained *somewhere*.

"So what's the next step? How do we find this bastard?" the one called Tag asks. He's just as good-looking as Rogan, but in a totally different way. He has a dark, aggressive look about him that reminds me more of Jasper. His hair is black-brown and longish, brushing the collar of his shirt, and his eyes are a stormy gray color. All three men are well over six feet tall, I'd say, and could probably win the heart of whomever they set their sights on, but my eyes are only for one of them.

Jasper.

His face, his eyes, his *intensity* draws me in a visceral way. It's like my body, my heart, my soul strain toward him, even in a room full of beautiful men. He holds my focus with a reluctant singularity that reminds me of a magnet, pulled to its mate even when it doesn't want to be.

"I won't rest until I follow this to the source," my father says.

"And I'll take care of it when you do," Jasper adds with a quiet ferocity that brings chills to my arms. I'm not repulsed or afraid. I can simply relate to the need to bring to justice those who took away what little he had left in the world. It makes *me* want to harm somebody, even though I'm still devastated over his deception. My heart isn't differentiating between the Jasper of today and the Jasper of tonight. It still feels only love. Hurt, yes, but also love.

"I wouldn't deny you that, Jasper," my father assures softly, setting his hand on Jasper's big shoulder. "We've all got a stake in this, though. We're all in danger and no one we love is safe until we put an end to the threat. So in the meantime, boys, do what you have to do to keep your loved ones safe. Be vigilant. Keep 'em close. Warn them if you have to, send them away if you need to. Just until I can get some answers. Jasper, since you're the only one still in the game, keep your ear to the ground and watch your back. Rogan, you're a pretty public figure. Hole up somewhere quiet if you can. Keep your head down."

"Done. Just so happens that's already in the works. Got a gig on a cable show. Quiet town, good money, hot chicks. I'm one lucky son of a bitch," Rogan replies.

"You'll be the primary contact. I think I can use your influence as an in. I know you've got some government contacts of your own."

"Yes, sir, I do," he confirms, nodding. "I'll use 'em however you need me to."

"Good. Tag," my father says, turning to the third man. "You're already pretty damn well hidden, geographically. Watch that mountain road that leads up to the vineyard. If I need a ghost to go in somewhere, you're it. You can blend in and slip through the cracks unnoticed among these high-society types."

Tag's laugh is mirthless and velvety. "Thanks. Just the talent I always wanted."

"You know to play to your strengths. Nothing wrong with that.

Also, I got us all new burner phones. Keep them with you. Expect a call. Jasper, you'll be the triggerman, but I'll use every damn one of you to get this done if I have to. We're going to finish this, one way or the other."

Both other men are nodding their heads, probably already making plans, but when my moving gaze settles on Jasper, his eyes are trained on me.

Nearly an hour later, after all sorts of unintelligible plans and decisions and codes have been established (at least they're unintelligible for someone *not* in their little group), the party breaks up.

Rogan stops at Jasper on his way through the kitchen to the front door. "Good seeing ya, man. I'll be in Georgia for a few weeks. Up in Enchantment. Doing that bit for cable. You should come up if you get a chance. It's been a long time."

"I'll try. I'll be in touch either way."

Rogan nods and they do that manly hug that men do, replete with hard slaps on the back that would probably break the bones of a less solid person. And then he turns to me, offering a hand, which I take.

He smiles and, despite my frustrating captivation with Jasper, my belly flutters a little. "Nice to meet you, Muse. You made this trip *very* worthwhile."

I can't help returning his smile. He's devilishly charming, that's for sure. "Is that right?"

"Gospel truth," he declares with a wink.

"I bet you're the most dangerous one of all, aren't you?"

"To you? Never," he replies, still slowly shaking my hand up and down. I think the most thrilling part is that I can feel Jasper's cold-as-ice gaze on us. It gives me a touch of satisfaction to know that he *does* feel, that he *does* react to me, and to others who might find me attractive. Under different circumstances, I might be tempted to flirt with Rogan and rub it in a little. But now's not the time for that.

"Better get on the road, Ro," Jasper says sharply, interrupting. Rogan raises his eyebrows and looks from me to Jasper and back again. He grins bigger and then walks away without another word.

Tag follows behind him, reminding me even more of Jasper when I see him walk. He's got a fluid way of moving that reminds me of a dancer. A dangerous, sure-footed dancer.

"Don't be a stranger," he says to Jasper, repeating Rogan's manly hug. "You're always welcome at the vineyard."

"Appreciate it. I'll be in touch."

Tag nods to him and then turns to me. His eyes are unnervingly direct and . . . admiring. They're like puffs of sultry smoke bottled in the orbs of his eyes, and they hold an intensity that might well rival Jasper's.

He leans in to brush his lips ever so slightly over my cheek. "It was a pleasure, Muse," he says in his gruff voice. And then he, too, is gone.

"I'll be back," Jasper tells me before he turns to follow them out.

When I hear the front door close, I relax onto a stool at the island, all the emotion, all the uncertainty, all the worry of the last few days coming together to just about put me on my ass.

"God, I'm tired," I breathe, my father approaching me cautiously.

"Muse, you have to know that I would never do anything to hurt you. I would never knowingly put you in danger."

I raise my prickling eyes to my father's and my stomach sinks. This isn't over yet. Nowhere close.

"Dad, can I ask you a question?"

"Of course you can."

I hold his gaze for several long seconds, taking in his casual expression, his attractively creased face. He controls himself almost as well as Jasper does, but I've known him my whole life. I think

I'd be able to tell if he was lying to me. As far as I know he never has, so I have nothing to compare it to, but still, I think I would know. I think I'd feel it somehow.

"Is there anything I should know about Mom?"

The change is so subtle, I could easily have missed it had I not been watching him so closely. But I *am* watching him closely, so I *didn't* miss the shift. His nostrils flared the tiniest bit before settling back into their normal state. It was a miniscule reaction, but a reaction nonetheless.

"What's got you thinking about your mother? She left a long time ago."

"Did she, Dad? Did she really just up and leave like you said? Or was there more to it?"

"What's this about, Muse?"

My heart, worn out from the events of the last few hours, isn't too worn out to accelerate, flooding my muscles with blood and adrenaline. "Tell me what happened, Dad. *Everything* that happened. The whole truth."

His eyes search mine. I wonder if he's looking for a weakness to exploit, some way to spin this that will make it more palatable. Because I know it's not. The fact that he's hidden something from me for so long tells me that it's nothing that I want to hear. But the thing is, I *need* to hear it.

"Before you go trying to soften the facts for my poor virgin ears, let me remind you that I have been through a lot in the last year. I'm done with blind trust. I'm done with partial explanations and being stuck in the dark. If you don't tell me what I want to know then I'll find someone who will. And that probably won't end well. We both know what could happen if I go snooping around in your affairs. Nothing good, I'd say."

I see his Adam's apple bob with his gulp and my nerves tingle with dread. His eyes never leave mine as he pulls out a stool and sits facing me. "Muse, before I answer your question I want to remind you that all I've ever done has been for the good of you or the good of this country. Sometimes both. There are things I'm ashamed of just because of the nature of the way they happened, but if I could go back and do it over, I don't think I'd change anything, because it's all been the right thing to do."

My breath is coming short and shallow. "Tell me what happened, Dad. Just tell me."

There's a long silence before he begins. "I met your mother when I was stationed in North Dakota doing some cold-weather training. She worked at a little diner there. Stole my heart the first time I laid eyes on her. We had only been dating a couple of months when I found out that I was being transferred to Germany. I couldn't stand the thought of leaving her, so I asked her to marry me. She said yes. We had a little informal ceremony and then packed up and moved halfway across the world.

"Things were fine at first, even after we moved back to the states two years later. Within a few months of coming back, she got pregnant with you, so I put in for a desk job in Texas. Anything to get out of the field, away from the travel. I wanted our family, especially you, to have stability and not have to move around so much.

"I was pretty sure I'd get the job. Even then I had a high clearance, but that position required top-level credentials, so they vetted me for it." His pause makes the bottom of my stomach drop. "That's when they found out about her."

My pulse stutters like a hiccup high in my chest. "Found out what?"

"She worked for an intelligence group that fed state secrets to a terrorist organization in the Middle East."

Sweet Jesus, will this day never end?

"M-my mother was a spy? Or a terrorist?"

At this moment, my father looks ten years older, his face that of a man who has seen more tragedy and heartbreak than I ever knew. He doesn't deny my deduction, but he doesn't address it either. He goes a different route.

"All you need to know about your mother is that she was the woman who gave birth to the most beautiful child in the world. She passed on only good things to you. Your green eyes, your quick smile, your art, your fierce loyalty. Your courage. I've never seen anyone as fearless as you when it comes to the people they love. I will always be grateful to her for giving me the best part of my whole life. You."

The lump in my throat is so big I fear that it might stop me from taking the deep breath that I so desperately need. "So what happened? Did she really just leave us? And you let her go? Or . . . ?"

A short, sad pause. "Yes. She *did* leave us. That was the truth. After I applied for the transfer, I think she knew it was just a matter of time before she was discovered. She knew they'd take us both apart before they gave me top clearance."

"Do you know what happened to her after that?"

His face blanches, and he looks down and away. "Yes."

When he doesn't continue, I have to prompt him. "And are you going to tell me?"

"Muse, I think it's better—"

"Dad, no! I need to know. I'm not a little girl anymore. You can't protect me from everything in life."

"But this is different. Knowing the details won't change the fact that she's gone, that she's no longer a part of your life."

"No, it won't, but I still want to know. I need to know the whole truth about my life, Dad."

"Muse, honey, please."

"No! Don't you do this to me. Tell me, Dad. Tell me right now. I need to know." I'm on the verge of some sort of conniption. I think he must know that.

He takes a deep breath. "They wanted her brought into custody for questioning. I knew what that meant, what they'd do to her." His pause gives me too much time to fill in the blanks, to complete the imagery with the most horrific ones that I can conjure. "No matter who she really was, no matter what she'd done, I could never let the mother of my child live out her life being tortured. No matter how short that life might've been. I couldn't do it. So I went after her. When I found her, she didn't try to run. I think she knew I couldn't hurt her. Not really. I told her they knew. I told her what they'd do. She just nodded. She knew, too. When she reached for my gun, I don't know if I thought she was going to kill me or herself. I don't know if she knew for sure either. We just stood there, staring at each other. My gun in her hand. When she raised it to her head, she said five words that have brought me more heartache yet more comfort than I could ever have thought they would." My father's eyes are distant as he looks over my shoulder, almost like he's looking into the past.

"What did she say? What five words?"

"'Don't tell Muse about me.' I knew then that she loved you as much as I did. I knew then that she was taking the only way out that could save us all, especially you."

"S-so what did you do?"

My question brings his sad, tormented eyes back to mine. "I . . . I gave her the only mercy that I could. I let her choose her own fate."

My stomach sloshes with a queasy feeling that only adds to my exhaustion from this day. My mouth is uncomfortably dry and my head becomes lighter the harder I try to think and process.

"You . . . you let my mother kill herself." Not a question. Not an accusation. A statement. An attempt to assimilate this information into the life I thought I knew, into the life I thought I was living.

"I had no choice. Not really."

I raise dull, watering eyes to his. "You could've taken us away. Far, far away. To another country maybe."

"They wouldn't have rested until they found her. Whether her people or mine, they never would've stopped coming for her. And that would've put you in danger. Every day for the rest of your life. She didn't want that. Neither did I. We couldn't risk you, honey. *I* couldn't risk you. Not my Muse."

My eyes sting with unshed tears. I don't *try* to stop them from falling. They just don't. I think they can't. Maybe I'm in shock. Or maybe I'm just all cried out.

"I hope you can forgive me for keeping this from you. I just didn't want you to have to live with that in your head. In your heart."

At this, I stand up, straightening my spine and raising my chin. "I'm stronger than you think, Dad."

"I never thought you were weak."

"Yes, you did. You just never wanted to admit it." He starts to argue, but I cut him off by moving past him. "I'm going to bed. If this is a one-bedroom, I hope you don't mind the couch."

With that, I walk numbly to the first bed I come to and I fall face-first onto it.

THIRTY-TWO

Jasper

Rogan and Tag have long since faded down the street, yet still I sit here in my car, thinking. Avoiding. Trying not to feel. Failing miserably.

I'm agonizing over what I have to do. I know it's the right thing to do. It's really the *only* thing to do. I never would've imagined myself in this position. I didn't think I was capable of . . . all this. But even if I *had*, I wouldn't have imagined it being this hard.

Finally resolute, I get out of the car and open the trunk, taking out the small black duffel. I never thought I'd use this in such a way either. These days "never" isn't as absolute as it once was.

I never thought I'd lose my mother the way I did. I never thought I'd have to worry about betrayal from one of my own. I never thought I'd hesitate to do my job. I never thought I'd meet someone who could make me *feel* so much—desire, frustration, guilt, regret. And probably even love. I don't want to start labeling things; it just gets even more complicated. Best not to go there. I just need to get this over with and move on. She'll be better off and that's what's important.

I walk quietly back toward the Colonel's little house on the hill and I mount the steps. I don't bother knocking, but I do notice the silence when I close the door behind me. I check the living room, which is empty, and then the kitchen, which is not. The Colonel is sitting at the island, toying with an old picture of a woman who looks remarkably like Muse.

He glances up when I stop in the doorway. We stare at each other, exchanging information without saying a word.

He glances at my bag. I heft it up as if to say *Yes, this is what I'm doing.*

He sighs and nods, knowing it's the right choice. The only choice.

"Afterward, get out of the country."

I nod in return.

He tips his head to indicate the space behind me. I turn to follow his silent instruction.

I walk to the first closed door I find and I knock softly. There's no answer, so I turn the knob and push until there's a crack big enough for me to see through.

Muse is lying facedown on the bed, unconscious. Her chin is tipped just enough toward me that I can see her relaxed expression. The other half of her face is buried in the comforter. Her fiery hair is spread out behind her like she's on fire and running as fast as the wind.

God, she's beautiful! I've never met someone who bothers me on so many levels. And I say bother because anything that upsets my carefully maintained existence is a bother. Or at least it was. Until I met her.

She's the most mind-blowing, body-quaking bother I could ever imagine meeting. I love so many things about her that I can tick off a dozen things without even having to think. I love the way she wholeheartedly throws herself into what she feels. She doesn't hold back. She just jumps. I love that I can turn her to putty in my hands with a simple touch or look. I love that she can stand against all my rough edges and never get cut. I love that she accepted who and what I am without all the lies I could've told her. And probably most *and* least of all, I love that, despite my resistance, she made me feel. She woke me up. She brought me to life.

But all good things must come to an end. And this is our end.

I look down at her peaceful face. Even though I want to touch her and taste her, to commit her scent and her feel to memory, I don't want to wake her. She needs the sleep, the rest. The escape. I walk to the bedside table and ease open the drawer. There is a notepad and pen inside, which I remove. I jot her a quick note and set it on top of the black bag, which I leave on the floor right in front of her. She should see it as soon as she wakes. And if she doesn't want to take my offer, her father will talk her into it. He'll help her see the wisdom in it.

As for me, I didn't get the good-bye that I'd like. Hell, I'd rather not say good-bye at all. But this is the best one I can give her. I just hope she'll understand it.

It's as I'm backing silently out the door that Muse wakes. She lifts her head a couple of inches and fixes her bleary eyes on me. I see confusion. When she speaks, I wonder if she's actually awake.

"Jasper?"

"Go back to sleep," I tell her softly.

"Don't go," she slurs, resting her head back in the same dip from which she raised it.

"I have to."

"Then take me with you."

"I can't."

"Please," she whimpers, her eyes drifting shut again, like the pull of unconsciousness is more than she can fight.

"I'm a killer. There's no place in my life for you."

"Then don't be a killer."

"It's who I am."

Her brow crunches up a little, but her eyes are still closed. I think she's already back asleep.

"You don't have to be."

I don't know what to say to that, so I say nothing. I simply wait by the door as her breathing returns to its deep, even cadence, and then I walk out of her life forever.

THIRTY-THREE

Muse

I feel like I've been run over by a Mack truck when I roll over in bed. Every joint is sore, every muscle is stiff and my face feels like it's been kicked a time or two—swollen and tight.

I manage to lever myself up onto an elbow and look around. It's daylight. I can see sunshine peeking around the closed blinds at the window. I smack my lips. My mouth is dry as a bone.

I move into a kneeling position, taking in the nearly untouched comforter. Evidently I didn't move at all last night.

As I go to scoot off the bed, I see a black bag sitting on the floor between the door and me. A narrow white paper is perched on top. I reach forward to snag it between my thumb and forefinger, plucking it off to read what it says.

The script is neat, bold and slanted. Without even looking at the signature line, I know who wrote it. It's as much Jasper as his tiger eyes and the scent of his skin when it's wet.

Go paint in Paris.
Start over.
Sarò sempre pensare a te.

—J

Sarò sempre pensare a te. I will always think of you.

That sounds final. Like the end. Like forever.

My heart lurches inside my chest as I consider that. Yes, I was (and still am) very upset with Jasper, and for good reason, but I never really thought that there would be nothing beyond yesterday. I never really thought that the things I said last night would be the only ones I'd ever get to say. I never really expected it to be over so fast, so suddenly. Like an unanticipated amputation. A clean, brisk cut. And then . . . nothing. Nothing except the phantom pain of what was. And what will never be again.

What did I expect? I don't really know. I only know that *this* wasn't it.

That's when bits and pieces of a conversation rush in. Did I talk to Jasper last night? Did I ask him to take me with him? Did he tell me that he can't? Or did I dream the whole thing? It's fuzzy and unclear, but something in my heart tells me that it happened, that Jasper chose the life of a killer over me. That he walked away from me. Permanently.

I scramble off the bed, throw open the door and go looking for Dad. He's in the kitchen nursing a cup of coffee like it's a glass of vodka, which, considering the events of last night, it might very well be.

"Good mor—"

"Have you seen Jasper?" I interrupt without preamble.

"Not since last night." His expression is tired and a little melancholy.

"Did he say where he was going? Did he say if he's coming back?"

"No. He didn't. He just left."

"So he—he might not be coming back? Like *at all*?"

"I don't think so, honey. He left that bag and took off. That was the best thing he could do for you and he knew it."

"But . . . but that can't be it! He can't just leave like that!"

My lungs are pumping harder and harder, my breath coming faster and faster. I feel frantic, desperate, like an addict who just lost her supplier in an unexpected drug bust. But he's not my supplier. He's my Jasper. And if he wants to be gone, there's nothing I can do about it. There's no way I can find him if he doesn't want to be found. Jasper is a ghost. He's trained to be invisible and has practiced it for years. If he leaves, that's it. I'll never see him again whether I want it that way or not.

"Muse, you have to let him go. Trust m—"

"Trust you?" I spit. "How the hell can I trust *anybody*?"

"I know you're upset, but when you calm down—"

"When I calm down? When I *calm down*? Then what? I'll go back to my blind ways? None of this will matter? I won't be heartbroken and devastated and betrayed by the people I love most? Is that what you were going to say? Because if it was, you can save it. None of that's true. Things won't ever go back to the way they were. They won't ever be the same again." My voice cracks and I feel tears coursing down my face from a well I'd thought was dry. "I finally found someone to love. Not someone who loved *me* enough, but someone who I *could love* enough. How can I just let him go? How can I just go on like everything is okay? How can I pretend that everything will be okay when *nothing will ever be okay again*? How, Dad? Tell me how!"

I'm nearing the point of irrational hysteria. I can feel it, winding up inside me like a toy monkey, cymbals at the ready to bang and bang and bang until I can't think or see or hear anymore.

Dad knows I'm on the verge, too. I can see it in the way he's look-ing at me, like I'm an escapee from a psychiatric ward.

"Muse, calm down. You're tired. You've been through a lot in the last little while," he says soothingly, reaching out to stroke my upper arms like he's pacifying a child.

"Stop it!" I hiss, throwing off his hands. "Stop treating me like an imbecile. You have no idea what you've done to me. What *all* *this* has done to me."

His eyes are full of remorse. "I never meant for you to get involved. I never meant for this to touch you. I never meant for this to be your life."

"Fat lotta good that does me now, huh, Dad?" I snap bitterly.

A pinch of guilt nips at my conscience when I see his expression fall. It's as though I physically slapped him across the face. It's not fair, of course. I'm just lashing out. I know he'd never purposely hurt me, and I know that this is all a by-product of his career and the way in which he has lived his life. It's collateral damage. *I am* collateral damage.

I close my eyes and take a deep breath. I need to get a handle on this before I say or do something else I'll regret.

"Look, I know you've always tried to live your life being good, *doing* good, making choices that have the right outcomes, but sometimes no one can see how far the ripples will spread. No one can know that. And you were no exception."

I can see that he's relieved by my composure. He's never known how to deal with a woman's outburst. I remember that well enough from my hormonal teenage years.

"Muse, you're smart and capable, resilient and one of the most talented artists I've ever seen. You'll land on your feet no matter what curveball life throws your way. I never worry about that. Even if that curveball is making some big changes, like moving again or taking on a different name, you'll take it all in stride. That's your nature. You'll still be *you*, Muse Marie Harper, no matter how other people know you. But what I *do* worry about is your safety. If it weren't for that, I'd never suggest you pick up your life and move it."

"That's why you let me believe moving to San Diego was for *you*, wasn't it? You knew I'd never go unless I believed I was protecting you."

That's the one thing I inherited from my father. I don't run.

His smile is sadly sheepish, one that says he's been caught red-handed.

"I know you well, Daughter."

"So it would seem," I reply. My part should've ended with "Father" as his ended in "Daughter." It's a simple way we've teased each other since I was a little girl. But today is not a day for teasing. Things are not the same as they were when I was a little girl. They may never be again.

He grips my shoulders, his fingertips digging in tight as he bends his knees a little so that he can look me square in the eye. "Everything I've ever done was to keep you safe. From defending this country on the front lines to working with covert teams to take out threats against it, it has always been with you in mind. Giving my baby a safe place to grow and prosper. I just never expected it to come to her door this way because of it."

I swallow my resentful retort. I know he meant well, but it still stings right now. Nothing but time and distance will change that. But right now, I can at least give him this. "You couldn't have known, Dad."

"Maybe. Maybe not."

I don't know what else to say to that, mainly because I don't know what the right answer is. All I know is that talking about all this isn't doing anybody any good. Trying to survive today and planning for tomorrow are the only things worthwhile right now.

I nod and attempt a smile, needing air and space and time to think and heal and go forward. I hike my thumb over my shoulder. "I'm gonna go look through what Jasper left me and get a plan together."

"No breakfast?"

"No, maybe later."

He nods, but his smile is strained, as is his expression. He knows me well enough to know that this is something I have to do on my own. He has to let me come to terms with it in my way, in my time. The days of him sheltering me are over.

I stop before I close my bedroom door, calling back over my shoulder. "Dad, could you find Jasper for me? If I needed you to?"

I hold my breath as I await his answer, the one I have a suspicion that I already know. The one I believe to be inevitable.

"No, honey," he replies soberly. "If he doesn't want to be found, there's probably not a person in the world who could catch him."

My heart sinks. "That's what I thought."

When I close the door, it feels like I'm closing the door on so much more than just a plain white hallway wall.

THIRTY-FOUR

Muse

I sit on the bed with the makings of a whole new life spread out around me—a new social security card, a new driver's license, a new passport with my DMV photo on it. It's even been stamped several times, like I'm an accomplished world traveler. All of them look slightly worn. Handled, like they would if they really were mine. And they're all in the name of Elizabeth Harker.

In the bottom of the bag sit several stacks of money in four different currencies, sunglasses, and a wig if I need them. Staring at it all makes me feel incredibly sad and heartbroken because it assures me that the life I've always known is over. Whoever is after Dad's team and their families put me in danger, too. There's no way he'll give me a moment's peace if I try to stay at this point. Jasper obviously agrees.

But buried underneath the sadness and heartbreak is a little bud of something . . . positive. Good. Hopeful, maybe. It comes from knowing that Jasper has obviously known for at least a day or two that he had no intention of killing me. Long before the ins and outs of his fake assignment were revealed. That much is clear.

The rest, however, isn't clear at all, but I'm learning that when it comes to Jasper, most things aren't. Like I don't know when he had time to get this together. He's so secretive and sneaky, it's hard to say. The one thing I'm not really surprised about is that he has these kinds of connections. I mean the guy is a government assassin. It's kind of like a job requirement that he has shady acquaintances. I guess the only thing that really matters at this point is that whether he'd ever admit to it, Jasper has feelings for me. Enough to make him forego doing his job in favor of letting me live. Even going so far as to make sure I'm started up with a new life and new identity. That I'm safe. And according to Jasper himself, his job has always come first. According to him (and his motto) he never thinks of his targets again. His own way of living with it, surviving it. Yet he made an exception for me. Surely that means something. It *has to*, right?

For the first time in what seems like years (although it's been nowhere near that long) I have hope. It's a tiny, fragile thread, but I can still feel it. That's why I take my time in making arrangements and picking a place to go. Maybe Jasper will come back. Maybe he will choose me over his old life. Maybe he will come back and take me with him wherever it is that he needs to go.

And I will go. I'm beginning to think I would follow him any-where. Because if he comes for me, it means he loves me. And if he loves me, maybe my fatal flaw isn't so *fatal* after all.

Saying good-bye to my father this time was a little different than it was last time. Although this time I'm moving farther away, we're parting on much more mature and advanced terms. And there's a lot more turbulent water under our bridge.

We both know the score, which is a first for me, and while learning the truth about so much has been a hard blow for me, it has also given me a sense of control that I've never had before. I don't think Dad is very fond of it, but he'll have to work through this his way because it's not changing. Things won't ever go back to the way they were before.

Of course we'll keep in touch. Regardless of my struggles with what I now know, he's still my father. I love him very much. So we've worked out a way to communicate via an online dating site for weekly updates and then postcards containing code that we'll follow up with the occasional phone call once a month or so. He also bought a burner phone. I am the only one with the number. It is only for a true emergency. We both agreed that hopefully I'll never have to use it.

In the event that something happens to him, God forbid, he's got a failsafe in place and I'll be notified via a phone call once I obtain a new cell and give him my international number. It's all very complicated and spy-ish, not at all as thrilling and satisfying as it's portrayed in the movies. Right now it only seems to intensify the feeling that my entire life is a lie. I don't know why that should bother me now. Evidently big parts of it have been for a long, long time.

Dad also promised me that either he'll join me or I can come home once all this is sorted out and taken care of. Part of me looks forward to that day. Part of me dreads it, as that will be the day when Jasper will truly be out of my life in every possible way. Until then, I'll hold out hope that he'll come to me, but I understand that things have to be this way for now.

For now.

Until then, I've got the clothes on my back and what few things Dad is having Miran ship to me to a hotel in Paris. Everything else will be stored until life returns to normal.

Or whatever new normal there will be in the aftermath of Jasper.

THIRTY-FIVE

Muse

I watch through the hazy oval window of the airplane as Paris comes into view. The glitter of a million lights sparkles below like a miniature Christmas village as we descend. For a second, I think I can even make out the Eiffel Tower as we pass over, heading toward Charles de Gaulle Airport.

I open myself to the awe of the moment, to the excitement of a future exploring such an amazing city. I let it wash over me, let it pour into my every inner crevice, hoping it will drown the ever-present gloom that has haunted my bones since the morning I woke to find Jasper gone. I've fought it with a variety of weapons. Everything from bitter rage to blind hope—each has worked exceptionally well for a brief period of time, but then, like a boomerang unerringly finding its way back to its starting point, I return to a semi-despondent state of emotional unrest. But at least I have those spots of freedom from my misery. If not for those, I'd have likely already gone totally off the deep end.

So tonight, I'm going to embrace Paris. I'm going to embrace the adventure of starting over. Few people get the opportunity to completely reinvent themselves, yet here I am staring one right in the face. As much as I can, I'm going to seek out happiness here.

In a land where I don't speak the language, where I don't know a soul, where I have no clue how to go forward, I think dismally.

Stop it! I reprimand my inner child firmly. *You can't think that way. You* will *survive. You* will *move on with your life. And one day, you* will *get to go home.*

That's what I tell myself, but I'm pretty sure not a single part of my tattered soul believes it.

Two and a half months later

The November evening wind is chilly on my cheeks as I ride my bike along the rutted road that leads from the train station to my cottage. Auvers-sur-Oise is my new home. It's less than twenty miles outside Paris, small enough to get around on a bike or on foot and, best of all, it's rich in beauty and art history.

As I ride, I take in the soothing landscape. I can call to mind a number of paintings that depict the narrow, winding streets and rolling, bungalow-dotted hills of a quaint French hamlet, but nothing compares to actually being here.

I chose a tiny village to put down roots for several reasons, but if I'm being honest, the fact that Vincent van Gogh is buried here might've tipped the scales. Regardless of the reasons, though, I'm glad that I followed my heart. For the first time in two long months, I've begun to think I could one day actually be happy here.

One day.

And I'm always holding out the hope that "one day" could be

tomorrow. Even though I feel like one day might never come. Life without Jasper isn't getting any easier. Or prettier. Or happier. And every day that passes, every day that goes by and he doesn't show up at my door, steals another grain of the optimism that I struggle so valiantly to hold on to. If "one day" doesn't come soon, I'll be a pile of ash that will simply scatter when it finally does blow in.

It's full dark by the time I park my bike under the overhang beside my front door. In most other places I might have to worry that it would get stolen if left unattended and unsecured out in the open over night, but not here. I could probably leave my door unlocked if I really wanted to. But I don't. I doubt I'll ever feel *that* secure. Too much has happened. I have too many bad memories.

As it does a thousand times a day, Jasper's mysteriously handsome face creeps through my mind. I take a deep breath and close my eyes, reveling in the sharp angles and planes of his bones, basking in the honey glow of his gaze, shivering under the remembered feel of his touch. I allow myself only a few seconds with him before I push him ruthlessly to the farthest corner of my memory. It didn't take me long to realize that's the only way I'll ever have a moment's peace.

"*Bonsoir,*" a smooth voice says from behind me.

I jump and whirl around, hand clutching my chest over my racing heart. I was so deep in thought I didn't hear Gerard approach.

"You scared the pee out of me!" I breathe.

"*Pardonnez-moi s'il vous plaît.* I did not mean to startle you, Elizabeth."

Gerard moves into the soft light spilling from the kitchen lamp that I left on until my return. It turns one half of his face to gold and throws the other into blackness. I study his good-looking features—light brown hair, gray eyes, classic bone structure, ever-smiling lips—and I'm reminded of the differences between him and Jasper. It's as though his face represents those disparities. Gerard is light and open, soft and welcoming, while Jasper was dark and guarded, cool and brooding.

Their interest in me is equally contrasting. Jasper wanted me as a woman. Gerard, sweet yet firmly gay, wants me as a friend and confidant.

"It's okay. What are you doing here so late?"

"I've been watching for your safe return since I arrived home from work."

"Is that code for you've got man troubles that you need help with?" I ask bluntly, smiling.

His grin is sheepish as he runs a hand through his hair, throwing spikes up all over his head. "Do you have the time?"

I study my friend. Today has been a hard day. Memories have been playing on my mind, causing the edges to turn black and curl up like burning parchment. As much as part of me wants to bask in the pain, to let it in so that I don't completely lose Jasper, another part of me craves the respite such a distraction will bring.

"Of course. Come on in."

With a smile, Gerard follows me in. He wipes his feet on the mat, leaving streaks of mud there. It clings to his feet when he walks down to my cottage. He lives just up the hill from me, which is how we met. He owns the charming little bungalow that I rent. It couldn't have worked out any better. He speaks excellent English (which is very helpful until I learn French), he has been a cheerful and informative tour guide and he provides a friendly face and a touch of security, which I desperately needed when I first got here. In fact, most days, I still do.

I dump my cross-body bag and the pack containing my canvas onto the floor by the door.

"Did you paint today?"

My smile is immediate and genuine. "I did."

"Will you show me? Or must I beg?"

"Maybe tomorrow? I'm pretty tired from my travels."

Gerard's eyes fill with sympathy. Although I've never confided in him, I think he knows there's more that bothers me some days than just fatigue or sleepless nights. "You need to rest, I can see. My troubles will wait until tomorrow. Dinner?" he asks, his expression that of an enthusiastic puppy when he hears the word "play."

"Tomorrow," I confirm with a nod, grateful that I don't have to show him my work tonight. I don't feel like reliving it. I don't think I have the energy.

With a quick kiss to both cheeks, Gerard bids me a cheerful good night and disappears into the darkness, leaving me to drag myself up the steps to change out of my paint-spattered clothes.

At the top of the stairs, I turn left and I flick on the soft overhead light to my bedroom. I stop in the doorway.

Jasper.

Sometimes I'm rocked by his presence when I walk into this room. The walls are dotted with oil and canvas reminders of him. He's everywhere I look, in the familiar landscape of the lake, in the familiar scenery of the woods behind his house, in the familiar angles of his face. My time with him has colored every piece I've created since I got to Paris.

I told myself I had to do it, that it would be cathartic. These were the only things I was inspired to paint, these were the only comfort I could find for weeks. I like to think it's helping, but there are still times when the sense of loss is nearly crippling, but it does seem to be getting better.

Maybe.

A little.

I hope.

Some days I think so, but others I fear that it will never get better. Not that it matters. When it comes to Jasper, I'm at his mercy.

Turning from the shrine my bedroom has become, I make my way into the small, attached bathroom. I splash cold water on my face and take deep, calming breaths until I feel a little more stable. As I stare at my reflection in the mirror above the sink, I notice the shelf behind me. My perfume bottle is in the wrong place. I turn to look at it, recalling my routine before I left the house this morning.

Littering the top shelf is the little wooden box that I keep my jewelry in when I take it off at night, a figurine of a painting girl that I picked up in Paris during my first trip into the city and, usually, my favorite bottle of perfume. On the second shelf are a few other odds and ends and a bottle of exotic French perfume that Gerard brought me. He thought it was "divine," but I prefer mine. The hint of lilac in *my* perfume reminds me of Jasper, so I wear it every day. It holds a special place in my heart *and* on my shelf.

Until today.

For some reason, the bottle is resting beside the only other bottle of perfume that I own. But I didn't put it there.

A niggle of unease slithers down my spine. After I use the bathroom, I walk back out into my bedroom, looking over every familiar detail of the room. It's the one room that I have poured most of *me* into, the one where I feel most at home.

Everything looks clean and orderly, just like I left it this morning. The bed is neatly made with a spring flower duvet cover that I found in Paris, the rug in front of the closet still holds my slippers, kicked off as I dressed this morning, and my curtains are still open to let in the warm sunlight while I was gone.

I try to shake off the unsettling feeling and chalk up the perfume bottle to me just depositing it on the wrong shelf by accident. I *did* leave in a hurry so that I could get back before dark.

Back downstairs, I search for other things amiss and I find none.

I don't beat myself up over my paranoia. I figure I've earned it and then some.

As I pass the front door, I pick up my portfolio and bring it back with me. I perch on the edge of the couch and unzip the padded sheath, revealing the dried watercolor that I painted in the grass beside a cafe today. I was determined to capture a little bit of Paris rather than spilling my memories onto the thick paper. I was successful, right up until the moment I looked up and saw the back of a dark head ducking around the corner up ahead. It reminded me so much of Jasper, like most tall, fit men with short, dark hair do (at least from the back) that I couldn't finish the painting without adding his vague shape to the background. In days ahead, that's what I'll remember most about today. The scene was beautiful, the weather perfect, the location exotic, but what will always stand out most was the jolt to my heart when I saw that dark head walking away.

THIRTY-SIX

Muse

Two weeks later

There's something enchanting yet downright depressing about the idea of spending the holidays in Paris. The city is so charming, as is this little town with all of its eight-or-so-thousand residents, that I can easily picture cozy nights indoors as well as festive dinners with friends. Only I don't have many friends. To be more precise, I have one. Ms. Etienne doesn't count, as she only speaks to me when she wants my help with something in her garden.

On the other side of that cheerfully imagined holiday coin is the one that shows me all alone in a foreign land, unable to hug my father, share a drink with an old friend or hold the hand of the man I love. I feel as though nearly every step of every day is some strange mixture of moving forward, yet not moving forward at all. I can't seem to let go of my old life, of my old hopes and dreams.

It's too soon, I reason, which is true. It's only been three months since I left. It's insane to expect to be fully healed by now.

But maybe just a little bit healed . . .

I shake off the thought. It *does* bother me that I don't seem to be doing *any* better. There are times when I think I am, but then I quickly realize that I'm not. Those short bursts of well-being are more like comets. They streak brightly, promisingly across the midnight sky of my life, giving me a few fleeting seconds of light and hope, only to disappear over the horizon. Sometimes they leave me in an even darker place than I was before.

I look up from my blank sketchpad when I hear a knock at the door. I don't have to wonder who it is. Since Ms. Etienne's garden is dead for the winter, it can only be Gerard. He's still the only friend I've made.

He's smiling broadly when I swing open the door. He bows cordially and hands me a small, white envelope. "I would like to invite you to a very special dinner tonight, Elizabeth," he says, pronouncing my name like *Eee-lees-a-beth.*

"Well, if this is any indication of what I can expect, I *know* I won't have anything appropriate to wear," I say, giving myself an immediate out.

His smile gets bigger. "Not to worry, *ma chère.* I have taken care of that for you."

I'm not as apprehensive as I would normally be when Gerard hands me a long box that he was hiding behind his back, likely because he typically has excellent taste.

"Gerard, you shouldn't have. I really can't—"

"Ah ah ah," he clucks. "I wanted to. And you really *can.*"

I gnaw my lip for a second as I think. I'm sure it's an extravagant gift, which would normally make me feel bad. But Gerard has money. Lots of it. Evidently he has several investments, including a lucrative development somewhere in Paris. There's probably no reason for me to feel guilty. He's my friend and I think he just likes doing nice things for people. So I decide right now to just enjoy it.

I take the box anxiously. I'm curious about the whole thing—the special dinner, the dress, the formality. He follows me in and closes the door before we go into the living room.

I set the box on the aged coffee table and release the big, beautiful blue ribbon before taking off the lid. Lying beneath a wisp of tissue paper is a beaded bodice in emerald green. I slip my fingers under the spaghetti straps and lift it out from its nest. Luxurious velvet in the matching jewel tone makes up the lower half of the floor-length gown. All I can do is stare at it for several long seconds before I look over the top of it to Gerard, who is smiling at me with twinkling gray eyes.

"You will look *tres magnifique* when you meet the gallery owners."

My mouth drops open. "G-gallery owners?"

"Yes. Gallery owners. Husband and wife. I own the buildings where they opened their first two galleries in Paris and Rome. I've known them for quite some time and I know they like to deal directly, as I know many executives do. Julienne saw your canvas on my office wall and would not rest until I agreed to bring the artist to meet her. So here I am, making matches."

Now I understand the twinkling eyes and grin that won't stop.

For the first time in months, I'm filled with excitement and anticipation. To have the work that I pour my heart and soul into appreciated by art lovers has been a dream of mine since I was a little girl. And the timing couldn't be better. I have pinched pennies to stretch the money Jasper gave me as far as I could, but I have been wondering lately where on earth I could get a job when I can't speak the language fluently yet. But this . . . this could be a godsend!

"Nothing to say from those beautiful lips?"

I blush, not because of the beautiful lips comment, but because I'm sure I'm being rude by diving into my own head rather than thanking Gerard.

"I'm speechless. I could never thank you enough for being such a good friend to me, Gerard. I don't know what I'd have done without you these last months."

He nods graciously, but I can see how pleased he is. Flattery works best on Gerard. "I believe in your work. I am happy to see when another does as well."

"And I'm meeting them *tonight*?"

"Yes, in two hours, but we're meeting in Paris, so you won't have that long to prepare."

"Then I'd better get started. I need to see if I've got shoes to go with this, too," I mutter absently as I carry the dress toward the stairs.

"Have you checked the rest of the box?"

I turn to find Gerard holding the white box out to me. As I approach I can see a bulge under another layer of tissue paper. When I peel it back, two silver sequined shoes are revealed. I take them out and place them gently on the floor, slipping one foot in to see if they fit. And they do. As perfectly as if I had picked them out myself. I suspect I'll find the same with the dress.

"Like Cinderella, my favorite," he says with a dreamy roll of his eyes.

I can only imagine that wearing such a beautiful dress, standing in such beautiful shoes, meeting with people who could make my dreams come true, I'll feel much like the fairy tale character. If only I had my Prince Charming to complete the picture. Cinderella wouldn't have her happy ending without him. And I know, deep down, that I won't ever have mine either. My painting could set the world on fire, I could move back to the states with my father, I could achieve every other thing I've ever wanted in life, but all of it would be slightly hollow without Jasper. *He* is where my heart truly lies.

"I will be back to collect you in one hour. Will that be enough time?"

I nod. "That should be fine."

I wait for him to cross to the door and I open it for him, leaving my hand on the knob. *"Jusqu'a ce soir."*

Until tonight.

Until tonight. When I take the first step into my future. Without Jasper.

I needn't have worried. Dinner was an amazing success and I'm practically walking on clouds when Gerard ushers me out of the restaurant. I don't even need a wrap. Wine and happiness are warming my blood.

I take a deep breath and stretch out my arms, spinning in a circle on the sidewalk. "That was incredible!"

Paris dips a little on my second spin. Gerard's arms keep me from busting my ass and tearing my beautiful-but-tight dress.

"Woops!" I chirp, righting myself and pushing back from his chest a little.

"Tonight *was* incredible, just as *you* are incredible," he says happily, his gray eyes sparkling.

"Gerard, thank you so much for this. I just can't tell you—"

My words are cut off by the chilling sensation that someone is watching me. It makes no sense at all. I can only attribute it to the moved perfume bottle and a heaping dose of paranoia.

"What is it?" Gerard asks, concern showing on his face.

I realize immediately how unlikely it is that I'm being watched. No doubt Jasper sent me to a place he felt was safe, but try as I might, I can't shake the feeling that there are eyes on me. Dark, menacing eyes.

I glance around surreptitiously, but see nothing suspicious, nothing nefarious like a black sedan with a hooded figure in the driver's seat or a man in a trench coat, smoking by the corner of a shadowed alley. Although I doubt anyone who could find me would be that sloppy in their surveillance.

Anyone who could find me . . .

Jasper.

Could he have found me? Would he have wanted to?

My heart leaps with a joyful relief at the brief thought that it could be him, that he might finally have come for me. But then rationale dashes those hopes. If Jasper *did* come for me, there's no reason whatsoever for him to stalk me in Paris when he could just catch me at my small-town cottage.

No, it wouldn't be Jasper. If he was watching me, I'd never know it. As much as I like to think I'd feel him, too, I doubt I would. He's like an apparition. Invisible. Fleeting.

"Nothing. It's just . . . nothing," I add with a reassuring smile. "I'm just ready to go home and let all this sink in."

He smiles brightly and loops his arm through mine as we start off toward the car. When Gerard opens the passenger door, I duck inside, searching the street and shadows for anything that appears out of the ordinary as I do. Nothing does, though. No stalker. No watcher.

No Jasper.

On the way back to our little village, my heart sinks with every mile we drive, every mile that brings me closer to my new existence. And farther from the man I love.

That brief, nonsensical thought that Jasper might've found me (and yet he hasn't) heralds a darkness that creeps over my life, over my days and nights like a storm cloud. Longing turns into bitterness, melancholy turns into anger. My frustration with myself for falling in love with a man who is so deeply flawed and inaccessible gushes out in a spray of venom and animosity that has one target and one target alone—Jasper.

It's easy to place all the blame on him. If it weren't for him, at least I'd still be in the states, I'd still be me, living a life that was just "okay" as I waited for something wonderful to happen rather than *this*. *This* life is, at times, nearly unbearable. The loss of so much—my home, my father, my identity—was bad enough without Jasper. Falling for him was like getting hit by a missile filled with fireworks. It was brutally wonderful, gloriously explosive, but, in the end, short-lived and empty. Now I'm left with only wreckage. No sparks, no light, no beauty. Just the scorched wrappings of what was and is no more.

I pack up my easel and a fresh canvas, along with some brushes and watercolors, angrily tossing it all into the basket on the front of my bike and tearing off down the lane. I don't even glance his way when the corner of my eye catches Gerard's car pulling up. I keep right on going as though I didn't see him at all. I'm not in the mood to deal with him, although I'll have to eventually. He's tried several times to talk to me since our dinner last week, but so far I've been successful in holding him off. I just don't want to deal with it yet. If he has good news from the gallery owners, it means I have to move on. If he doesn't, it means I might never be *able* to move on. I'm not sure I can deal with either path right now.

I travel the familiar road that leads to the river. Even though I'm hissing hostility like a busted radiator hisses steam, something in me yearns for the "homeyness" of the river. It's the closest I can get to Jasper right now, and even though he's the source of my current disgruntled state, I follow my instinct and go toward him anyway.

When I get to the river, I'm glad to see that the bank I like is empty except for a few birds. They fly when I wheel my bike to a stop in the grass.

I engage the kickstand and pull out my supplies from the basket, hauling it all to a sunny spot near the water's edge. With the ease of someone who has done it dozens of times, I set up my easel and place my canvas before taking out brushes and digging out my tray of watercolors. When it's all ready and a brush is gripped firmly between my fingers, I take one look at the bright, happy scene before me and I begin to paint.

Thoughts about my new life, about my old one as well, circle my mind like a predator, waiting to attack. I think about how I used to think I was happy. I think about the way I felt like I was flying when I was with Jasper. I think about how nothing else mattered when I was in his arms, drowning in his kiss. Not the world outside, not the people within it, not the past or the future, not right or wrong—nothing mattered except Jasper and me and the electricity that was between us. And I think about now, today, and how I'm one step closer to giving up. How I'm sinking deeper and deeper into hopelessness and misery. It's with all this swirling through me that I paint.

Emotion pours from me like blood, black blood spurting from a mortal wound in some unfathomable place. The trees that take shape are dark and pointed, their branches more like thorns than foliage, and the sun never appears. It's hidden by thick, rolling clouds that speak only of warning, warning of unpleasantness to come. And the water . . . the water looks nothing like what's in front of me. The water on *my* canvas is turbulent, churning, its surface anything but placid and sweet.

I lash at the canvas with my brush, unaware of the tears streaming down my face until another chill seems to freeze them on my cheeks.

I gasp this time, dropping my brush and whirling around like someone tapped me on the shoulder. I look about, three hundred and sixty degrees, but don't see even one sign of another person.

Eyes still watering and chest now heaving, I reach for my brush, carefully examining this odd sensation that has come over me for the second time. What am I feeling? Anger? Pain? Loneliness? Desperation?

Yes. To all of them. But why? Why would I get such a sudden burst of sensation out of nowhere? I have experienced most of these feelings practically every day since I left America, but never like this. Never all at once and so poignantly that it's physically startling.

When I turn back toward my painting, I see the unrest of my soul. It's coloring everything around me, stealing beauty from the beautiful. I know I shouldn't let this happen, shouldn't let this go on. But I just don't know how to stop it. I'm not sure I even *can*.

I wake hours later, at home and feeling exhausted. It's still dark outside, well before dawn. I consider just lying in bed, wallowing in my misery, although I know sleep won't find me again.

Frustrated, I throw back the covers and make my way to the en suite bathroom just off the master. I cut on the faucet and run fairly hot water into the tub, adding just enough bubble bath to give me a nice thick, scented foam. I stretch my arms up over my head, noting the sting of the muscles in my neck from painting for so long yesterday. So long and so angrily. Maybe a hot bath and some soothing aromas are just what I need.

I light three candles and then switch off the overhead light. After stripping off my nightclothes, I step into the tub, hissing when the nearly scalding water hits my cold feet. It takes a few seconds of adjusting before I can lower all the way down, resting my legs along the still-cool ceramic of the old claw-foot. But when my skin stops complaining, I relax my head back against the little pillow and let the steam carry every troubling thought up into the hazy air.

I'm drifting in that place between fully awake and half asleep when I hear a muted thump. It's so soft, I might never have heard it if I weren't awake and quiet in the middle of the night. My eyes fly open as the fog clears from my muddled brain and I strain to listen, not certain my overactive imagination didn't manufacture the sound.

I hear the telltale creak as weight eases onto the platform at the top of the stairs. There's no place to step that the boards won't groan. It's like a hidden alarm. And I'm alarmed. Every muscle in my body clenches. I gasp quietly, holding my breath as I debate the wisdom of trying to get up and alerting someone to my presence, or keeping quiet and hoping the intruder doesn't come into the bathroom.

My time quickly runs out as the muffled fall of nearly silent footsteps rustle on the carpet, drawing closer to the bathroom door. The hard, rapid thud of my heart is almost painful in its intensity, but still I remain calm and silent. My eyes search the immediate vicinity for a weapon of any kind. When they fall on the wooden box that I keep my jewelry in, I run through a quick plan on how I'll jump up, grab it, bash my interloper in the head and then bolt down the stairs to the kitchen. Where the knives are.

Provided that I could even escape him in this manner. I think of trying to get the better of Jasper. In *any* situation. I know I couldn't. Few, if any, probably could. He's the best for a reason. I can only hope that whoever is breaking into my home is a long way from being as good as Jasper.

I listen closely for the approach of my creeper. The only sound I hear is the delicate crackling of the bubbles bursting all around me. I'm staring at the doorway, my heart in my throat, when a dark figure suddenly appears.

I scream, shooting to my feet and reaching for the box, slinging it with all my might at the head looming in the shadows. I leap from the tub, my wet foot slipping on the tile and sending me lurching forward. Luckily, my attacker wasn't expecting that and I'm able to lunge past him and out the bathroom door.

I'm barely aware of the cool air hitting my skin as I tear through the bedroom. I'm nearly to the door when steely fingers grip my arms, jerk me to a stop and lift me off my feet to throw me onto the bed. A heavy body falls on top of me, pinning me down.

"No reason I can't have a little taste before I slit your beautiful throat," a voice growls in my ear. I open my mouth to scream just as a big hand that smells like grease and smoke clamps down over my lips. "But if you're determined to scream, I can always cut your throat first. Makes no difference to me."

I stare at the ceiling, at the silvery moonlight that pours in through the part in my curtain as I digest his words. My mind races for options, *any* options, yet it finds none. If I scream or fight, he'll probably kill me. But he's going to kill me regardless and I'd rather be dead when any man besides Jasper touches me. In fact, I think I'd rather be dead than live this miserable life without him anyway. Does it matter who does it or when?

I realize that it doesn't. It will simply be a relief, a respite from the constant heartache that I can't escape. That's why, in an attempt to provoke him, I sink my teeth into the fleshy part of the palm that silences me and I flail wildly, bucking my body and straining with every muscle in my arms and legs. I feel flesh give way from bone. I taste blood. But my attacker will not be moved. He doesn't even make a sound until I hear the wet sound of his kiss against my cheek.

"Have it your way, princess."

And then I feel the prick of a knifepoint at my throat.

THIRTY-SEVEN

Muse

I lie quietly, awaiting the cut that will end my life, when the crushing weight on my chest suddenly disappears. At first, I think he's merely leaning back to shove a knife into me, but then I hear the scuffling of clothes, the whisper of two bodies grappling in the dark.

Instinctively, I roll off the bed, sparing only a quick glance into the shadowed corners before I scramble down the steps, my only thought now of escape. I don't know what happened and I don't care. I only know that I have to get away, my instinct to survive now in full swing.

A loud crash has me screaming and turning to see a man toppling down the stairs behind me, head over heels. He lands with a shoe-clattering thump at the bottom, a few feet from where I'm crouching.

I struggle to understand what is happening until I see another shape appear in the slant of light that cuts across the stairwell. It moves like water and triggers an instant spark of recognition in my heart.

I know who it is before his face is revealed. My body, my soul, my every cell and nerve react to him as profoundly as ions react to electricity. And when I see his face, God help me, I think for a moment that I'd trade my life and every breath I have left for just one more day with him.

Jasper.

My Jasper.

He came for me.

I watch him until he reaches the bottom of the steps. He pauses in front of me, his eyes scanning me briefly in a quick assessment of my current state of injury. Ostensibly determining that I'm not hurt, he turns his focus to the half-conscious man on the foyer floor.

Jasper's voice is a deadly growl when he bends to hiss into the man's ear. "You would rape this woman? You would take from her what she doesn't want to give?" The disgust, the fury in his voice is nearly palpable. He pulls the man to his feet, wrapping one thick arm around his neck and twisting the guy's arm behind his back before slamming him, face first, into the wall. The door rattles on its hinges. "You would die to taste her? Because I would die to protect her. Which of us do you think has the better chance of surviving?"

The man says nothing, but turns until his cheek is pressed to the wall and he's facing me. I see one eerily calm blue eye staring out at me, promising that if he gets loose, he'll hurt me in ways that I can't even imagine. My blood runs cold.

"Who sent you?" Jasper asks, shoving his weight into the man's back. I hear a grunt, but no answer. "You'll tell me. One way or the other, you'll tell me."

The guy laughs, his eye still trained on me.

"You may not have realized when you took this job that it would be your last, but it will be. You're going to die tonight. How you go is up to you. If you tell me what I want to know, I'll be quick. If you don't, I'll make you wish you were never born."

Jasper's coolly venomous words echo in the quiet that follows. They've fallen to the floor, where they taunt the intruder until he finally breaks his silence. "Get on with it, then," he goads, his expression never changing, no fear ever registering.

"I've killed better men than you, but I've never enjoyed it. Until tonight. Until you. I'll get what I want and then I'll watch the life drain out of you. Because nobody comes after what's mine. Nobody."

Jasper reaches out to twist the doorknob. Without looking at me, he mutters, "Stay here. I'll be right back," and then he disappears into the dark.

THIRTY-EIGHT

Jasper

My hands are shaking as I haul him away from Muse's front door. I'm controlled. Always. Until tonight. I've never experienced rage like this. It's like an all-consuming fire I can't push through, a red haze I can't see past. I can only feel the heat. I don't bother to fight it. I just let it burn right through me.

As soon as my foot hits grass, I pull in and up with all my might, dislocating both shoulders of the man who was going to rape and kill Muse. He makes no sound, as I knew he wouldn't, but I know he's in pain. I've had more dislocated joints than I can count. They hurt like a bitch until the numbness sets in.

With a foot to the lower part of his back, I kick out, sending him reeling forward, unable to catch himself with his useless arms. When he hits the ground, I follow him down, rolling him onto his back and smashing my boot heel into his kneecap, crushing it so that he's further incapacitated. I take the knife from my waistband and I jab it quickly into the meat of both thighs, careful to avoid his femoral arteries. I can't have him bleeding out before I get my answers. I just don't want to make it easy for him to fight me. I want to be able to look into his dead eyes until they're just that—dead.

"Give me a name. That's all I want and then I'll put this knife in the base of your skull. I'll give you that—a quick death. No more."

In the dim light, I can see his face as he stares up at me. His eyes are those of a killer. I wonder if that's what mine look like to others. If that's what they've always looked like. If that's what they always *will* look like.

He says nothing. As I expected. I won't get information from him. He's trained to take his secrets to the grave. It's what sets men like us apart from a legion of other hired guns. This is the code we live by.

I lean in and press my elbow into the deformed ball of his shoulder as I reach between us to feel his pockets. I don't really expect to find anything, but I'd be remiss not to at least check.

I'm surprised when I find the hard, rectangular bulge of a phone in his front pocket. At least he's smart enough to keep it there where no one can easily lift it from him. Rear pockets are easy to pick. Front ones are not.

I wiggle my fingers in to retrieve it, pulling it out and flipping it open. It's innocuous looking enough. Like an old flip phone. But I'm not deceived. It's a high-tech satellite phone with encryption and a built-in voice synthesizer. This guy must be freelance, which tells me that whoever is after us must know that the government web is compromised. They know we're onto them and they've moved to private contractors, men who cut ties with legit assignments and work only for the highest bidder. No conscience. No affiliation. No loyalty. Just greed, blood lust and lethal skills.

The screen is locked, of course, so I reach for the guy's hand. I press each finger to the screen until it unlocks and a series of letters and numbers flash in neat rows from left to right.

"I'm a little disappointed. You're sloppy. I wouldn't be caught dead on the kill with my phone in my pocket. Of course, I wouldn't get caught," I tell him as I wait for the phone to initialize, grinding my elbow into his shoulder again.

When it does, with the bluish glow of the screen to illuminate his face, I ask him about the first name I see in his contacts. There is no reaction. No twitch, no rise in pulse, no pupillary reaction. Not to the first name, the second name or the third.

With my fist, I thump him in the wound on his right thigh as I tap the screen over a secure text file. It appears to be just letters and numbers again, but I quickly use one of the ciphers that we used in Saudi to decode it. It's a simple directive. To kill Elizabeth Harker, aka Muse Harper. Below it there is a single word: "Napalm."

"What's 'Napalm'? Is that the operation or your contact?"

I get no answer, but I see the slight dilation of his pupils, telling me that whatever or whoever Napalm is, it's sensitive. Protected. Important.

Something occurs to me as I watch this man. "Why aren't you fighting me?" Despite his wounds, a man like this—men like *us*—wouldn't stop fighting. We'd push through the pain. We'd use it like fuel. Only he's not.

One side of his mouth quirks up. "Is there any reason to? I know who you are. You're a soulless bastard, like me. And this is all we've got. We wake up every day ready to die. Nothing else to live for, so just get it over with."

I know I'll get nothing more from him, just like I know that he'll never stop coming after Muse as long as there's a price on her head. Or on mine. It's with mixed feelings that I lift his head and push the tip of my blade into the indention at the base of his skull. I thought I would enjoy this more, and part of me does. Part of me wants to punish him for what he intended to do to Muse. But part of me sees too much of myself in him—a man with nothing but death and loneliness to keep him company for the rest of his life.

I know as I carry his limp body away that I'd rather die tonight than spend the rest of my life like this man. Alone. Without Muse.

THIRTY-NINE

Muse

I stand with one foot outside, listening for several minutes before the cold manages to penetrate my strange stupor and remind me of my nakedness. Reluctantly, I step back inside and close the door. I start to turn away, but I can't. I can't bring myself to leave this spot, leave the door. I'm too afraid that Jasper won't come back through it.

A couple of times I think I hear a grunt or a scuffle, but it's hard to make out much from in here. My ear is pressed to the wooden panel when it swings open, knocking me in the side of the head. I barely feel it. I'm experiencing too many jumbled emotions for it to register.

Jasper steps through, his bulk filling the entryway. His amber eyes find mine immediately and they latch on as he closes the door behind him. He turns the lock on the knob and then flips the deadbolt. He doesn't say a word. He doesn't take his eyes off me either.

He's still for a few seconds before he slowly approaches me and stops within an inch. He smells like the night—cold and dark. But his scent, his face, his very presence warms me like nothing else can.

With purposeful, measured movements, he bends and sweeps me up into his arms. Gazes still locked, I wrap my hands around his neck as he turns to mount the stairs. He carries me through the bedroom and back into the bathroom, where he sets me on my feet. I watch as he pulls the plug from the tub and turns to exit the room.

I stand and wait, listening to the muffled sounds of material shifting from the other room. When he returns, the last of the water is circling the drain.

Jasper turns on the faucet and resets the plug, reaching into the corner for the bubble bath. He pours a capful under the stream of hot water and then recaps and replaces it.

When he straightens, he faces me. His eyes click to a stop on mine and we stare at each other. Still neither of us speaks. I don't know what's going through *his* mind, but I'm too afraid of ruining this moment to utter a single word. I'm too afraid that I might be dreaming and I'll wake up. Or that he's an apparition and he might disappear. *That's* what's going through mine.

The moment stretches on, tight as a drum, until the tub fills. Jasper reaches down to turn it off and then lifts me off my feet again, setting me in the gloriously hot water. I hadn't realized how cold I was until the heat hits my skin. I did, however, know how lonely I was, how desperate I was for Jasper. Now that's all the more apparent.

Eyes locked together, Jasper pushes up the sleeves of his black shirt and takes the washcloth I'd set on the edge of the tub earlier. He wets it, lathers it with my soap and then with a gentleness that melts my heart, he starts to wash me. He drags his hand under my chin, down my chest, circling my breasts several times before he applies more soap and starts again. He follows the same path, only this time takes his cleaning down my stomach where he circles and circles and circles.

I study him the whole time. I watch his face, a face that has always been hard to read, but is now showing me a sea of distress.

"Jasper, what's wrong?"

His eyes are intent, focused on his hands, but I don't think he's seeing them. He seems to be looking somewhere else. Inward maybe.

When he repeats the same steps again, making his way to below my navel this time, I finally understand what this is about.

He's washing away what just happened. He's doing the only thing he can to take away the trauma of what I almost experienced, the horror of being that close to rape. And to death.

"If I'd been here, he'd never have gotten that close," he finally says in a softly haunted voice. It slides over my skin like velvet and moves over my heart like silk.

I catch his wrist and bring his hand up to my chest, where he can feel the thud of my heart beneath the bone. "Do you feel that, Jasper? That beats for you. I feel like it hasn't beat since the day you left. I'd risk losing my life all over again if it meant you coming back to me."

Jasper drops his head and rests it along the edge of the tub. Slowly, I sit up, reaching forward to cup his face and raise his eyes to mine. Now is not the time for second thoughts or stubborn pride. I may never get a chance like this again. I have to make the most of it.

"Jasper, I love you. I've loved you from the second you walked into my life. And I never stopped. Not for one minute. Nothing else matters. Nothing. And no *one*. All I want, all I *need* is you. Just you. And you're here. Finally," I tell him, happy tears blurring his face in front of me. "You're finally here. You came for me."

I watch as Jasper's eyes turn to dark gold. I hear his shaky breath as he exhales. I feel the tremor in his hand where it rests against my skin. We stare at each other, something more powerful than words, more powerful than the electricity swirling in the air around us. It triggers a shiver that skitters through my muscles, my body responding to the unspoken, to the undefined.

My stomach twists into a knot and my chest swells with emotion. I gasp. I can't help it. I want this man. I want everything he can give me, however much for however long.

"Don't do that," Jasper whispers.

"Don't do what?" I breathe, my insides jittering.

"Don't make this harder than it has to be."

"Make what harder?"

"Me keeping my hands off you."

"I never asked you to keep your hands off me."

"But after what just happened . . ."

"It *didn't* happen. And I can't think of anything I want more right now than to have your hands on me, erasing the touch of anyone else."

"Muse, I—"

"Make love to me, Jasper. Please." I move his hand down my body. I guide it between my legs. The thought that someone else might've forced himself on me only makes me want Jasper that much more. The touch of the man I want. The touch of the man I love. The touch of the man I think loves me.

He holds perfectly still for a few seconds until I press one of my fingers onto his and guide it between my folds. Tentatively, he rubs me, his eyes never leaving mine. Long ovals, fluid, teasing, until my stomach tightens with a different kind of emotion.

Jasper lengthens his stroke until he is moving ever closer to my opening. When he reaches it, he eases a single finger inside. Sweetly, tenderly.

Desire gushes through me and I feel my muscles clamp around his digit. Our eyes are still glued together. Inseparable. Desperate. Jasper brings his thumb into play, massaging me with it as his finger gently explores me from the inside. He increases his rhythm just enough to take me up to the next notch. I press the back of his hand with my own, a silent plea for more.

Jasper wets his lips and slides another finger into me, thrusting deeper, yet still only slowly forcing me higher and higher. My breath is coming faster. My hips are moving against his hand. Jasper's eyes are darkening and the world around me is fading.

Then, with a growl that thrills me and movements so fast they surprise me, Jasper lifts me to my feet to stand in the tub in front of him. He leans forward and buries his tongue between my legs, like he couldn't wait another minute to taste me. A starving man offered a feast, and he accepted.

The heat of it, hotter than the bath water. The wetness of it, wetter than the bath water. I fist my fingers in his hair and hold him to me. He curls his arms around the backs of my thighs and nudges my legs apart before pulling one up onto his shoulder, opening me to him so that I am at his wonderful mercy.

Like a man possessed, Jasper devours me. His hunger is so voracious, it sizzles in the air around us. I've never been so wanted. And I've never wanted so much.

With swirls and licks and thrusts of his tongue, Jasper pulls me apart at the seams. My straining body convulses and my locked knee buckles. But I don't fall. Jasper supports me with his strong arms and his relentless tongue.

When I can neither stand nor speak, Jasper rises to scoop me into his arms and carry me purposefully into the next room. In one smooth motion, he turns me toward him and sits on the end of the bed. Just as I'm noticing that all the sheets are in a pile on the floor, I hear the zip of a zipper and then I'm being impaled on him.

My body responds as if we weren't separated all this time. After a moment's adjustment to his gasp-inducing size, I stretch around him and take him into the very center of me. All the way in.

I throw back my head, air lost in my lungs, speech lost on my tongue, and I just feel. My arms are draped around Jasper's shoulders, nowhere near touching in the back, and I feel him tremble again. When I open my eyes to look at him, his hot whiskey gaze is fixed on me.

The longer we watch each other, the more pronounced his tremor becomes. My heart and mind are intent on him, but my body is thinking more about where he's seated within me than anything else that's happening.

"Jasper?" I ask, my voice coarse and rough, even to my own ears.

He closes his eyes and I see his jaw clench. "Just give me a second."

"Is something wrong?"

At this, he opens back up and looks at me. "You're perfect. I just want to enjoy this. Just . . . *this*."

"Does that mean you're not already?"

"No. I just don't want to go too fast and risk—"

He stops abruptly, provoking my next question.

"Risk what?"

A fine bead of sweat is breaking out on his brow.

The pause is long before he answers. "Risk hurting you."

I take his face in my hands, my eyes boring into his. "You won't hurt me. You never have. I want all that you have to give, Jasper. Rough or gentle, sweet or dirty. I love it all."

I sit up slightly and then ease back down onto him. Jasper grabs my hips to still me, air hissing through his teeth. "Muse, I'm warning you . . ."

I smile down at him, pushing at his shoulders so that he'll lie back. Reluctantly, he does. I lean over him, letting him slip nearly all the way out of me. "Consider me warned," I say just before I press my mouth to his and move back onto him.

There is another pause, this one shorter, just before one big hand cups the back of my head to crush our lips together and the other one splays at the top of my butt to hold our bodies tight while he grinds his hips up into mine.

With a guttural grunt and the thrust of his tongue, Jasper pulls out of me and pumps back in. I know instinctively this is the moment he's giving up his fight. Seconds later, with a near-violent abandon, he begins to ravage my mouth, both hands now at my hips, guiding me into a wild, hard rhythm on him.

He moves me on him, grinding and sliding, the friction unbearably delicious. When his hand slips between us and his finger finds my folds, I tip over the edge I was so precariously clinging to.

"J-J-Jasper," I half pant, half moan.

"God, you're amazing," he growls, rolling over until he's on top of me, pounding his body into mine.

Sensation ripples through me in explosion after explosion. His thick, rigid body inside mine, his lips sucking at my nipple, his hand wrapped around the top of my thigh, holding my hips up and keeping me open.

And just before I catch my breath and begin my descent, I feel Jasper stiffen in my arms as his cock pulses and throbs within me. Heat pours into me and I take it all in, hoarding it greedily and milking him for more.

"I can't be without you again," he breathes into my ear in a harsh and winded voice. "Ever. Not ever, Muse. Do you hear me?"

He flexes his hips, spurting the last of himself into me just before he tips me up to take him a fraction deeper. Like he wants to bury himself in me as far as he can. And I want him to. I want anything he'll give me. And I don't ever want to let it go.

I wrap my arms around his shoulders as far as they'll go and I hold Jasper to me. We are as joined as two people can be, the indelible bond we share transcending even that which just happened between our bodies. I know this moment has changed everything. I don't know what tomorrow holds, I don't know what heartbreak might lie ahead, but I don't care. I *can't* care. He is the ocean that swallows my emptiness. He doesn't *fill it*; he makes it as though there was never a space there. He is a part of me and with him it's all or nothing. And I've had the nothing. I've lived with the nothing for months. I'm not interested in one more minute of it.

"I love you," I mumble, my lips pressed to the salty skin of his throat. "Iloveyou Iloveyou Iloveyou."

FORTY

Jasper

I have to make myself pull out of Muse, regret setting in once my mind returns. I roll away and sit up, running my hands through my hair as I think of the best way forward.

I feel the bed shift as Muse sits, too. She presses her front to my back, draping her arms around my neck. I can feel the delicious points of her nipples pressing into my shoulder blades and my mouth waters reflexively.

I stand, breaking free of her hold as I pace to the other side of the room.

"I'm sorry," I confess, unable to look back at her. I can picture perfectly what she must look like, sitting on her haunches, legs spread to reveal that beautiful pussy, lush nipples now a darker pink from the assault of my mouth.

"Why?" Her voice is small. Hurt.

I turn to find her head downcast. "I let you go so that you

wouldn't get hurt, so that *I* would never hurt you, and yet here I am . . ."

"You didn't hurt me, Jasper," she says, raising her liquid green eyes to mine. I can see the glitter of them in the moonlight streaming through the window behind her.

"I came inside you, Muse. What if you get pregnant? Do you think you'll ever be able to get rid of me then? I took your choice away from you tonight."

"No you didn't. I *let* this happen. I was here, too, you know. And I don't *want* to get rid of you. I want you here. With me. Always. And I thought that's where you wanted to be."

I say nothing. She's right. I knew what I was doing. And I knew I didn't want her to have a choice. I want to be bound to her forever. And her to me.

"Your last painting," I begin. "I saw the hurt in it. I saw the pain and the anger. *I* did that."

"You've been watching me." Not a question. A statement.

"Yes."

"I hoped you were."

"You did?" That surprises me.

She nods. "I also hoped that one day you'd let me see you."

"I had no intentions of that ever happening, but when I saw him on you . . ."

My blood boils instantly. I curl my fingers into fists so tight my joints ache.

"If you had no intention of ever being with me or letting me see you then why did you come? Why do that to me?"

"I wasn't doing it *to you*, Muse," I snap a little more harshly than I mean to. "Don't you get it? I've never loved someone before. Not the way I love you. I can't sleep. I can't think. I hardly eat. For months, I prayed to go back to the way I was, when I didn't feel. Didn't want. Didn't love. But it wouldn't go away. The more I tried to run from it, the worse it got. Nothing could make me forget you. Not drinking, not drugs, not other women, not—"

"You were with other women?"

"I tried to be, but damn you, I couldn't do it. They weren't you. They didn't smell like you, didn't taste like you, didn't *feel* like you. I couldn't get past a kiss, a simple touch. But God, I tried." I'm out of breath. Bitterly angry. Frustrated. "So I'm here now. To overdose. You'll either kill me or heal me. Either way, I can't live like this anymore. Without you."

Muse gets up and walks to where I stand in front of the other window. "But I don't want you to. I don't care about the danger or what *might* happen. My life isn't worth living without you, so I'll take the risk. *That's* what you saw in the painting. You saw how miserable I was without you. You saw that there was no sun even on a sunny day. You saw that the beauty around me wasn't beautiful anymore. But now it is. You're here. With me. And I don't want to spend another minute of another day in that kind of misery again. I knew if we'd ever have a chance, you'd have to come to me on your own. You'd have to be as ready for me in your life as I am for *you* in *mine*."

"I'm ready. I'd give up everything I am to be with you. Staying away didn't help my mother. It didn't save her. It only hurt her. And me. If you'll have me, I'm yours. I think I have been from the day I met you, when the man I've always hated started to die. You showed me love, real love. The kind that changes you from the inside out. I just didn't know if *you* could still love *me*, after all that's happened."

"Like I said, love doesn't let you go. And neither will I. I'll hang on until I draw my last breath, whether you do or not."

Hearing that brings me an odd sense of relief. It's almost an assurance that when Muse loves, she loves forever. No matter what happens, no matter who you turn out to be. She just loves. Even the monsters.

"So you aren't upset that I was watching you?"

"*Now* I'm not," she says with a grin.

"I felt like a creep."

"Doesn't look like that stopped you," she teases, dragging her fingernails up and down my biceps. They tense in response to her touch. That's all she has to do—touch me, smile at me, walk too close, the smallest thing and it's all over with. I'm done. Or maybe *undone*.

"I needed it. I needed *you*. A little bit of your heart, your soul. Even a glimpse of it—through your paintings, through your window, through the crowd on the street—just to keep me going. To keep me putting one foot in front of the other."

Her expression takes on one of sadness. "It didn't have to be that way."

I smile. "I had to *try* and let you go. For your sake. So I did. I tried like hell, but God! Every time I tried, I didn't get more than a hundred miles. Before I knew it, I was on my way back. Back here. Back to you. I didn't want to be anywhere that you weren't."

"Please don't leave me again, Jasper," Muse pleads, her eyes glistening, her chin trembling. "I don't think I can survive it again."

"I won't. I *can't*. I'm strong enough to kill, to maim, to survive things that would destroy other men. I'm strong enough to do whatever it takes to keep you safe, to protect you. As long as it's not from me. The one thing I'm not strong enough to do is live without you. *Sarò sempre pensare a te.*"

"You don't have to *think of me* anymore. I'm right here. And I always will be. Wherever you are."

"I want you to know that I will do anything to make you happy as long as you never ask me to leave."

"Then you're already making me the happiest girl in the world."

She rises up on her tiptoes and presses her lips to mine, her lush breasts dragging over my chest. My cock stirs to life, nudging her soft belly.

"There's nothing 'girl' about you," I say, reaching between us to palm the firm mounds.

"Mmmm," she moans against my lips. "Nope. All woman. And all yours."

I wrap my arms around her waist and pick her up to carry her back to bed. "I like the sound of that."

EPILOGUE

Muse

Four months later

"Are you sure I look okay?" I ask for the twentieth time at least.

"You look edible. Maybe you *should* change."

I tilt my head to give Jasper a withering look, but my lips are still curved in a smile. "Not a chance, buster, because after this, *you* get to take *this* home and eat it up."

A laugh bubbles up in my throat when I see his eyes darken to the color of light molasses. "You *do* want me to go in with you, right? Because if you keep saying things like that, what I'm thinking will be very apparent to everyone in the restaurant when I walk in with this."

He points to his lap and I can already see the growing bulge. My insides heat and contract, and I actually consider a quickie before we go inside.

I close my eyes and turn back to face the windshield. "Okay, okay, okay. Fooocus. Fooocus."

Jasper's long, warm fingers wind around mine and give them a little squeeze. "Come on. This is more important that your fiancé's libido anyway."

I open my eyes and meet the gaze of the love of my life. "*Nothing* is more important than you. No dream, no job, no art exhibition. Nothing."

"Well, I'm looking at it this way. Later, you ought to be so wound up after signing a contract to get your work on display in a famous French art gallery that I can just sit back and enjoy the ride. It's win-win."

I laugh. "You make an excellent point, Mr. uhhh . . ." I have to pause and think about his name. Jasper picked a new identity, too. We started over. Clean slate. Completely blank. *Blank.* The only thing we brought from our old lives was each other. And my father, when we get a chance to meet up with him. "Mr. Blank."

"Besides, soon-to-be *Mrs.* Blank, I wouldn't miss this for the world."

I lean my temple against the headrest as I consider the man before me. More handsome than anyone I've ever seen, more fierce than anything I've ever known and more mine than I ever thought he could be. "I wouldn't miss *you* for the world."

He leans forward to take my lips in a kiss that's both sweet and passionate. There's enough electricity passing between us to give light to a small country, and within seconds, it crackles into something that nears the "wild and hungry" side.

Jasper pulls away, his breathing harsh and heavy. "Unless you're up for attending this meeting with a sweaty dress and smeared lipstick, you'd better stay on that side of the car. That or we'll have to skip it altogether."

His smile is devilish and I actually consider rescheduling. But then I remember how important this is, not just to me as an artist, but to our future. Jasper told me we need not worry about money, that he had made some good investments, but I want to be able to invest in our life and our happiness, too.

I sigh loudly. "Fine. I guess we'd better get in there."

His smile is crooked, and I wonder how I got through the first part of my life without it. "We can just . . . postpone *this*. How about that?"

"Maybe call it 'dessert,'" I suggest.

"I'll bring the syrup. And the ice cream," he says in a voice that sounds like caramel. His words alone conjure an image that affects me in a very visceral way. Muscles low in my belly clench spasmodically. I can all but feel slick syrup and cool cream being dribbled all over my body and then licked off by Jasper. I have to stop myself after I imagine the second swipe of his tongue.

"You're evil," I tell him breathlessly.

"I'll show you just *how* evil later."

With a quick peck to my lips, he gets out and comes around to my side, opening my door and taking my hand like a perfect gentleman, like he didn't just nearly cause me a hands-free orgasm in the parking lot of a restaurant.

When I'm standing beside him, he looks down into my eyes, staring into them like they hold a thousand wonders. "Have I told you how beautiful you look tonight?"

I nod, my mouth so dry my tongue is stuck to the roof.

"Have I told you how incredibly talented you are? And how much you deserve this?"

Again I nod.

"And have I told you how lucky I am to call you mine? No matter what tomorrow holds?"

I nod and smile, my skin warming as though I'm being bathed in sunlight. And that's about right. That's what it feels like to be loved by Jasper. It's sometimes rough and fast, sometimes sweet and languorous, but always bright and hot.

"I love you, baby."

I feel tears prickle. I will never get used to hearing those words from his lips. Nor will I ever get tired of it.

Before I can respond, Jasper tucks my hand in the crook of his elbow and we make our way into the crowded restaurant.

We are greeted immediately and taken to a private dining nook where Hugh and Julienne await us. They both rise when we appear, both kissing my cheeks before greeting Jasper. I can tell by the look on Julienne's face that her appreciation for art extends to my jaw-droppingly gorgeous man. I smile. It doesn't make me jealous. It makes me proud. So proud that he's all mine. Although he's polite, the greeting he gives her pales in comparison to the look he slants my way after he pushes in my chair.

Conversation is easy and light, the food exquisite and expensive.

"I have Gerard to thank for introducing me to this lovely woman's work," Julienne says.

"Obviously he had a good eye," Jasper says mildly.

"Did you know him?"

"Not really. We only met once."

"A pity we couldn't all be here tonight. I have a feeling business will be very good," she says, winking at me.

"I'm sure he hated to miss it," I add.

Gerard sold his house and moved to Italy within a month of Jasper and me moving out. Jasper wanted to choose a place that was more to his liking. In other words, some place that no one could find us until my father finds out who's behind Napalm.

In the last four months, he's been able to uncover a few details about Napalm. It's a covert operation, not sanctioned by the government, that appears to lead right to a senatorial committee. Every day he gets one step closer to putting an end to all this so we can go home. He's got Rogan in the wings, waiting for another name, another connection so that he can work his own sources. Until then, we're making a home where we can. With each other. We're healing more and more, learning to love and be loved. Jasper is putting his old life and all its nightmares behind him and reaching for a future with me. He even grieved the loss of his mother, shedding a single tear that I caught before it could touch the ground. With each day, we're growing closer together and farther from the pain of the past.

Jasper mentions one of my newest pieces, effectively bringing me back to the present. Under the table, he takes my hand and squeezes it. He's always attuned to me, always sensitive to my moods and my thoughts, it seems.

They finally get around to making me an offer that makes my head spin. I feel giddy and light, my laugh sounding more and more like Julienne's champagne-soaked one. But my bubbles come from within. This news makes an already wonderful day *perfect*.

My mind reels as I think about the other news I got, news that Jasper has yet to find out about. I'll be telling him later, when we're alone. Until then, every time I think about that little plastic tube that's in the trashcan back at our new place here in Paris, I feel giddy. It read positive this morning. The pink plus appeared almost immediately. I knew it would. Something in my gut, something in my *heart* told me that it would.

Jasper will be thrilled. He tries to act nonchalant about me getting pregnant, but he's as disappointed as I am when the test reads negative. So tonight, we'll be celebrating more than one dream coming true. After a lifetime of tough blows and bad dreams, I want Jasper to have his every heart's desire, starting with our baby. If it's within my power to make him happy, I'll do it. I'd do anything for him. And he'd do anything for me. That's why I don't worry about tomorrow. As long as I've got Jasper, I'll be more than okay. I'll be perfect.

Turn the page for a special excerpt from the next
Tall, Dark, and Dangerous novel by M. Leighton

TOUGH ENOUGH

Coming soon from Berkley Books!

PROLOGUE

Katie

Something is prodding me to wake up. Like an insistent finger poking my shoulder and someone whispering, "Wake up, wake up, wake up."

But I don't want to. I only want to hide. Hide from the light, hide from the world, hide from reality. I turn deeper into unconsciousness, but there's no rest for me there.

Wake up, wake up, wake up.

A dull pain begins to spread down my left side and sounds that were a distant backdrop only moments before come closer, closer, closer. One by one, I can make them out.

Sirens.

Metallic clattering.

Strange voices.

Screaming. Awful screaming.

It sounds so familiar, that scream. That voice, although I can't figure out why. The answer is fuzzy, like the face that swirls behind my eyes.

Distorted. Mocking. Cruel.

It's Calvin.

Panic swells within me, forcing me toward wakefulness. I don't want to go, don't want to wake. I claw and scratch. I dig in with my heels, with my hands, but nothing can stop my ascent.

Agony rushes in. It steals my breath and sweeps over me like flames, licking at my skin, turning the air to napalm.

More screaming, only this time I recognize the voice. I know it. I've listened to it my whole life.

It's mine.

And then I remember.

Just before the blackness welcomes me back.

I rouse again, despite a gut instinct that tells me not to.

I wake to harsh voices, shouted commands and muffled road noise.

The face is still there, still there behind my eyes. Taunting me, haunting me. Satisfied.

Horrific pain radiates from the left side of my body. It sears its way across my nerves, gaining strength, gaining momentum until I can't fight the blackness.

So I don't.

My eyelids flutter open. I see white metal above me, the dark head of a man beside me. I'm lying on my back. He's sitting to my right. I don't know who he is or what he's doing. I don't even know where I am. All I know is that something is wrong. Terribly wrong. I know it. I can *feel* it, like frantic fingers picking at my consciousness, picking away the scab. Tearing away the blindfold. Luring me into awareness.

I turn away. Back into the nothingness.

Seconds, minutes, hours pass. Time has no real meaning. It's only a series of disjointed sights, sounds and feelings. Fear. Dread. Pain.

Excruciating pain.

And aloneness. Even though I know I'm not alone; I'm far from alone.

I hear dozens of different voices now. Beeps. Thumps. Scrambling. And I can smell. Something awful, putrid even, mixed with the chemical scent of a hospital.

But the pain is what overwhelms it all. It's nearly unbearable, like my left side is trying to secede from the rest of my body. Nerves tearing away from nerves, muscle ripping away from tendon. Flesh falling away from bone.

So I run.

I run into the deepest part of my mind, the part that refuses to participate with the outside world. I hide there until the pain stops.

Only it never stops. It never stops stalking me from the shadows.

ONE

Katie

I haven't been so aware of my shortcomings, of my fears, in the two years that I've been here. Each time I ask myself *Why today?* I can come up with only one answer, but really it's no answer at all. It only spurs another question. *Why him?*

"You're not *the least bit* excited to be putting makeup on *the* Kiefer Rogan?"

We slow our walk as we approach my "office," which is basically four thin walls that house a makeup chair, a bank of lighted mirrors and a wraparound counter topped with a bunch of shelves. And on those shelves are the supplies of my trade—a wide array of everything from pancake makeup to prosthetic noses. It's not fancy, but it feels as much like home as any place does.

I turn my eyes to Mona's cornflower blue ones. She is the only person who might even *come close* to being called my best friend. Am I oddly nervous? Yes. Am I extremely uneasy? Yes. But am I *excited*?

"Not even a little bit," I reply sincerely.

Her full lips fall into a disbelieving O. "Wow! I can't even imagine not getting excited over a guy like him."

"He's just a guy," I declare with a shrug. I wish I *felt* as casual as the gesture indicates. Kiefer Rogan *is* just a guy, but guys like him spell trouble. For that reason alone, I can't *really be* as nonchalant as I pretend to be. I try to change the subject, turning the conversation back to Mona and her man. "Besides, why should you care anyway? You've got a boyfriend."

She grins, which makes her look even more innocent than her platinum hair and eyes that are too big for her face. Physically, Mona is the perfect split between a Barbie Doll and a Precious Moments figurine, all with a touch of clueless porn star thrown in for good measure. She can work her assets like nobody's business, but she does it in such a way that doesn't make her detestable, which is quite a feat. She's very genuine, too, which is one of the things I like most about her. That and the fact that we are polar opposites in practically every way.

Mona is tall and fair and beautiful with a sweet, outgoing personality. I am none of those things, but we both seem to be okay with that. It's probably why we get along so well.

"White's great, but he doesn't look like *that*." White Bristow is the executive producer of the show. He's fairly good-looking, but nothing like the guy Mona is talking about, Kiefer Rogan. White's a total player like Kiefer allegedly is, too, but Mona loves him enough to overlook it. No matter what else he's doing (or *who else* he's doing), he always comes back to Mona. I guess maybe he loves her in his own way. "God, I wish he did, though."

"Looks aren't everything," I remind her softly.

Her expression falls into one of regret and sadness. She reaches out and smoothes the hair that I always keep swept over my left shoulder. It can always be found draped around my neck to hide my scars. She's one of the few people who know what lies beneath the swath of hair. And how sensitive I am about it. "No, looks aren't everything, but if they were, you'd still be one of the most wanted."

I smile. That's Mona—always seeing the best in me, whether it's accurate or not. "That's sweet, but you and I both know that's not true."

"Oh, but it is. Look at you, Katie. All this thick, wavy auburn hair, those big, dark blue eyes. And you're so tiny! I'd give anything to be petite like you."

"Mona, you're like a living, breathing Barbie Doll. If I were you, I wouldn't want to change a thing, not even your Amazonian height," I tease. She's not the least bit insecure about her five-foot-eleven frame. In fact, she'd be the first to tell you that it's her unusual stature and legs that go for miles that helped her get the attention of White, who is the person pretty much responsible for bringing her into the Hollywood world.

I stop in front of my "office" door and turn to face her. Mona leans up against the jamb, her eyes going all dreamy. "I wonder if Rogan likes tall women," she muses.

Back to Kiefer Rogan, I think with a deflated sigh. I won't be able to avoid him much longer, so why do we have to talk about him now?

My bitterness surfaces and I let it flow. Maybe it'll prompt her to stop bringing the conversation back to him.

"From what I've read in the tabloids, he likes anything with boobs. But I think he's into the divas mostly, which would count you out. Thank God!" I, for one, am glad that Mona isn't conceited about her looks or her position here at the studio. She's utterly guileless and happily clueless, and I like her just the way she is. With a diva *not included.*

"I could be a diva," she says, straightening, her expression turning enthusiastic. "I could totally be a diva. If it meant having those flirty green eyes and that drop-dead gorgeous smile turned on me, I'd be whatever he wanted me to be."

Her little-girl giggle belies her words. She could never be a diva. "You don't have a diva bone in your body. Besides, why would you want a guy like that? He dates the most horrible women and he goes through them like water. I mean, look at Victoria," I say, lowering my voice as I scan the hall left and right to ensure we aren't being overheard. "What kind of a decent person would date her? She's awful!" I go on cynically, finding some strange comfort in pigeonholing him, calling a spade a spade. Hoping that maybe if I build up my armor against him, I won't be swayed by his pretty face. "I bet he's a conceited jerk, who only cares about what his arm candy looks like."

"Guys who look like him can be *annnything* they want, as long as they stay hot."

"Well, he's all yours, then. I don't have room for cocky, obnoxious, selfish sleazeballs in my life." I glance at my watch. Six fifteen a.m. Mr. Rogan should be here by six thirty, but I won't be holding my breath. "I bet he doesn't even show up on time. Jerk!"

Mona sighs, tilting her head, a faraway look in her eyes. "I'd wait all day for a guy like that. He makes my special places shiver."

"Well, you and your special places are welcome to him. I don't see what the big deal is," I reply, turning into my office. "He's not even *that* good-looking."

I take two steps and round the corner, my eyes falling on the chair that should be empty. I stop so suddenly that Mona crashes right into my back, pushing me sharply forward. I brace myself, keeping us both upright as we stare at the man smiling casually from the makeup chair in front of the lighted mirrors.

Settled in with one ankle resting on his other knee, looking highly amused and like he's been here for a while, is none other than MMA champ and up-and-coming Hollywood sensation, Kiefer Rogan.

The guy I was calling cocky and obnoxious and selfish while standing just a few feet away.